TALO

Lily stared at her c
mander's order. She
of definite concern. "There's someone out there," she said.

LePetit blinked. "What do you mean?"

"Well, unless there's a microwave tower that we haven't destroyed—"

"There isn't," snapped LePetit.

"Then someone on the ground is sending microbursts to a satellite somewhere near us. It's rolling across the frequencies. Do you have somebody else working for you that I should know about?"

"No. Whoever's out there is someone we haven't met before. What are they saying?"

Lily shook her head. "That's going to take time to decode."

LePetit said angrily, "Dammit, we don't— Who the hell is sending the message?"

"This is very sophisticated stuff. Way beyond what I'm doing. *Nobody's* that good on this island."

LePetit stared hard at the computer, and felt a tiny pinpoint of fear enter his heart.

"Somebody is now."

Also in the TALON Force Series

THUNDERBOLT

MELTDOWN

SKY FIRE

SECRET WEAPON

ZULU PLUS TEN

TAKEDOWN

Cliff Garnett

A SIGNET BOOK

SIGNET
Published by New American Library, a division of
Penguin Putnam Inc., 375 Hudson Street,
New York, New York 10014, U.S.A.
Penguin Books Ltd, 27 Wrights Lane,
London W8 5TZ, England
Penguin Books Australia Ltd, Ringwood,
Victoria, Australia
Penguin Books Canada Ltd, 10 Alcorn Avenue,
Toronto, Ontario, Canada M4V 3B2
Penguin Books (N.Z.) Ltd, 182–190 Wairau Road,
Auckland 10, New Zealand

Penguin Books Ltd, Registered Offices:
Harmondsworth, Middlesex, England

First published by Signet, an imprint of New American Library,
a division of Penguin Putnam Inc.

First Printing, September 2000
10 9 8 7 6 5 4 3 2 1

Printed in the United States of America

People sleep peacefully in their beds at night
only because rough men stand ready
to do violence on their behalf.

—George Orwell

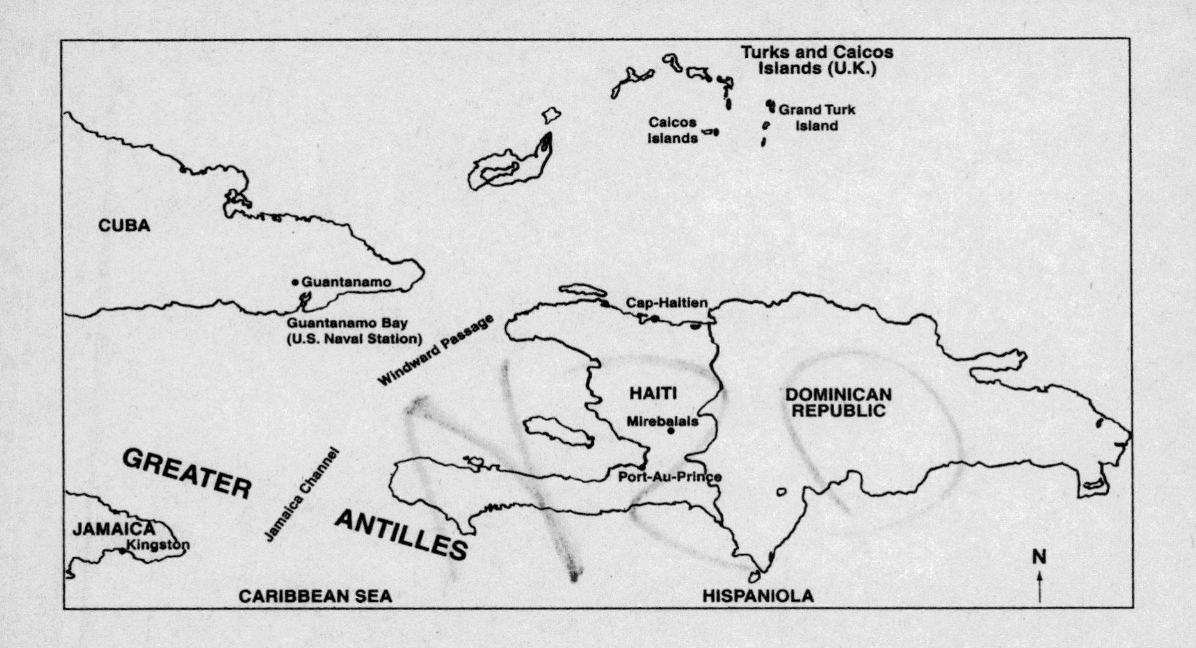
Turks and Caicos
Islands (U.K.)
Grand Turk
Island
Caicos
Islands
CUBA
Guantanamo
Guantanamo Bay
(U.S. Naval Station)
Windward Passage
Cap-Haitien
HAITI
Mirebalais
Port-Au-Prince
DOMINICAN
REPUBLIC
GREATER
ANTILLES
Jamaica Channel
JAMAICA
Kingston
CARIBBEAN SEA
HISPANIOLA
N

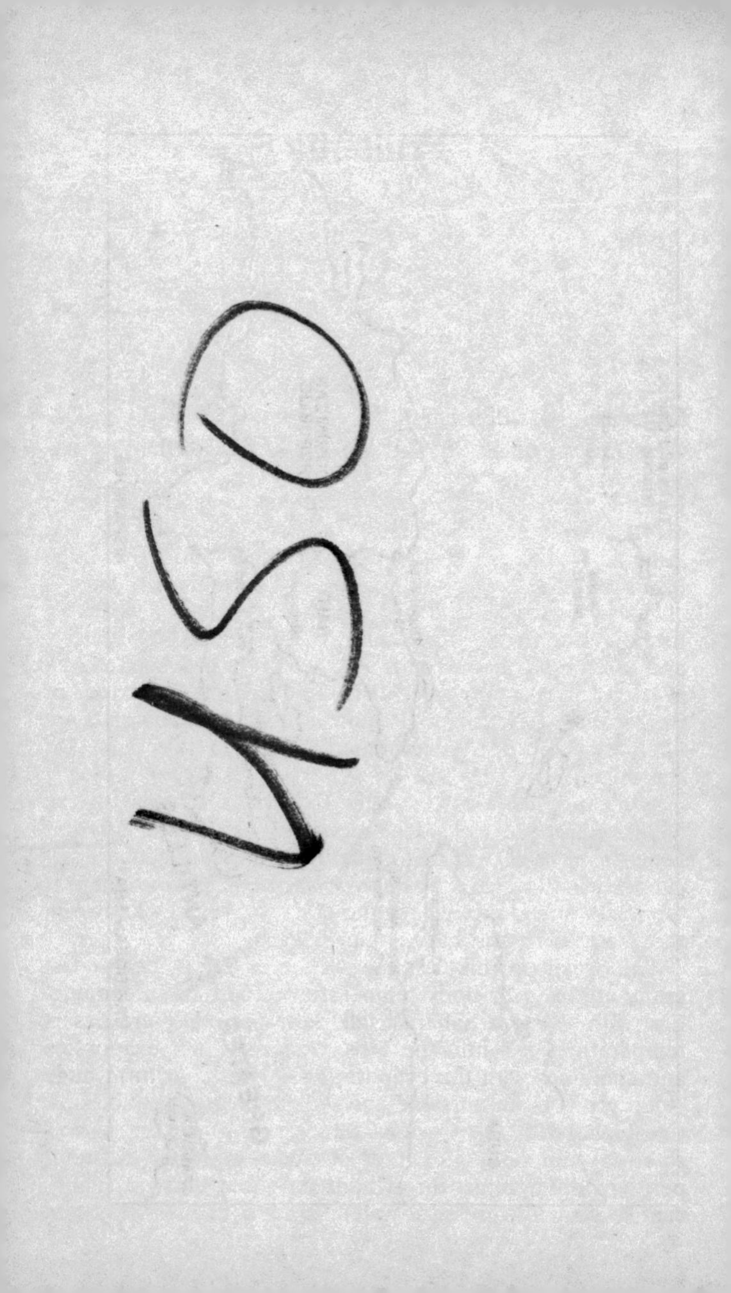

Prologue

September 14, 0824 hours
West African coast, 28° 31' West, 24° 51' North

On the northwest coast of Africa lies a land few know exists. The Western Sahara—bordered on the west by the Atlantic Ocean, the north by the Quarkizz and Oued Draa Mountains, and the south and east by barren desert—exists in a geopolitical nonstatus. Claimed by Morocco, its neighbor to the north, and Mauritania to the south—and abutting Algeria to its northeast—it has been called Western Sahara only since 1975. Its residents, a mixture of Berber and Bafour people now called the Saharawi, are nomads who roam the scorched deserts as they have for centuries.

While few concern themselves with the struggle of the Saharawi people for independence, a movement that has gone on for well over half a century, in certain climatological circles, the area is infamous. For the Western Sahara is the fecund natal ground for the massive cyclones known in the Western Hemisphere as hurricanes.

The ocean off this desolate section of the African coast easily attains near body temperature readings. In conjunction with Western Sahara's fall rainy period where desert temperatures run into the 140s, what rain falls evaporates and combines with the evaporating seawater to form huge cloud growth and unstable and violent weather conditions. Combined with the Coriolis force (caused by the earth's rotation) and varying degrees of prevailing wind and temperature differentials throughout the air column, a significant swirling low-pressure system forms as the storm system moves off the coast and builds in strength over the ocean; feeding itself on water, wind, and heat.

The NOAA's National Hurricane Center in Miami, Florida—a repository for information received from an army of satellites, radar, earth stations, ships at sea, and aircraft—was the first to observe the low as it swirled and grew in strength, making its way deeper into the Atlantic. The nascent storm was named Lily, and it was the twelfth major low-pressure system of this year's hurricane season. It soon ceased to be called a "low" and achieved full hurricane status when the winds reached over seventy-four miles an hour while it was eight hundred miles east of the Caribbean Basin. Lily stood tall over the Atlantic. The eye was already well formed and Lily crested at stratospheric levels: as she assumed the hurricane's characteristic anvil shape she reached seven miles into the atmosphere.

Fed and pushed slightly southeast by a combination of the Canary Current and a high-altitude wind shear, it was accelerated under the impetus of an unusually strong—and somewhat farther north than usual—vector of the Northeast Trade Winds. The hurricane fed off the warmth of the North Equatorial Current and whirled itself tighter and tighter, increasing in power on an hourly basis.

Slowly it started the patterned curve of nearly all tropical systems emanating out of Africa and gathering even more strength; its winds increased sharply. The eye, when viewed by various passing weather satellites, assumed sharp and perfect symmetry. Lily remained compact—perhaps 250 miles in diameter—but was a fast and fierce mover. Already a Category 2, it retained its compact size and headed inexorably for someplace to vent it fury.

"This is going to be a kick-ass storm if the winds go any higher," said Professor Robert Hughes, as he read the data sheets about Lily. "She's nowhere near the Bermuda-Azores High but she's acting like she is. Doing a perfect drop and curve heading for the Antilles. What are the models saying?" he asked the grad student seated across the room.

"Right now looks like growth to a Cat three or four. There's enough gas in the atmosphere and, well, the water's still up a few degrees higher for this time of year compared to the mean."

"Not good, not good," replied Hughes. "Okay, Tom, start getting advisories out."

As the mechanism that tracked hurricanes and provided every level of government, military, and civilian authority with forecasts, updates, propensities, possibilities, and probabilities leapt into action, Lily grew in strength. And grew.

The warning system that predicted Lily's track wasn't far off. Nor was the emphasis on the danger of the storm, but none of that helped the impoverished citizens of the western side of the island of Hispaniola.

It was December 5, 1492, when Christopher Columbus first spied the island he would name four days later *La Espanola*. That the indigenous population already had a name for the island—*Quiesqueya*—made little impression on neither the swashbuckling explorer nor any others whom claimed "discoveries" in the New World. But that was the way things were done in this era of adventure and discovery; the era of the conquerors and the conquered.

Hispaniola lies just across the Windward Passage from the southeastern tip of Cuba. This third largest isle in the Caribbean is divided into two parts; two-thirds of it is the Dominican Republic.

The eastern third of the island came into being as a separate entity by virtue of the Treaty of Ryswick in 1682 between the countries of France and Spain, but it wasn't until 1804 that the words "Republic of Haiti" burst upon the geopolitical scene. With the formation of the republic, Haiti became the first independent republic in Latin America (second in freedom only to the United States in the entire hemisphere). Haiti also had the fortune—or misfortune—to be the first all-Black republic anywhere, and the first where the slaves overthrew their masters by military force.

Since then—and perhaps because of that—things have not gone so well for the Maryland-sized country. And Hurricane Lily was just another in a series of natural and man-made disasters to hit Haiti with an iron glove.

Lily came ashore outside the town of Jacmel about thirty kilometers southwest of Port-au-Prince, Haiti's capital. She was a solid Category 4, pushing winds over 135 miles per hour, its power virtually undiminished by its run-ins with the smaller islands it had encountered on its way.

If a storm could have a purpose, it seemed Lily's was dedicated to reaching Haiti and finishing off what man, geopolitics, racism, colonial arrogance, slavery, cruelty, and neglect had missed. Lily was very successful at her job.

The storm surge that first battered the south coast was in excess of twenty-five feet. A hundred-plus foot intercoastal freighter was shoved so far up into the town of Jacmel, that it looked like the ark on Ararat. Shanties were whirled down the crowded streets like Auntie Em's house—when they landed they killed just the same, though there were no wicked witches, just humble, hardworking people beneath them.

As Lily made her way to Port-au-Prince, the storm system drew sustenance from the Baie de Port-au-Prince and the Golfe de la Gonave and maintained her steady rhythmic pace of destruction. Trees—a commodity in Haiti, where firewood was always at a premium—either broke or uprooted, pulling the ground up with them and slamming into any manner of building or shack that was near. Telephone poles toppled in comic order like a well-planned layout of dominos, the weight of wire and energy toppling each in succession.

Some areas saw ten inches of rain in the hour the worst of the storm lasted. Drainage ditches and streets flooded and swept the unwary—human and animal—away. The wind smashed windows, by itself or aided by airborne detritus. Winging sheet-metal signs decapitated some people, smashing others viciously. The wind was powerful enough to surge under five-ton trucks and topple them to their sides.

Even praying wouldn't stop Lily. As she roared out of Port-au-Prince and the calm of the eye passed over the city, she gathered her skirts for an assault on the hinterland. While the wind after the eye rose in crescendo, Lily's leading edge reached a small town just north of the capital called Bon Repos, where over a hundred souls had gathered for shelter and prayer in the local church. Lily tore the church's steeple apart and collapsed the building in on itself. Sixty-three people died while speaking to their maker.

Heading into the mountains the storm followed a wobbling track as if looking for someone to vent her fury on. Interior Haiti is an area of small scattered towns and outcroppings of civilization, but that would have to do.

Mountainsides collapsed under the weight and suddenness of the assault of drenching amounts of water and crashing winds. Mud slides—twenty-foot high walls of viscous, red muck—-took the lives of hundreds throughout the craggy, rough Haitian interior. Rivers swelled to heights few of the country's old-timers could recall and wiped everything clean as the water swelled from the heights and made its way back to the sea. What crops there were, were destroyed in the half hour the storm spent crossing any given area.

By the time Lily crashed into the homes of the wealthy in the heights around Cap Haitien, she was winded, but far from done. The homes there were bigger, more modern, and more expensive, and while they were not blown flat, none were left to resemble their former glory. Roofs were sent sailing, windows were blown in, and those with the beautiful views of the sea beyond often joined those waters as the hillsides let go. Much of Haiti's tourism was centered on Cap Haitien, and the hotels that dotted the landscape and provided some form of living for the local populace were victims of the storm as well. Lily was, if nothing else, an equal opportunity destroyer.

To add insult to injury, she veered northwest off of Cap Haitien and jogged a short distance up the coast. Just far enough to beat the coastal city of Port-de-Paix into submission before dealing Cuba's southeast coast a glancing blow and heading east searching for more.

By the time the storm finally departed—as a mid Cat 3 having vented its spleen on the Black Republic—Haiti was finished. In the future it would be estimated some fourteen thousand people had died in the storm and another four or five thousand as a result of it, either through starvation, injury, or disease.

But Haiti's problems were far from over.

Chapter 1

September 15, 0100 hours
A small clearing in the Chaine des Cahos,
south of Fort des Bayonnais, Haiti

The people had heard of the man who was the *lwa*—the spirit—of Louverture, and they had come to see and hear him for themselves.

The interior of Haiti was a land closer to the magic and mysticism of the Vodoun; while those in the more urban areas also believed in the religion of spirits, possession, good, and evil, it was the populace of the countryside that was the cathedral of Vodoun. The true believers lived here and experienced the world through Vodoun on a daily basis. An enemy could be made to die, good deeds were rewarded, bad ones punished, and all was right with the world for those who were faithful.

Raoul Louis Bata was a *boko*, a Vodoun priest. The *boko* held mystical and magical powers in the Vodoun religion and could work for either good or evil. He could send the spirits of the departed to help those he chose, and also send spirits to wreak havoc. This was also how the *boko* made his living, and Raoul Louis Bata was one of the better known *bokos* in this section of northwestern Haiti. He was here at the *Kalfou*, this sacred crossroad where the human and divine worlds intersected, on behalf of a regular client, a man whom Bata was not really sure needed his intercession. He had heard the man speak and had witnessed his power but once, and the experience had given him pause. The man had promised that Martine Chaffard would be punished for stealing the wife of Andre Cheverny, and no one had seen Chaffard since. Chaffard had even threatened Bata himself, so the *boko* knew he had been a very evil person.

Bata poured cornmeal in an intricate pattern on the ground to form the *veve*, the drawing that invited the *lwa* to descend and join the ceremony. If all was in order, and all the participants' hearts were pure, tonight those assembled would be introduced to the future of Haiti.

As the people sat and stood around the torchlit clearing, the *yan valou*, a solemn beat kept by three different drums following the lineal ringing of an iron bell called an *ogan*, began.

As the tempo of the drums increased, the normal reaction of the gathered assemblage would be to translate the pulsating beat into dances that would eventually allow the *lwa* of the summoned personage to enter the bodies of the supplicants and communicate with them in a tangible way. But Bata had been asked to perform a special ceremony to summon only the spirit of Louverture to commune with the people through the physical body of only one man. Jean-Guy LePetit.

The music soared to a feverish pitch and a man stepped into the circle the now-fervent worshippers had formed. Two men clad in camouflage fatigues but bearing no weapons parted the crowd, and as the drumming quieted the man strode into the circle and stood before the *boko*. LePetit looked down at the old priest and nodded his head, the motion barely detectable.

The ceremony to invest Jean-Guy LePetit with Louverture's spirit—a rite that had already occurred in a hundred clearings throughout the mountains and villages of Haiti—began.

September 16, 0320 hours
Massif des Montagnes Noires, outside the city of Mirebalais, Haiti

The idea had been born with his father's death and had matured into a workable plot to assimilate himself into the democratic process that currently ruled Haiti by intertwining the Haitian belief of Vodoun and the spirit world into a strong power base that would allow him to take over the country. The elections were to be held in December and now was the time to move. The hurricane had been an added bonus and merely accelerated what LePetit planned.

While incorporating his late father's existence into his own had been a stellar idea, Jean-Guy was most proud of his resurrection of Louverture, the George Washington of Haiti. A whisper that the spirit of the great man, the man who had first established Haiti as a free republic, spoke through Jean-Guy was all he needed to insure the loyalty and fealty of much of the populace.

Jean-Guy simply wanted to control Haiti. He didn't want to resort to the thuggery of many previous Haitian rulers, only for the reason that it became self-defeating. Instead, he had quietly spent the last ten years observing his plan slowly evolving into something that nearly had a life of its own. Ambitious, to be sure, but as time had passed Jean-Guy's original idea became more attainable with every passing day. The idea had grown from one that would provide Jean-Guy with the ability to make his own life as easy and comfortable as possible to one that brought that concept to its nth power. Why not become the leader of *all* of Haiti and reap every benefit?

Lily Rebuffat was a key, and the hurricane of the same name was a stroke of good luck that would make it even easier to attain his goal. It had to be an omen that both the young computer genius and this massive storm were of the same name.

The young, oh-so dedicated, oh-so Haiti-for-Haitians Amarilla "Lily" Rebuffat, a twenty-something raven-haired cover model cum college student was the epitome of what was so intriguing and beautiful about Haiti. While LePetit, even at the ripe old age of thirty-six, was enamored by her stunning body and looks, it was a singular other skill that made her so necessary to the cause. Lily Rebuffat was the best computer hacker in the Caribbean and possibly anywhere north or south of the equator. Lily had hacking—from government mainframe computers to satellite navigation systems—down to a science. It seemed that no matter what was put in her way, she was able and capable of finding a way around it. And with that skill, LePetit was on his way.

LePetit looked at the young woman as she paged through a manual of charts and numbers and formulas. She's so damn intense, he thought, but that's a good thing for now. I wonder if she realizes exactly what we're doing?

Haiti had far too many mouths to feed and Hurricane Lily would be a mechanism that could take the lives of many if he could just keep the do-gooders who'd basically ignored Haiti all these years from stopping mother nature's culling. Famine, pestilence . . . if he could just delay help for a week or so, there'd be hundreds of thousands (he fervently hoped) less people to deal with. And every little bit helped in a country as overcrowded as this. Since much of the population was concentrated in conditions of abject poverty—even for this island—in the two main cities of Port-au-Prince and Cap Haitien, the devastation the hurricane had caused there should kill them off like the flies they were. LePetit needed the government "aura" intact, not the government or populace itself.

It was classic "thinking on his feet." Even though the hurricane had brought undue attention to Haiti at a time when he least needed it, he'd use the storm to further his cause.

With Lily already in all but complete control of the communications system of the island, all he had to do was jam up the ports with some well-placed wrecks and ensure the main airports—the three paved ones, anyway—remained inoperable. The rest of the plan was merely to lead the populace down the path he'd chosen, and the years in the mountains had provided him with celebrity to do so. Most of the islanders had heard of him for nearly fifty years. That it had really been his father was somehow ignored by the superstitious.

Jean-Guy had recruited some five hundred young men and women, people who showed the spark of cunning that hunger, poverty, and life at the bottom of the totem pole bred. He reactivated the specter of the MPP—Mouvman Peyizan Papay—the people's movement that had been the *lavalas*, the grass-roots organization, that had held the promise of democracy in the post-junta period. Using this armed and—eventually well-trained—force, along with the Vodoun mystique, he was able to extract concessions, money, and finally collaboration from the drug lords, the businessmen, the *meriken* capitalists, and more. All quietly, all under the subversion of the Vodoun beliefs, and the application of violence when necessary. Violence had been surprisingly less necessary than he'd first supposed, because Vodoun was alive and well in the ruling class as well, and the drug lords were—regardless of their money—peasantry of other countries with similar fears and superstitions. The *merikens* had been less pliable, but since all of their help was Haitian the point became moot.

Where the *meriken* DEA and military had been consistently unsuccessful in interrupting the flow of drugs through Haiti with their satellites, electronic eavesdropping, helicopters, radar blimps, and money, LePetit's burgeoning organization—and nearly an entire island of informants—had much success. Then again, he wasn't trying to stop the flow. If the *merikens* wanted to use drugs, it was fine with him. His benevolence stopped there, however. He'd had to execute two of the MPP for the same reason, but the point had been made. If the *narcotrafficantes* wanted their ingress and egress through LePetit's island all they had to do was pay. Eventually—businessmen that the drug lords were—they saw the benefit of siding with him.

And then he'd met Lily and the last key fell into place. If you can control communications, you can do anything you want, and Lily knew how.

"I've been able to stop any electronic traffic in or out of the American Embassy," said Lily. "They're not very happy about it, and they did manage about three hours worth of transmissions before I could access the satellite." She turned back to the laptop keyboard as the screen danced with characters. "They're trying again," she said to LePetit as she peered at the screen. Her fingers flew over the keyboard.

"Explain this to me a—"

"Jean-Guy, you'll never understand it."

"Humor me *anon, mon cher*."

Lily shook her head. "The Americans are bouncing their signals off satellites that patrol overhead. I wrote a program that can access the satellites. The small antenna outside is what transmits and receives the signal. They send their encoded messages in a burst transmission. While I can't read the transmissions—"

"So there is something you *don't* know how to do," said Jean-Guy.

"I *know* how to, but I'd need a bigger computer and considerably more time. Besides, you don't care what they say. We *know* what they're saying."

"*Oui.* Help is what they are saying."

"Right," said Lily. "And I'm sure that messages got back to their superiors in Washington before I finally broke into their system. There have been overflights of military planes from the American base in Cuba already, but I've been able to stop them from speaking to the embassy as well . . . and I've been able to interfere with their navigation too."

"And you do that . . . ?"

"Essentially the same way, just with different satellites and ground stations. That computer," Lily pointed to a second laptop, "deals just with ground-based navigation, DGPS to be specific. If they want to use satnav, which most of the aircraft and many of the larger ships do, I use this computer. If a signal is accessing any of the orbiting or static satellites, the scanner attached to this computer will let me know. In a few more hours, I'll probably even have it down to specific bandwidths. They only use certain ones, but the program can keep scanning across the dial, so to speak, in case they try—"

"Enough," said Jean-Guy. He pointed to the second laptop. "The small corner screen?"

Lily quickly moved over to the other table. "I wish I had a damn office and a rolling chair instead of this handmade—"

"Soon, my dear. Soon, you will have all the computers and equipment you will need."

"Hmmm," said Lily as she typed into the screen. "Well, Jean-Guy, here is your chance to prove that your men are as good as you say. A freighter heading for . . ." She tapped some instructions rapidly and watched as the screen changed. "Sea lanes. Approach. Let's see . . ." Lily continued in this vein alternately keying and talking as she went. "Okay.

This ship . . ." She interrupted herself and typed more on the keyboard. "Okay. Yes. Here's your first one. A freighter out of Miami. It must have been loaded and left right after the first calls from the embassy went out. Very fast. People are very anxious to help us, I think," she said with some surprise in her voice.

"No one wishes to help Haiti unless they can profit from it, *mon cher*. If they are anxious to help it is only because it costs them money. When we have the country, we shall see who our true friends are," said LePetit. "What can you do to the boat?"

LePetit listened as Lily explained her actions, then continued watching as she returned to her computers. After a moment of thought, he walked out of the cave and looked around. He spotted a man sitting against a rock about twenty feet away. "You," he said calmly, but loud enough to be heard. The man started and swiveled his head round. When he realized it was LePetit he immediately jumped to his feet and hurried over. "Go, tell Henri to come here." The man sped off.

As Jean-Guy strode back and forth in front of the cave's entrance the man returned. "Louverture?" said the man accompanying him.

"Henri. Climb to the top of this hill and radio our people in Cap Haitien. Tell them that it is as we planned and to be ready shortly."

The man nodded and ran off.

LePetit rolled his head on his shoulders and then looked up into a sky that still scudded with clouds from the storm. It starts, he thought.

Chapter 2

September 16, 0549 hours
Aboard the freighter *Scylla* approaching
Cap Haitien, Haiti

"Still nothing from the portmaster, Cap'n," said J. B. Bailey, the ship's first officer.

"I did this run once several years ago, but I sure would like to get a pilot aboard," mused the captain, Doug Scholz. "They responding to anything at all?"

"Nada. Even tried a cell phone, but I guess that storm really kicked some ass."

"The damn following sea all the way here nearly kicked *our* ass," responded Scholz. "That was a fast moving storm, but it sure left some crap in its wake. I can't recall seeing so much flotsam and jetsam in the water."

"Yeah, and the color was really off. Even the deep water was pretty roiled. Glad we were in port, and glad it veered out to the east."

The *Scylla*, out of Norfolk, Virginia, was one of that rare breed, an American merchantman. The ship had been named after the Greek goddess the Sea Nymphs were said to protect and was a 270-foot general cargo freighter that had been sitting in Port Everglade waiting out Hurricane Lily. Already loaded with foodstuffs, medical supplies, building material, and three containers of off road motorcycles, she'd been originally scheduled to run to Honduras—which was still trying to recover from a hurricane from last season—with the medical supplies, foodstuffs, and half of the building materials. The rest of the load was scheduled for offloading on the huge six-mile pier that extended off the coast at the town of Progresso in Mexico's Yucatan. A general call for merchant shipping had been received by the home office in Norfolk, and after perusal of the load, the *Scylla* had been chosen to head for Haiti as a relief ship.

Scholz had been the *Scylla*'s captain for three years and this was the third time he'd had a sailing preempted for some kind of government job. He'd started wondering whether there was any connection between his company in Norfolk and another "company" in suburban Langley, Virginia.

"Damn spooks," he said aloud.

"Cap'n?"

"Nothin' J. B. Just thinking aloud. So." He turned to the radar, then to the DGPS. "Nothing out there," he noted. "Punch in the way points for access to the port. Maybe when they see us glowing in the dark they'll get the idea that we're inbound."

Bailey worked on the navigation computer and Scholz looked down the length of the ship toward the land he saw only as a black irregular lump standing above the sea. "Not a damn light to be seen," he said aloud. "They got trashed."

Scholz felt a shudder. "What the fuck . . ."

Bailey looked up wide-eyed. "Shit, Doug, we're in deep fucking—"

Another shudder and then both men were sent flying forward, as the ship slammed onto the sand, rock, and coral of a reef.

Below decks, the chief engineer, whose nose and arm had been broken in the impact, struggled to his feet and managed to disengage both props, then start the engine shut down procedure before passing out.

Bailey had slammed his rib cage into the nav console and broken three ribs. Holding his arm tightly to his chest, he crawled to where Scholz lay on the floor of the deckhouse. "Doug, Doug." He grabbed the captain's arm and shook the man, who moaned, then rolled over, revealing a puddle of blood on the floor.

"Shit!"

The captain groaned but remained unconscious.

Bailey struggled to his feet, grasping the steering station

then pushing himself to the rear wall and the commo gear. He closed his eyes as a black-spotted lens slid over his vision. "Shit," he moaned. He stood still, his hand grasping the microphone of the boat's internal speaker system, then suddenly turned to his right and puked. The force of the contraction made him grasp his rib cage tighter and he fell to his knees, one arm bracing him from falling flat on his face. "Oh, God," he moaned.

As Bailey tried to recover enough to stand and find out what had happened to the *Scylla,* a forty-foot cigarette-style boat with the name *Lady Luck* emblazoned the length of its hull idled alongside the grounded freighter. One of the men on board stood on the bouncing deck, his feet wide apart for balance, and whirled a grappling hook in increasingly larger circles before letting the hook fly toward the *Scylla*. The hook snagged on the first throw, earning the man a "good shot, brudduh" yell from the pilot of the *Lady Luck*.

The man drew the knotted line as tight as the bouncing *Lady Luck* would allow, and two men dressed in camouflage fatigues and carrying CAR-15 automatics strapped to their backs jumped onto the forward deck of the *Lady Luck* and started to climb the rope. The first man disappeared over the freighter's railing before the second started climbing.

As the second man reached the railing, the first man's head appeared about fifty feet forward on the freighter and he whistled loudly. The pilot of the *Lady Luck* turned, waved, checked to make sure the second man had cleared the rope, then yelled to the man on the deck to kneel. He pushed the throttles forward and the *Lady Luck* leapt hard over starboard before returning to an idle and drifting back to the *Scylla*. The man who had whistled tossed down a traditional wire and aluminum-step boarding ladder, and the remaining seven men—all armed with twelve-gauge, twenty-inch barrel, pump shotguns—climbed the ladder and fanned out throughout the ship.

The two men in camouflage headed aft on the freighter toward the towering pilothouse. The one who had thrown the boarding ladder down to his compatriots yelled sotto voce at the other, "Jobo, mon!" The man called Jobo spun around and nodded as the first man indicated for him to go up the starboard side of the wheelhouse. Both started up the outer stairs to where the captain and first officer lay.

Jobo reached the door to the wheelhouse first and looked in through the window. One body lay on its back beneath the large forward windscreen. Jobo undogged the door and walked in.

"Oh shit, what the fuck happened," said J. B. Bailey to Jobo. "We were dead in the middle of the fucking channel, what the . . . ?" Bailey stopped and shook his head, then peered at the man standing before him. "You coast guard or . . . what the fuck is that in your hand?"

Bailey didn't see the man's hand move, but he felt the impact of the machetelike bush axe as it severed his jugular and nearly his C-4 vertebrae. His eyes went wide and he was as good as dead and well beyond feeling when the second blow removed his head from his neck. The body remained kneeling for several seconds, blood erupting from the severed arteries before it toppled over to the floor.

"She-et, mon," said the other camouflaged man, Erla, who had watched Jobo at work. "That's wha' de gives you dis fock-een gun for, nigguh." The man held the CAR-15 in one hand and pointed it at the prone body of the captain. He fired a single round into his head. Scholz's body spasmed once, then lay still. "You a fuck-een savage, brudder."

"I save my bullets for the HNP, Erla," said Jobo. *"Yozesi."*

"Oh yes," laughed Erla. "They *very* surprised, mon."

0645 hours
Cap Haitien, Haiti

The *Lady Luck* returned to Cap Haitien less than ninety minutes after it had left and nine of the men headed off into the city to spread the word. Louverture had provided the first of many good days for the people of Cap Haitien. There was plenty of food on board, plenty of material for shelter, even motorcycles for those that cared. Plus there was all the fuel the boat carried and anything else the people cared to take. The ship was the first gift of Louverture to the faithful. There was no one aboard to say no or to make people pay for the supplies. Louverture had brought the boat to the Haitian people and just left it in the sea for them. All they had to do was help themselves.

Word moved throughout the town's stricken citizens in a laser-fast geometric progression. First hundreds, then thousands moved to the beachfront, searching for any form of transport to reach the boat that could now be seen just sitting two miles off shore. Louverture would provide.

Chapter 3

September 16, 0555 hours
Special Operations Training Camp, Hostage recovery area, Fort Bragg, North Carolina

These guys were pretty good, all things considered, acknowledged Lt. Commander Stanislaus Powczuk grudgingly. Then again, I guess I shouldn't be so surprised. After all, they *are* Navy SEALs, thought the bearded SEAL . . . simply the best of the best.

With the difficulty most people had pronouncing the Cs, Ws, and Zs in Powczuk's name, those in the unit who liked him referred to the number two of TALON Force's Eagle Team as Stan. Those who didn't like him had names that were somewhat longer and considerably more scatological.

The SEALs didn't know Powczuk's name or the name of any other member of the Eagle Team. The "enemy" were members of SEAL Team 6 in this TALON Force–requested exercise. There were seven members of the TALON unit . . . seven my ass, thought Powczuk when he thought of the unit's commo expert, Sam Wong. Jeez, if that little computer geek didn't have DuBois to haul his ass around . . .

A slight movement in the absolute-no-moon darkness stopped his train of thought. The movement blended artfully into the tree just about fifteen feet away. To Stan, it appeared as if the guy had jumped up, waved his arms, and yelled, "Come get me." Stan was good. Behind the legendary Dick Marcinko of Red Cell fame, who Stan resembled in all but height and ponytail, he was the best to come out of the SEALs. Neither Stan, nor anybody but a TALON operative, would have ever gotten this close, nor seen the other man had it not been for the small monocular BSD eyepiece. The Battle Sensor Device was attached to Powczuk's helmet and provided him with a holographic image direct to his retina; it worked better in zero visibility than a Baghdad searchlight. This was the first of the bad guys in the exercise to make a mistake and, small as it was, he was history.

Stan kept his XM-29 at waist level and looked at the target. The BSD computed range and, with about two pounds of pull from Stan's finger, the custom-made "smart rifle" fired what would have been a 5.66mm round that would have literally blown the heart out of the enemy soldier. Since this was an exercise, however, it merely transmitted a laser beam from its millimeter wave sensor aiming device to a receiver on the SEAL's body. To keep the exercise as real as possible—the XM-29 naturally would have been silenced—only the target would hear or know he had been hit. Stan pulled the trigger, saw the SEAL stiffen slightly acknowledging his "death," then relax. He was out of the exercise.

"Down," he mouthed.

"Confirmed, Short Round," came a voice in reply. Sam Wong's.

Stan stiffened worse than the SEAL had. That little geek is gonna pay for that, he thought angrily.

"Cut the crap. Anybody think this is funny?" came the voice of Major Travis Beauregard Barrett, who, on this particular exercise, was monitoring rather than participating.

Good, thought Stan. Travis'll ream his Oriental ass.

If you weren't a TALON Force member, you'd have thought yourself a paranoid schizophrenic. Voices coming out of thin air and all that. And while no one within earshot would have heard Stan say "down," no one would have heard Sam Wong's acknowledgment—or wise crack about the XO's height—either. This was due to a micro-cybernetic implant chip located behind Stan's—and every other team member's—ear. In conjunction with the Battle Sensor Helmet, it transmitted and received messages and a wealth of other data seamlessly.

Sam was one thousand yards removed from what was going on and simply tracking all the TALON operatives. The reports started coming in as the teams converged on the small blockhouse holding the "hostages."

Messages were extremely brief. Sam's equipment tracked each of the five in the field, so identification was not required. A series of messages streamed in as the timed exercise drew to its inevitable conclusion.

"Down." Captain Hunter Evan Blake III's target did the same stiffen-relax jig.

"Down," said Lieutenant Jennifer Olsen.

"Down," came Captain Sarah Greene.

With Greene's message, vox commo ceased. Jack DuBois hadn't signaled a hit.

The team waited anxiously. Even if this *was* a training exercise, thought Stan, no TALON member had ever . . .

"Down," Jack said.

Stan looked into his eyepiece for time confirmation. Eight seconds off. If Jack . . .

Sam's voice came into their heads.

"Wildcats rolling. Take it."

There were five outrider guards—now officially deceased—and three more near the house guarding the hostages. One of the SEALs thought he saw a shimmer move from the woodline, but before he could click his night vision goggles into place, a helmeted shadow stood before him. He, along with his colleagues, were dead before the simulators blew what would have been the doors and the windows off the house. The flashes and deafening explosions of the stun grenades hadn't cleared when two other equally ephemeral armed soldiers went through the doors and windows.

The shimmer had been real and had the SEAL taken it under fire, perhaps he would have scored a kill. But it was beyond even a SEAL's need-to-know of the existence of the LOCS technology. LOCS—Low Observable Camouflage Suite—was a bullet-proof battle dress uniform of the TALON team that, chameleon-like, automatically sensed its surroundings and rendered the wearer practically invisible, save for some heat-wave-like blurring. By the time the SEAL recognized the human form as such, it was far too late. His comrades never even noticed the shimmer. They just "died."

Hostage rescue—a specialty of TALON Force—worked on several general principles. Intelligence obviously, but also knowing the location and layout of target and hostages, and neutralization of enemy personnel were paramount. Recovering the hostages, limiting their injury, and then getting the hell out of Dodge in one piece were the main objectives.

An added factor of realism, four screaming and yelling hostages—unfortunate basic trainees who had done something to *really* tick off their drill instructor—made the recovery exercise as difficult as it would have been in real life. The four were roughly grabbed and shoved out the door as two TALON Force XM-77 Wildcat armored cars roared up to the house. The hostages were unceremoniously thrown in, and the vehicles roared away. The actual recovery operation, from putting the three close-in guards down to vehicle exit had taken twenty-eight seconds.

The five team members shepherded their hostages from the CO's 'Cat. The trainees had been "kidnapped" about three in the afternoon as they approached the mess hall where they'd been sent—ostensibly for backup KP duty—and spent most of the evening being kicked, shoved, pushed, and gleefully abused by the SEAL "enemy."

They'd been gagged and hooded with hands tied behind their backs for that time; none had the clearance to see anything that had happened to them and they'd remained blindfolded throughout the exercise. The SEAL "enemy" simply disappeared after the exercise; they knew that secrecy was the primary rule in the covert-ops business, asked no questions, and "told no tales." It was riskier using the trainees to a certain extent, but Major Barrett had insisted on taking that chance.

"Get them out of here," said Travis as the "hostages" exited the Wildcat.

As it turned out, all the trainees really knew was they'd spent one *very* scary and uncomfortable evening with what seemed like some *very* bad dudes, been rescued by some *other* bad dudes, been thrown in a vehicle, then dumped unceremoniously on a road about ten miles from their camp, according to the road sign that was the first thing they saw when they'd finally freed themselves.

One later thought a female trooper had placed an Army-issue knife in his hand, but wasn't sure. With much fumbling, they'd set about freeing each other, found themselves on the dark, wooded road, and had been standing there rather stunned when the pre-planned five-ton "happened" upon them. They'd also ended up with a much better appreciation of the dangers of military work and would, quite certainly, try extremely hard not to annoy their staff sergeant, John Berkowitz, any further.

Berkowitz had the rest of his platoon out in front of the barracks in formation when his prodigals returned. He dismissed the platoon to mess and hustled the four disoriented trainees into the barracks' latrine.

"Listen mutts. And listen good," he said to the four exhausted "hostages." "That was your E and E course. You get a pass on the escape and evasion exercise in week six, got it? You get a three-day pass instead. Any questions?"

"That was bullshit, Sarge!" popped one of the dumber-or-braver-take-your-pick trainees. "Those guys or broads or . . ."

There's always that 3 percent who don't get it, thought Berkowitz. He didn't know exactly what his shaken charges had been involved in, only that a message had come down to him to provide the meat. The DI glared. "Watch my lips, dumb ass," he enunciated the five words quite carefully and ominously. "I don't know what you did, an' I don't wanna know what you did. I don't care *who* you thought you were with. I don't wanna hear a thing. Understand? You got two choices. Say 'Yes, Sarge,' and rack out for four hours or spend the next four years—if you don't get recycled—in Greenland guarding empty boxes of flyboy equipment. Period. Got it?"

They did.

While the trainees were being "debriefed" by their DI, TALON Force Eagle Team was going through a similar, but less pleasant procedure. The TALON soldiers prided themselves on perfection. Although hostage recovery was part of their SOP, they thought it should have gone smoother. Delta, SEALs, Recon, PJs, Rangers, SAS, SBS, GSG9 . . . they were all good outfits and the cream of their various militaries, but TALON was the crème de la crème of the covert-ops world. And in that world execution often meant the difference between success and, well, execution in a different sense. TALON operation execution had to be precise, and none of the troopers brooked any variance from that.

Major Travis Barrett looked bigger than he was, and that was saying something. Barrett was a ramrod straight six foot-two, but his bearing, build (three hundred sit-ups and push-ups a day will do that to you), and close-cropped military buzz cut made Travis seem even larger. A Texan by birth, his neutral voice made it hard to discern whether he was pleased or displeased with the exercise.

"Gentlemen." Regardless of the fact that two of the team were women, all were officers and Travis addressed them all as "gentlemen." "That was not what I expected. Sam. Screw around in training again you're out."

Captain Sam Wong thought the threat somewhat empty, but shrugged his shoulders in apology anyway. You could never tell with Travis.

Sam was, literally, a genius when it came to electronics, computers, encryption, and communications. If it had to do with bytes or radio frequencies he knew it, did it, invented it, perfected it, or advanced it for Eagle Team. He also knew that he was the weak link in the superbly fit and trained TALON Force, though he assured himself they couldn't do it without him. Well, at least he didn't think so.

Stan smiled at the little wiseass.

"Stan?" quizzed Travis at the smile.

"Trav?"

"Where'd it go wrong?"

Stan started scanning the exercise in his mind. "Well, there was a slight time lapse in the take-outs, and we didn't go. My guess we were five seconds off at the start." He said this without looking at anyone other than Travis.

Captain Jacques Henri DuBois, the largest member of the team at six-foot-five, cleared his throat.

"Sorry, boss," said the giant, black, one-time Force Recon

team leader. "My take-downs have gotten a bit sloppy with the technology, sir."

"And that means . . . ?"

"I slit his throat, sir. It took an extra beat or two to cover the ground unobserved. Jesus, Travis, I gotta keep in practice. This battery-operated shit . . ."

Travis often thought that a look from Jack might kill a man. He fought off the barest trace of a smile. "We have the stealth technology," he said. "Use it. Anything else?" he asked.

"Well," said the XO, "I know we were going for realism, but if we hadn't had to keep the hostages' hoods on—I realize we had to for security—we could've shaved probably eight to ten seconds off the recovery, from recovery to load to egress."

"Fair enough. Jen?" asked Travis.

The stunning blonde trooper had her helmet off and was shaking her hair out of a French braid. "Yes?"

"You left your gloves on my Cat when you returned the hostages."

"So?"

"Did they feel your hand when you gave them the knife?"

"Those bozos? Not a chance!" said the team's intel specialist. "They were yapping a mile a minute and shaking like leaves. They couldn't have felt their own . . . well you get my point." Olsen was the resident Mata Hari; an actress who could become that "special" woman to anybody or everybody as required. Whether it was coquettish co-ed or stiletto-heeled working pro, any man who'd met Jennifer Margaret Olsen saw her exactly as she wanted them to. She realized she'd made a mistake, a rarity for her, but a mistake nonetheless. Olsen—or any member of the team for that matter—abhorred mistakes.

"All equipment stays on until debrief. You know it. Don't do it again."

"Yes, sir." She batted her eyes at the boss, but knew it would have less meaning for him than a glance from that mutt, Alamo, Barrett's real best friend and favorite Texas bloodhound. Damn.

"Speaking of equipment, Travis," said Sarah Greene.

"Sarah?"

"Ah jeez," said Sam. "Not that again. Lookit, we can't get the BSD to work with cyber commo units in a soft hat. Not yet anyway."

"None of us have ever liked the helmets, Sarah," said Stan. "Hell, I hadn't worn one since OCS . . . but even this little nerd here can't get all that technology into a boonie hat."

"Don't need the technology if you're good," offered Jack.

"Yeah, right, you big gorilla," said Sam. Sam and Jack were best friends, an odd couple if ever there was one. No one in or out of his right mind would ever refer to Jack with any other address than "sir" otherwise. "Tell me you don't wanna wear . . . hell, love . . . your BSD and LOCS."

"They're great," said Jack, "but they don't make up for lack of skill. Hell, we all know that." He finished with a big grin.

Sarah jumped back in the repartee. "Look. We have auto trauma packs and health status sensors. We've got more microchips implanted than a damn white mouse, and you're telling me you can't get sensors into a boonie hat? You're supposed to be the damn commo genius." Sarah was the team's doctor, surgeon, and CBW expert. Her left ear had enough holes to whistle when they HALOed, and there were bets among the male members of the team that the granola-eating Meg Ryan–with-black-hair lookalike had a belly-button ring as well. Money was she did, but the payoff was waiting confirmation.

"Another time," said Travis. The conversation stopped. "Hunter. Anything?"

"Hell, nothing with wings or rotors involved," said the team's aviator. "What do I know? I point the XM-29, the guy drops, I shoot anything else that moves, grab a hostage, and go home." Hunter's attitude went along with his *GQ*-good looks, but was belied by his incredible expertise with virtually every manner of craft that defied gravity. Plus, the male members of the team were betting on him to solve the Sarah Greene–belly button mystery.

"And that's supposed to mean . . . ?" asked Stan.

"Sorry, Stan. I had some problems with that new gunship

targeting system . . . when? Er . . . last night and was right in the middle of it when I got the call from Sammy boy here. I'm a little ragged right now."

"Rough life for the flyboys, huh, Blake?"

"Well it ain't exactly as easy as driving a damn boat," returned Hunter.

"Stow it," said Travis. "Okay. That's a wrap. Everybody back to their bases. Sam, what are you doing?"

"Ordering transport, boss."

"Okay."

"For D.C."

Six heads snapped to the small commo expert. "I got a message coming in from the capo."

The feigned indifference and casual mien of the team instantly disappeared. Brigadier General Jack Krauss, the TALON Force *capo de tutt capi*, as Wong referred to him, was their boss's boss. And you never heard from the famed one-handed brigadier unless it was serious.

Chapter 4

September 16, 1400 hours
Office of the Chairman of the Joint Chiefs,
the Pentagon, Washington, D.C.

The two TALON Force commanders entered the room and snapped to attention. Even Stan Powczuk, who was a bit more casual about military courtesy than his commander, fired off a near perfect salute. Regardless of the fact that the TALON Force troops were about as special as any *could* be in the Big Green Machine, one simply had better be as strat as a recruit when the audience consisted of a four star, a two star, and a one star general, all of whom held as impeccable and battle-earned credentials as any soldier that would ever report to them.

It was a normal TALON briefing. Travis Barrett knew all three generals, though he was least familiar with the Chairman of the Joint Chiefs, General George H. Gates. Travis knew the other two on a more personal level. He had been recruited from his beloved armor (Travis was a third generation tanker) into the 5th SF by the commander-in-chief of the Special Operations Command, Major General Samuel "Buck" Freedman. He'd been Buck's number two on a couple of hawkeyes into that almost-thermonuclear mess in the Kashmir. No one ever knew how close things had been to having several million Pakistanis, Indians, Chinese, and assorted Asian Russians turn into glow-in-the-dark corpses. And like most covert-ops missions, no one ever would.

Travis's immediate boss, the TALON Force commander, was Brigadier General Jack Krauss. Krauss looked every bit the same as his contemporaries in the room except for the single black glove he wore. Krauss had lost his hand during an insertion gone awry in some unnamed action in some unnamed place at some unspecified time in the past. Travis had heard it had been a mis-rig on a rappel rope that had ripped the general's hand off. There was also a rumor that it was the result of poor intelligence, a bad mission briefing, and an action that resulted in the loss of three-fourths of Krauss's team on a lrrp into North Korea. No one really knew the actual story and, needless to say, no one had the temerity to ask The fact that Krauss had returned to duty handless was also said to account for the reason that no one, regardless of rank, political position, or connection challenged Krauss (more than once) if he said his men weren't going in.

While artificial limbs had come a long way in the past twenty-five years, they still couldn't function with the facility of a natural hand, and thus Krauss's black glove. Travis thought there was a bit of ego and affectation involved in the black glove as well, though he'd never come close to suggesting that to his boss.

Besides, when you're missing body parts—regardless of how it happened—the military is done with you and it took something along the lines of a presidential order to change that fact. Apparently *some* president of *some* administration had issued such an order in regard to General Jack Krauss.

"At ease, gentlemen," nodded Gates, returning a less crisp salute than he'd received. Gates was instantly aware of what he'd done and realized these men didn't deserve that. Spending too much damn time with politicians, he grumbled to himself.

"Pardon me, General?" asked Stan, drawing an inaudible but nonetheless obvious growl from Travis.

"Nothing, nothing, Commander," said Gates, missing the point. "Sit down, both of you."

"Thank you, sir," said Travis. He snapped a glance at his number two, who affected a "What did I do?" look.

Military courtesy, especially at senior levels, is extraordinarily complicated and governs virtually every aspect of interaction between ranks, whether social or business. But it was all based on respect. Sometimes Stan's lack thereof, whether feigned or intentional, put Barrett off. It was a common trait in the special-ops community. Rank meant little to men whose safety and lives depended on one single thing: the ability of the men they worked with and for to do the absolute right thing at the absolute right time. Respect was earned on that basis, and not given as a result of rank. This was one of the real reasons why few senior military ever stayed in special operations for very long. You punched your ticket in spec-ops and got out while you still had a career. That, of course, assumed you wished to join the rarified atmosphere of multi-star generals.

Travis knew of Gates's history in the very bad mountains of Yugoslavia, northern Greece, the Kuriles, and Kamchatka, and on the most dangerous battlefield of all—that where American politicians tossed booby trap after booby trap at the armed forces. Gates could have easily retired, but instead he accepted the appointment to the JCS and consistently and successfully fought to maintain the integrity, strength, loyalty, and commitment to the men and women who served. If ever a medal was deserved or respect to be given, it was to Gates, thought Travis.

"Okay, gentlemen. Here we go." Gates would start the briefing with the political ramifications and basis for the operation then would probably leave for other duties. The CINC SOCOM would then brief on the overall military picture and then Krauss would hit particulars. Plus correct any of the prior—and senior—generals' remarks should they err.

"This is an odd one, both politically and militarily, because we're not quite sure if it is a TALON Force–required mission."

This was a first for Travis and Stan and they glanced at each other.

"A little background. Haiti. I'm sure you all have heard of the Haitian Vacation, back in the mid-nineties, correct?" This was how the ground forces had referred to a military incursion that had established a democratic political regime in Haiti. "While it did put Aristide—he was the president-elect who had been dumped by a junta, what a surprise—

back in power and it did make things work for a while, it would seem the situation has changed somewhat of late.

"Haiti has been pretty quiet for years. There're still the usual human rights abuses, the DEA still tries to interdict cocaine coming through there, and we keep an eye on it because it's practically swimming distance from Guantanamo. Hell. Even Fidel's slowly but surely heading the way of all dictators.

"There are no more death squads, the poverty level has finally passed that of Rwanda, and there are some functioning schools. In other words, gentlemen, Haiti has—somewhat uncharacteristically—remained the Haiti we all know, yet has failed to draw the eye of those magnificent purveyors of truth and justice, the Fourth Estate. If it bleeds it leads, and if nothing's bleeding they don't care.

"I'm not making a social judgment here. If you've ever been down there . . . well, it is still the second poorest country in the world, but by and large democracy seems to be working, somehow. Probably because we and every other world power have pretty much left them alone for a change.

"Over the past year some blips have been popping on the radar. Those geniuses over at Langley sent a French-speaking operative down and he came away with nothing since only about ten to fifteen percent of the population can speak French.

"Didn't know that did you, Travis?" asked the general in response to Travis's upraised eyebrow.

"That's a new one on me, sir. It *was* a French colony, but . . ."

"We've been teaching that it was a French colony since before I was a pup, but the fact of the matter is that only the upper class speaks French; and damn few of them since Aristide got back into the mix. They started developing a true national identity by making Haitian Creole a national language. And hardly any of the French speakers are truly bilingual. Most of the population, figure about five-and-a-half to six million of them, speak Creole and nothing else," acknowledged Gates. "That's only half of it. There's a fair bit of racism in the country and it has everything to do with why that damn poor place has had such trouble over the years. There's quite a bit of cultural and political tension between the older mulatto elite—this has nothing to do with PC, mulatto's how they refer to themselves—and the black middle class. And any of the folks who live in the cities consider the rest of those in the rural areas as 'outsiders.' " He shuffled through some papers. "Let's see . . . *moun andewo*. Outsiders."

"General, this is all very—"

"Keep your shorts on Stan. I said this was unusual," replied Gates. "Turns out that Langley had an asset down there anyway. They're more screwed with politics than we are, and somehow they missed him. He's worked for them since back in the old Bay of Pigs days."

"Bay of Pigs!" said Travis. "The man has to be seventy if he's a day! What good will that do?"

"That's Langley's problem, not ours, but Langley turns up nothing. By the way, Jack," Gates said to General Krauss, "you do know that Eagle Team's Force Recon element is fluent in Creole . . . both American *and* Haitian?"

"Yes, sir, I am aware of that," replied Krauss. He glanced at Travis.

"Sir, if all you need is an interpreter, then I'm sure Captain DuBois will be happy to TDY to whomever," said Travis.

"Were it ever so simple. We can't find anyone in the service who speaks Haitian Creole except him. And by the way Travis, you might want to amend his two fourteen. It doesn't note that he speaks Haitian, only the Louisiana version."

"Then how . . . ?" asked Stan.

"One of my ADCs was in Force Recon with him and recalled that someone he knew possessed the skill. We tracked it down. Regardless." Gates cleared his throat. "This isn't about an interpreter. It's much more involved than that.

"The blips. First we lose what may or may not turn out to be a dirty DEA agent. Meticulously done with a silenced .22. Most of the drug-trade people are, I'm told, much messier. Then some drug people start disappearing—well, turning up dead mostly in the mountain towns; the odd Jamaican, Colombian, Dominican, usually with some portion of his anatomy mutilated. Hearts, eyes, hands, etceteras, missing. Then there's some noise being expressed at our consulate about some banditry in the hinterlands—which in Haiti means pretty much everywhere except Port-au-Prince and Cap Haitien. Then our ambassador calls State and demands that we send some specialists down, as the Haitians—the Port-au-Prince ones—are sure there's a guerilla war brewing in the mountains.

"Then, three weeks ago—and no one knows this—there's a very professional effort undertaken to snatch the ambassador. The Marine unit accompanying him smells the ambush just ahead of time and manages to get everyone out with not much more than the usual amount of bullet and shrapnel damage to the transport. The gunny's a thirty-year man, and he called it one of the better executed ambushes he's seen, and the man has as many decorations as—no offense gentlemen—an Army man."

The general smiled. There was an almost-to-blows rivalry between any Marine and any member of the Army regarding the awarding of citations. Marines felt, and there was some basis for this, that medals were given out like popcorn in the Army. The fact that the gunny was so well decorated indicated a thirty-year career of considerable amounts of successful combat.

"So. So far nothing that warrants your unit's infiltration, Major Barrett. Do we agree?" The general looked around the table and watched as each man nodded.

"Here's where it gets curious," said Gates. "When we add these incidences up to quite a few smaller but equally skillful military or paramilitary operations that have happened throughout urban Haiti—a bank heist here, a kidnapping here, an assassination there, little things that individually wouldn't warrant attention—we find that there is overwhelming evidence of something, or someone, professional behind it. The NSA can't tap the phones because there's still essentially no phone system in the country worth a damn. We can't get any hard intel through ground agents, sat-intel is virtually worthless unless you like pictures of the jungle or shots of Colombian boats running to and fro, there's nothing coming out of the Dominican Republic, and, believe it or not, nothing out of Cuba as far as the NSA can determine. But something's going on. And that's where things stood until earlier today."

Gates looked at his watch just as a full colonel knocked on the door then entered the room.

"General," said the colonel.

"Gentlemen, I have an appointment on the Hill, and then a briefing with the C-I-C. You now know what he knows, what I know, and what the Secretary of State knows. The C-I-C is adamant that Haiti continue on its own democratic path and that nothing change that. General Freedman will pull the strings together for you. Buck, you're up."

The four men stood and saluted the Joint Chief—who this time returned it as crisply as a Ranger lieutenant straight out of OCS and walked out—then sat down and waited for General Freedman to begin.

1430 hours

"As you may be aware, there was a hurricane down in the Carib last week," started General Freedman. "After reading up some on Haiti I have to agree on General Gates's take. That is one bad-luck island. Hurricane Lily bounced out of the south Atlantic, smacked into the Windward Islands, but remained offshore and outside pretty much. It traveled north along the Lesser Antillies, smacked the hell out of St. Kitts and then Nevis. Then it jumped into the Caribbean proper, bounced off Puerto Rico—apparently there was some extensive damage along the south coast—then jumped to the DR's southern coast and literally bounced off it and headed south. Not bad. Then it did a one eighty and ran full bore into Haiti south of Port-au-Prince and just tore the coast *and* interior a new asshole before pretty much destroying both Port-au-Prince and Cap Haitien. It clipped Cuba, then headed east for the Bahamas. As of this morning it is—so far—headed out to the mid-Atlantic."

"Sir?" interrupted Stan.

"You've been extraordinarily quiet, Stan," said Freedman. "What may I do for you?"

"Are we going in or aren't we? I mean, I realize we're just supposed to do the 'cool' missions, but it's been awhile and we could all use some action. I know you're never supposed to volunteer, but—"

"That'll be enough Commander Powczuk," snarled Travis. "We could *never* use some action. You read me?"

Stan did a mental gulp.

"Sorry, sir," he said rapidly. "That's not exactly what I meant, but—"

"No buts. End conversation. Sorry, General."

One thing you learned in special ops was that there were no easy missions. To be sure there were missions where nothing happened, where everything went as planned, where no one died. But the entire concept of special ops was based on the fact that small units could go in and do what bigger units were intended to do by virtue of cunning, quiet, skill, and surprise. More than that—and rarely spoken except in command circles—was the fact that the small-unit concept was based on manpower expediency. It was *always* better to lose six or seven men rather than a platoon or company. Expendability was a rarely spoken word in the special-ops business, but one that every volunteer lived with. The ramifications of expendability were morally neither justifiable nor acceptable but they *were* a fact. If you went on a military operation somewhere with a small group of individuals, at any given moment the entire operation could go to hell faster than you could blink. This was regardless of training, equipment, or circumstance. It would just happen. It was also the reason why General Krauss guarded the deployment of the TALON teams so fiercely and why Travis had snapped at Stan's cavalier statement of "needing action." In his earlier days, Travis earned a Silver Star and a Purple Heart in Somalia pulling out nineteen dead Rangers from a mission they'd had no business being sent on. It had been a mission that required massive internal firepower that could sustain a long period of engagement. The Rangers weren't designed for that type of battle and had paid a horrific price because someone else had the idea to "send in the Rangers." That would never happen on Travis's watch, and any suggestion along those lines brought back the images of the dead and mutilated Rangers and their support pilots. Those men had died literally fighting to the last bullet because someone used them politically and improperly.

"General? Excuse me, but I'd like to apologize for that last statement," said Stan. "I should know better."

"Relax, Commander," said Freedman, looking at Travis, who nodded to his number two and hit him on the arm with the back of his hand.

"Stan, sometimes . . ." said Travis, shaking his head.

"Yeah, yeah, I know."

Both Krauss and Freedman allowed themselves a small smile. All had "been there, done that" and were part of the special ops *very* private fraternity.

"Back to Haiti," said Freedman. "Lily hit Haiti three days ago. We got a Navy Sea Knight out of Guantanamo down to the ambassador, and the film and commo we got back is pretty impressive. Huge mudslides and massive flooding in the interior. They don't have a very good road infrastructure, but what they had they don't any longer. The cities look like a trailer park after a tornado. Needless to say, no water or electricity. Medical service has always been sparse at best in-country and we've been told it's virtually nonexistent now. The bodies are piling up, so we've got the whole disease process starting. There are three airports with paved runways, but only one can handle C-17s. We're going to throw some old Hercs and 141s in but the lift capacity just isn't there. A Pathfinder unit is ready to go in and try to get things rolling at Delmas, which is about thirteen kliks out of Port-au-Prince. There are eleven other brush strips that are essentially gone. It's going to require an awful lot of rotor equipment to resupply and we just don't have it like we used to. Ah, the peacetime military.

"Anyway, everything's being mustered, and the first merchant ship—we chartered it—was dispatched from Port Everglade two days ago with medical supplies, water purification equipment, basic food, tent cities, etcetera. We haven't heard from it since."

"What do you mean, General?" asked Krauss incredulously.

"Just what I said, Jack. We have a satellite pic of her yesterday evening. Then the satellite didn't take pics anymore. All the DEA radar and whatnot is kaput because of the storm. We've had no radio communication. She disappeared. NSA says someone's been able to access the only comsat with picture capabilities and is shutting it off as it passes. They're trying to re-route some of the ones that shoot Cuba, but they say they're having trouble with jamming."

"If this is going to be a shipboard takedown why not let the SEALs . . ." Travis stopped mid-sentence. "You mean we don't know where it is, period?"

"Exactly, Major. And then the ambassador reported he received a missive of sorts; a rock thrown through his window yesterday morning. Hit one of the maids who actually read it—there's only about a fifty percent literacy rate in the country. She up and quit on the spot. It said—and please, bear with my pronunciations—*Sango has joined force with Ogu Badagris. The mon is mine. Ayiti Libere.* It's signed *Louverture.*"

"Sorry, General," said Travis. "And that means?"

"We didn't think anything of it until the ship disappeared. The Haitian amabassador—who, I'm told got a bit nervous when he was read it—said that *Sango* is the god of the sea in the voodoo religion and . . . I mean Vodoun, not voodoo. Anyway, *Sango* is the god of the sea, *Ogu Badagris* is the god of war. Gentlemen, please suspend credibility for a bit. *Ayiti Libere* is Freedom for Haiti and *mon* is the mountain interior of Haiti."

"And the guy who signed it, Loova whatever?" asked Stan.

"That one is a bit curious, militarily," noted Freedman. "First off, Louverture's been dead since the early 1800s. Second, he was quite the general apparently. He freed Haiti with a guerilla army he raised, trained, and led himself. They say that Napoleon's invasion of Egypt was sort of inspired by this guy since he was the man who drove the Brits out of Haiti."

"Hell, I didn't even know the Brits were there," said General Krauss.

"This Louverture character killed twenty-five thousand

along the way, which was a number that wasn't surpassed until the Huns got hold of the Brits in the First World War. Our people say yellow fever had a lot to do with it, but still . . . twenty-five thousand is quite a number back in 1804."

"But he's dead . . ." said Stan.

"Gentlemen. The national religion with just about any Haitian, Catholicism aside, is Vodoun. Life after the grave, the living dead. Zombies, gentlemen. Zombies. You're going to have to deal with this as part of the mission and while I'm not saying you have to believe it, you'd better accept that most of those you'll encounter *will* believe it at some level or another. I realize it's the twenty-first century, but apparently this old-time religion is still practiced by some seventy million people worldwide. Don't make the mistake of ignoring it or forming opinions based on 'civilized thought.' Remember, placebos work, so it's simply mind over matter. Never ignore someone else's reality."

Stan started to speak, then shook his head and with a hands-out-to-his-side gesture indicated the floor was Travis's. Travis returned the gesture.

"All this goes along with what the general was telling you. There is a sophisticated setup existent in Haiti that no one knows, knew, or could imagine existed. Somebody really knows what they're doing over there, and our guess is they're using the storm to come out in the open. Probably fortuitously, but regardless, something serious is brewing in the Black Republic, and it's going to be your job to find out who, what, and why. There're several things we're concerned about. We need to find out if this is a coup in the making. If it is, we need to know who and why; the Haitians don't need another Papa Doc or the like. They seem to have finally been getting things in order. Secondly, whomever is doing this has the intelligence-slash-electronic capability to mess with our eyes in the sky and that is unacceptable. Third, we've got to be able to get relief supplies in and ensure they go to the right people. We can't be held for ransom, real or imagined.

"Here's the pitch," said Freedman, standing. "These people have a long, arduous, nasty history of suffering and it would seem they're starting to come out of it. Mother nature deals them a bad blow, and now someone is cashing in. We have to know who and why. And stop them regardless."

"General Krauss will give you the rest of the details, and I want an ops plan outline on my desk by 1800," finished Freedman. "As always, you want it, you get it. Any problems, get hold of Colonel Morrisey in my office. This is on a need-to-know as always. You've got carte blanche. Gentlemen."

The three remaining officers rose and saluted as Freedman left the briefing room. Krauss walked to a wall, pressed a button, and a holographic map of Haiti appeared on the wall. "Would you believe we didn't have anything but paper maps of this country until about six hours ago?" he said to Travis and Stan. "General Gates had DoD mapping working on this since we got the ambassador's call about the note. Seems like nobody but this Louverture, a hurricane, and a bunch of sneaker manufacturers have any damn interest in that country."

"Sneakers, sir?" asked Stan.

"It's irrelevant now," said Krauss. "There is no infrastructure of any kind left, so it doesn't matter. Travis, what do you see this as?"

"Sir, this is a different one if everything you've told us holds." Travis stood and addressed the general. "What I see is an island operation on terrain that is essentially mountainous. We've got an unknown force whose politics we have no idea about. We don't know size, we don't have any idea on his AO other than the entire island. We're not sure if he has a force and we don't know what his SOP is. Hell, we don't even know if it is a he. We've got a country that—from what you tell us—is almost in stone-age ruin, and wasn't too hot to begin with. There's a possibility that all our com could be intercepted and apparently it'll be primarily a foot mission since there weren't any roads to begin with and what there was may be pretty much destroyed."

"And," added Stan, "if the fact that this map just came down from DoD is any indication, it would seem that we're going to have to rely on a lot of physical on-site looks rather than map or satnav work. Are the charts of the coast any good?"

"As far as NOAA, Navy, and DEA can determine, the coastal charts are okay," answered Krauss.

"Do we have any assets in-country at all?" asked Barrett.

"Well, yes. There is a small military presence at the embassy. There's DEA, but they're out of the loop on this one, though they'll probably be a source of info at least as far as smuggling goes. Where there's drug money, there are usually guns, so there is the possibility of some connection. There's also an American doctor that General Gates knows who has been working the interior of the country for some years. He suggested you get in touch with her."

"A her, sir?" moaned Stan. "Not one of those do-gooders who hates the military, the U.S., and sees a conspiracy under everything?"

"The general seemed to respect her, though he wouldn't say more than that she'd be a good source of information," answered Krauss.

"General Krauss." Travis turned to his commander. The formality was not lost on either man. "I don't like the idea. This is—if you'll pardon the expression—piss-poor intel. This is a long-term ops that requires a long-term commitment of men and material. That's not our job. You know that, sir."

"Okay, Travis. I agree. Now, don't tell me what I know, don't tell me why it shouldn't be done. Tell me how you're going to find a needle in the haystack that is essentially holding eight million people hostage. I've thought this over carefully. TALON goes in. None of the other spec ops have the talent or training for this and it would take too long for the RA to get anything accomplished. This situation has to be rectified and rectified immediately."

Stan eyed his CO and stood. Both he and Travis knew an order and dismissal when they heard one. They barked "Yes, sir," in unison and saluted. General Krauss glared up at the two men. God, but it was good to be involved with men like this.

"Relax gentlemen," said Krauss. "Travis. Stan. This is serious, but well within the realm of your SOP. Do it. Head down to the SOCOM's office, do the ops plan as best you can, and get your men at Bragg organized. General Bartlet over at Fifth knows you're en route. That's all."

The two TALON Force commanders saluted again. Travis donned his beret, Stan his cover, and the two men left the briefing room.

"Damn," muttered Krauss. He stood and turned to the map and stared at the topographic details. "Damn rough terrain," he said aloud.

Chapter 5

September 16, 1940 hours
Aboard a Warthog C-type, 18,000 feet,
en route to Simmons Army Airfield, Fort Bragg,
North Carolina

Travis Barrett held his chin with his thumb in his own version of the classic thinker's pose as their transport approached Simmons Army Airfield at Fort Bragg.

When TALON Force moved, they did so surreptitiously, but speed was as important. Rather than commandeer a very senior officer's Lear, Travis and Stan traveled in a C-version Warthog. The venerable—ugly to some, but beautiful to any ground troop who's had it flying cover in battle—ground support fighter's cargo version held three people in addition to its pilot. It was fast and drew little attention.

The rest of the team were all assembled at the team's ex-officio headquarters building that stood innocuously on the airfield's perimeter road.

The building's outer facade belied its interior by a factor of about one hundred. A normal concrete block and tin-roof, medium-size, hangarlike structure, circa the Vietnam War era, it was both soundproof and temperature controlled. The interior featured the kind of lighting no military man had ever seen; soft, indirect, but bright enough for any type of work; an office ergonomist's dream. There were windows, but they were merely cosmetic. Any curious, avoiding-duty trooper who peered in the windows would see nothing beyond an empty hangar, courtesy of the images of a permanent hologram security system. If the curious trooper was to think the hangar an ideal place for grabbing some sack time, he would find the only personnel entrance doors locked shut, and a twenty-foot high hangar door seemingly rusted to its runners. If the trooper was seriously intent about entering, he'd find that nothing short of some well-placed plastic shape charges could break the locks or glass. Not even the best of B&E skills would gain entrance, and while the individual involved was frustratingly busy working away with lock picks, crow bar, hammer, or rock, he would find himself set upon by three irate 82nd Airborne Division MPs. Being tired would then become the least of the trooper's problems.

The interior of TALON HQ, one of several scattered on military bases throughout the country, was the epitome of future-tech. Static roof antennae grids covered 360 degrees of the sky and allowed communications every and anywhere without any telltale signs to draw attention to the otherwise empty-appearing hangar. These in turn were wired to a not-too-far-below-CrayVII-like computer system that did everything but think—though listening to Sam Wong have conversations with the various VDUs often brought the computer's supposed lack of life into question. Each of the seven Eagle Team members had an individual work area and locker system for working on his private specialty and storing his personal gear. There was also a briefing area composed of six chairs behind a long wood table facing a large HDTV screen. The table had six pop-up computer stations. Behind that was the long rigging table for parachute packing. A common area, complete with a decent array of exercise equipment and a well-appointed, militarily speaking, kitchen completed the HQ.

Stan's work area—called the coffin by the rest of the team—was the only one separated from the others. His "office" was an interior block house made of titanium, steel, Kevlar, and concrete that could contain virtually any explosion should the commander err so dramatically. It wouldn't save Stan, but it would protect the rest of the team and the equipment in the hangar.

The remainder of the team's transport and heavy armament—Wildcat armored cars, IA-Hummers, cruise missiles, and a V-22 Osprey among others—were housed at another innocuous field-side hangar at Pope Air Force Base, always serviced and ready for rapid deployment.

The C-10 Warthog taxied to an unused hangar—the field was actually home to the 18th Weather Squadron—the cargo door opened, and Travis and Stan got out, automatically holding their headgear as the plane revved, spun, and taxied away. A regular Army Hummer pulled up; Stan jumped into the back, and Travis sat next to the driver.

"What's the story, boss?" asked Lieutenant Jennifer Olsen.

"Save it. Let's get to base," answered Travis, making a chopping motion with his hand at the windscreen. Five minutes later they arrived at the HQ. Jen lifted a small wooden square—it appeared to be a wood patch on the metal door—placed her hand flush on the screen that appeared, and, after a brief moment, the door slid open, and they walked in.

The four team members in the hangar—Hunter, Jack, Sarah, and Sam—gathered around. Stan walked to his area, disrobing as he went; he hated formal mufti, but loved the comfort of BDUs. Travis removed his jacket as he made his way to the briefing area, the rest of the team behind him.

"Sam, get the latest downloads from JTF and SOCOM. The situation was still fluid when we submitted our ops plan to Generals Krauss and Gates. There should be more info ready by now."

Five sets of eyes and eyebrows went through various contortions at that little tidbit. It was a rare occasion when Travis worked on the fly—at least insofar as briefings went. Once you were on the ground, well that was an entirely different ball of wax.

Travis walked to a refrigerator in the common area and withdrew a quart bottle of water, twisted the cap off violently, and took a deep swig. He placed the bottle on the briefing table and started loosening his tie.

"Stan, c'mon," he barked. "Let's get this show on the road."

"Right there, Travis," came a voice from the other side of the hangar. Acoustics had also been attended to in the construction of the HQ. Stan could have participated from where he sat lacing up his jump boots.

Stan strolled over, smacked Sam in the back of the head for the hell of it, and caught an elbow from Jack for his pains.

"Okay, okay," said Travis in preamble.

"You guys are gonna love this one," said Stan. Travis's head barely nodded in agreement with his number two.

"Sam. Downloads?" asked the big Texan.

"In about three-oh seconds, boss," said the NSA expert.

"You're gonna have a lot to do with this one I think, lightweight," said Stan to the electronics expert. His hand was at waist level as he leaned back in his chair and he made a pointing motion upward with his finger. Sam did *not* like airborne insertions, and an airborne insertion was what was in store.

"Screw you swabbie. Sir," answered Sam.

"C'mon guys. We got enough shit going on here," said Travis tiredly. "Downloads?"

"Here ya go boss," he said, handing him four sheets of paper. "There's also a hologram, loaded and ready for the screen."

"Punch it up," said Travis as he read the pages carefully. A detailed three-dimensional map of Haiti formed on the HDTV. As Travis perused the updates, the other six activated their individual screens and the map image appeared there as well.

"For starters, folks," said Travis, "you'll need full portability, Sam. And I mean full. Problems to be encountered may consist of: no power, no internal uplink facilities that we'll have use of, possible intercept of all uplinked material—"

"What!" yipped Sam. "What the hell—?"

"—electronic jamming capability," continued Travis barely missing a beat. "We'll want to use a full complement of UAVs. Have at least two Predator Fives ready to drop at a later date. Bring two 'Birds and I want everyone to have access to 'Flies." The UAVs—unmanned aerial vehicles—were portable eyes in the sky. The Predator was the length of a motorcycle with wings, the Hummingbird was a model airplane–size rotary wing craft, and the Dragonfly was a palm-sized video-only UAV.

"Boss, if we're . . . I mean if I'm jumping in . . ." started Sam.

"Can it. We'll cover that in the ops plan."

Travis turned to Stan. "I need to have two go-fast boats on alert and ready to either drop or cargo in. Don't know where or when."

"What about we take two assault RIBs and have three flying boats on call instead. If we need to move fast we can drop the flyboats and two-man them to destination."

Travis thought. "Okay. But make sure the RIBs are gunned for bear. I doubt we'll use the flying boats, but Hunter, have the techs spec 'em and have 'em ready to load anyway. Pilots'll be Hunter with Stan, Jen with Jack, Sarah with me. Sam you're grounded—or backup—if that comes into play.

"Sarah. Malaria treatment, dengue fever, the water's bad, there'll probably be typhoid outbreaks among the indigents. God knows what else. Arrange a rock-solid support package—not tons mind you—but enough to help the locals should that option occur. So far it looks like the only opposition armament is small arms . . . though bows and arrows aren't going to surprise. You shouldn't have any mass trauma problems. You know the rest of the routine. Oh, and load everybody up on the stay-awakes.

"Jen. The only thing I can think of is you might have to pass for black."

Jack choked. "She's a goddamn Swede," he said in between laughing spasms. The rest of the crew grinned as Jack spit soda out of his nose and dug in his pockets for a handkerchief. "Jeezus, man, she's good, but how the hell is she supposed to pull *that* off?" Jack was still laughing.

"From the sounds of this I don't think she'll need to, but who knows," said Travis.

"Well," said Jack, finally serious. "If we're going to Haiti you better do a quick Web search on Vodoun . . ." The blank stares made him explain. "Voodoo to you white folk, but it's spelled V-O-D-O-U-N. Maybe you'll get some ideas there. Ya' never know," he said shaking his head.

"Hunter. Aside from the flying boats. This is an MFF ops: HALO, full rig. Mountain DZ. We'll discuss HARPs later, but it won't be HAHO. Make sure the Osprey's ready to go with follow up gear. Get with Sam and see what kind of ADC you two can come up with.

"Jack. Get over to Third SF ASAP. See Mike Clancy, he's the CO. Tell him I gotta have anything he's got on Haiti. Go now. If he's got anything, it'll be part of the briefing when you get back."

"I'm outta here sir," said the huge black Marine.

"Er, Jacques Henri?"

"Oui?"

"You do speak Haitian Creole, correct?"

"I get by in it pretty good. My momma's girlfriend used to baby-sit me and that's all she spoke. Played hell with my language skills for a looong time," he said smiling.

"Good. Anybody Clancy turns you on to, get the juice out of them. You got two hours."

"Will do, boss."

"Stan. No hard targets that we can tell, right? Lots of plastic, good amounts of det cord. Mix the fuses. We'll use what indigenous stuff we come across.

"Okay folks," said Travis as he clapped his hands. "It's 2015 hours. Three ninety maxes on your equipment loads. HALO. Expect a lot of heat and a lot of humping, we're gonna be walking this one. Full combat packs. Everyone back here at"—he looked at his watch—"2245 hours for briefing. We're at Go Minus 6."

2020 hours
TALON Force HQ,
Fort Bragg, North Carolina

TALON Force was aptly named. And while the troopers were grateful for the combat systems it provided, they often made fun of what the unwieldy acronym stood for. Currently, Sarah's and Jen's Total Assholes Low On Nerve was the female troopers' favorites, while Jack's Testosterone Armed Ladies Occasionally Nude, was the male troopers' answer.

Regardless of in-house banter, the Technologically Augmented Low Observable Networked Force was just that, however. In an era when virtually everything was computerized and silicon chipped down to the proverbial pinhead—an inappropriate euphemism since memory chips were now atomic-size—TALON Force had access to the most compact, advanced, and working technology available.

The advent of the DUT-HA (Danish University of Technology–Hydrogen Atom) chip technology, where a single hydrogen atom bounced back and forth creating the on and off states of a computer chip, had truly ushered in a new age of miniaturization. Along with Texas Instrument's Oh-7 transistor technology—a transistor that was smaller than .07 microns (a thousand times thinner than a human hair), miniaturization had reached an all-time low, so to speak. With the money—even in so-called peacetime—that the military had access to, it was able to reap the extraordinary benefits of this movement to the infinitesimal.

Foremost in the TALON arsenal was their camouflage BDUs—the Low Observable Camouflage Suite (LOCS). Microsensors were woven into a tough bullet-proof fabric that automatically sensed its background and blended into it. While it didn't necessarily render the wearer completely invisible, it provided a heat-wave-like shimmer that matched the surrounding flora and took more than a casual glance to spot. A foe who thought he had seen something moving would nearly always rub his eyes, assuming a natural blur of vision. By then what he "thought" he had seen either was gone . . . or the foe was. A thermal imaging unit could make the suit more apparent and distinguishable from its surroundings, but in the type of missions TALON Force carried out, it was rare to run into that sophisticated a foe. The suit ran off a power pack that held a seventy-two hour charge, and also powered other equipment, but would deplete all juice if run continuously for more than six hours straight.

As electronic based as much of the TALON equipment was, there was the need for a power source above and beyond what was inherent to the various technologies. A hypercapacitor belt that contained charged cells of microconducting materials acted as a backup system for the entire battle ensemble. It could run selected portions of the system or power the most power-hungry system, the LOCS, for approximately thirty minutes.

The Battle Sensor Helmet acted as ballistic protection, as any helmet should, and it also acted as a satellite transceiver. It not only provided communications but also any information that was digitally transferable; i.e., just about everything. It beamed voice commo from the under-the-skin biochips via a network of comsats to other members as well as to Joint Task Force headquarters. Regardless of terrain or line-of-sight restrictions, TALON Force remained in constant communications with each other and their HQ.

Another unique weapon was the nonlethal RF Field Generator woven into the BDU's wrist. It generated electromagnetic pulse bursts that rendered most electronic devices inoperable. It could also short-circuit the LOCS for several minutes, something Hunter discovered on a mission, much to the chagrin of the suddenly quite visible Jack.

There were several other biochips implanted in all the troopers that performed full-time health status checks as well as directing an Automatic Trauma Med Pack (ATMP) woven into the BDU to perform wound cauterization and administer necessary drugs or fluids if a TALON member was wounded.

Most of TALON Force had gotten over the "bionic man" psychological phase after a month or two; it was a pre-enlistment psych requisite that they would be able to handle this less-than-personal invasion of their bodies. Besides, once the kinks had been ironed out and they were trained in the use of the equipment, everything actually worked the way it was supposed to.

The team members in the HQ were busily packing their gear. Though each had specialty equipment to be concerned with, the overall layout of the equipment they wore was identical. Since they were packing for a HALO insertion, they would all be wearing insulated jump suits and therefore their combat packs, which would be carried in front-mounted equipment bags that quick-release-clipped to their parachutes, had to contain their ground wear as well as their mission equipment.

Stan busied himself with an explosive kit; Sarah checked

everyone's trauma kits and handed out nutrition supplements and amphetamine additions to the kits. Hunter loaded the UAV control unit, while Sam hemmed and hawed over computer gear that he and Jen would share the weight of.

Time flew past as every piece of equipment was checked by each individual, swapped, and re-checked by someone else, then checked again. There was no room for error.

Chapter 6

September 17, 0538 hours
Aboard a 23rd Air Force, 1st Special Operations Wing C-141, 31,000 feet over the Caribbean

Sam started hearing the humming as soon as the cabin depressurized and the team went on oxygen. The temperature dropped and even the exposure suits they wore wouldn't keep the chill of the minus-80 degree air out for long. The seat heaters were typical military; they had relatively little effect on comfort, though Sam wouldn't like to be in the plane without them. But that damn humming. Where the hell was it coming from?

Maybe I'm getting a buzz from the O_2, he thought. He looked across the cabin at Miss Goody Granola. Sarah's pretty green eyes were sparkling, but Sam figured that was from the super oxygenation the breathing system was supplying. The humming was getting louder.

"Anybody hear that?" he said. No answers came back, and he realized that none of them was wearing their BSHs. Damn.

Sam reached to pull off his O_2 mask then realized the stupidity of that. Besides, it would be breaking stupid Army SOP for HALO ops. What the *hell* was that humming? And it was getting louder.

He saw Sarah elbow Hunter and caught the twinkle in his eye. Maybe they were all tripping away on O_2 hallucinations.

Voom, voom, voom, voom.

Sam looked down his stick and noticed that everyone seem to be breathing harder.

Voom, voom, voom, voom.

A voice suddenly stood out over the hum, and immediately was joined by several others. They sang to the tune of the "Battle Hymn of the Republic":

> "*He was just a rookie trooper and he surely shook with fright*
> *As they fastened his equipment and made sure his pack was tight*
> *He had to sit and listen to those awful engines roar*
> *And he ain't gonna jump no more.*"

"Gaaaahdamn you guys!" yelled Sam into his mask. Sam didn't like jumping out of perfectly good airplanes and fully subscribed to the theory of every ground-pounding military person when it came to parachuting: the only thing to fall out of the sky was bird shit and idiots. The fact that parachutists voiced the same sentiments as often as nonjumpers merely indicated that jumpers were seriously impaired psychologically. And this stupid song that they all sang whenever there was anybody around who had the slightest sane, normal, and sensible trepidation about relying on some diaphanous material to save his life was merely another indication of intellectual deficiencies—and not physical superiority.

The song was *the* hymn of U.S. paratroopers everywhere and chronicled a rookie's first jump into oblivion. The refrain was three lines of "Gory, Gory, what a helluva way to die" with a final line of "And he ain't gonna jump no more."

Sam knew all the words and knew the rest of the team—even the boss—would sing the entire damn song, right down to "*He hit the ground, the sound went splat, his blood went spurting high . . .*" etcetera, etcetera.

The song continued and Sam found himself, as usual, finally singing along as well. It *was* a catchy tune.

Sam had the least amount of jumps of anyone on the team. He hated jumping, thought it tactically inefficient, militarily as passe as cavalry, and considered it a pure waste of endorphins and adrenaline that could be better used down the line. After all, a man only had so much courage.

And after the near disastrous jump into northern Iraq strapped to Jack DuBois, Sam had been ordered back to jump school.

The fact that Sam now had over 250 free falls and 75 HALOs and HAHOs had done little to change his opinion of jumping. He hated it as much today as he did the first time he stood on the cables at Benning and the first time he heard this ridiculous song. Of course, after the song was done no one was going to give him the option of leaving like they did on that first day. That had amazed Sam. After the song, a black-capped jumpmaster climbed the podium and in the silence that had followed the song's conclusion, announced that anyone who didn't think they had what it took to be a paratrooper was excused. Fifteen people out of the three hundred soldier class left. Sam often pondered what had made him stay with the rest. He, after all, was supposed to have a brain.

Perhaps it had been the look that Sergeant First Class Dick Ma had given him that day. Ma was the largest Asian person Sam had ever encountered in his life. Sam had been the only other Asian in the class and naturally Ma singled him out. He'd made Sam's life as miserable as possible for the four weeks of jump school, but he'd also been the jumpmaster who pinned on his wings and who watched over him at post-graduation "prop blast," the object of which seemed to be to get as drunk as possible. Sam did, and remembered nothing more of that event other than noticing he'd awakened neatly tucked into his bunk the next morning. He'd run into Ma again at HALO school and noticed the pride with which the big sergeant had saluted him when they met. Ma was also their jumpmaster for this mission.

HALO'd been so much different than jump school. Even though most of the paratroopers had tremendous amounts of jumps under their belts, this was an entirely different ball game. It was like the difference between scuba diving 180 feet on air and 600 feet on mixed gas. Same idea but the consequences and eventuality of a screw up grew geometrically. Some troopers washed out—an amazing thing to Sam—but he hadn't. He hated every jump and would always hate jumping, but he always jumped. Never once had he frozen in a door.

The theory behind HALO was simple. When all went well it provided a means of insertion that followed the "no trace in, no trace out" concept of small unit covert ops. Only extremely alert radar operators could discern the drop, and they rarely did. The transport always flew commercial routes at commercial levels, twenty-five thousand feet and above. No matter what the country, somebody's commercial aviation overflew it. The insertion transport tucked in the commercial plane's radar shadow, with or without prior permission, flew its route, and dropped its load. A half-dozen unrecognizable-from-the-scatter blips weren't going to be picked up. You tracked to your insertion point and pulled your chute under the radar for an unseen touchdown. Theoretically.

HALO jumpers had knocked each other unconscious (a real bloody mess at speeds of 180-plus miles per hour), passed out from equipment malfunctions, had auto openers fail, missed targets woefully, drowned, crashed and burned, and, the scariest of all, had misreads of their altimeters. The speed of the jumper's fall created a low-pressure pocket above the altimeter, causing it to read higher than it actually was—not a great idea if you're going into a very hot place with a very low opening, and a *really* bad idea in mountainous DZs. No, HALO was a completely different ball game.

Personal equipment loads had to be light. The RAPs had come a long way, but the total suspended weight limits were still governed by physics; you couldn't exceed 390 pounds total suspended weight even with today's chutes. You had to factor in body weight (Sam, Sarah, and Jen had a leg up on this over their compatriots), oxygen gear, your LOCS and BSH, weapons, and equipment. Even though TALON had the ultimate in miniaturized equipment, it still was gear-intensive, and it all had to be factored in. If you had a water-ops it was even more equipment intensive, since you required breathing apparatus and more.

Each team member looked like a walking pile of dark-colored junk. There was no discernible human shape, except for a head, and even that was helmeted and masked.

The only time anyone looked somewhat human was during freefall, when arms and legs were splayed in that familiar arched crucifixion look that maintained body stability. You had your main wing and reserve, an eighty-pound combat pack or kit bag where your lap should be, XM-29 down your left side, O_2 unit side mounted, and more. Everything had to be easy to completely jettison or deploy down a tethered line before touchdown—or you had a tendency to hit the ground a lot harder than your body's SOP could take.

"Ten minutes to TOT [time on target]," said Jumpmaster Ma, interrupting Sam's reverie.

Shit. Here we go.

The atmosphere in the plane turned all business as the team prepared for the insertion. Eyes were generally straight ahead as each jumper did a hand check of equipment. If you had to look at something to figure out where it was or how it worked or where it was rigged, you were out of luck in a jump. Everything had to be in a certain spot, rigged a certain way, and available and operable by touch—and experience—alone. The entire team rigged alike. Any modifications to SOP rigging had been put through a test procedure before being incorporated. Any equipment accident or mishap was investigated and if it turned out to be a rigging problem, the rigging was changed, simplified or modified as need be. Then it went through a test procedure before the adaptation was okayed and shared with all HALO jumpers.

"Check oxygen," said Ma.

This command was issued at least twice, but always immediately after the ten-minute TOT warning. Sam considered it redundant. If it wasn't on, I'm out cold already, he thought.

The seven jumpers signaled an okay to the jumpmaster.

The jumpmaster conferred via his helmet com with the pilots. He turned to the jumpers, gave them expected wind speed, then called for them to arm their ARRs (automatic ripcord release). Each jumper pulled the pin, arming the auto-canopy release; if they passed the pre-set deployment altitude without opening, the ARR was supposed to take over. No one liked to think about what would happen if it didn't.

Travis, Hunter, Jen, and Sam were seated along one side of the craft, with Stan, Jack, and Sarah on the other. Sam looked diagonally across at Sarah and she winked at him. He nodded his head in response. Jack looked across at Sam and gave him a thumbs-up, which he returned with two thumbs. The big man smiled through the oxygen mask.

"We're depressurizing, gentlemen," came Ma's voice. The ambient noise grew, everybody's ears popped, and the cold increased tenfold.

"We are at three minutes."

Eyeballs locked on other eyeballs. Sarah's eyebrows rose, twisted, and torqued in silent communication with Jen across the cabin. Stan's gloved fingers wiggled like Willy Sutton's getting ready to crack a safe. Jen's legs pistoned on the balls of her feet. Hunter yawned . . . not an easy task through the oxygen mask. Jack rolled his head as much as possible on his shoulders. Two of Travis's fingers were making a cutting motion; he wanted a cigar. Sam stared across the cabin at the hydraulic lines; he'd mentally made his jump already and was centered in some very calm place—on the ground.

Ma held his mask to his face. "Stand up."

The seven rose and checked the equipment of the man in front of them. When finished, he patted the man on the head. The last man turned and was checked by the jumper he'd checked. Jen tapped Sam, Jack tapped Sarah. They also faced the jumpmaster. All of them had their left hand on their oxygen bailout bottle valve and their right on their flow meter.

"Move to the rear."

The cargo ramp lowered, revealing miles and miles of nothing. Zip, zero, nada. If HALO wasn't extreme enough, try it at night.

Each parachutist tightened the combat pack straps around their legs, adjusted their goggles one more time, turned the valve on their bailout bottle, checked the flow meter, then disengaged from the plane's oxygen console before moving to within three feet of the ramp.

The jumpmaster switched to hand signals and signaled

"Stand by." All seven jumpers returned the signal. They were about fifteen seconds from go. Ma looked at everyone's face, gave a quick nod to Sam, and then quickly threw both arms with fingers pointed down toward the floor. The team nearly mass exited.

The buffeting is what you first notice when leaving a plane at high altitude, then the cold and the speed. It always reminded Sam of those winter days when he was a little kid and the cold was just too much. It was the kind of cold that ate at you when you'd spent the entire day sleigh riding, were wet, exhausted, and heading home just as it turned dark. It got so cold you didn't think you'd ever be warm again and all thoughts of the fun you'd had, the trouble you were going to get into for being late, the homework you had to do was all gone. There was just you and a frozen face, numb toes and fingers, and a time-warp long walk home towing a sled that got heavier by the minute. The cold wouldn't go away, wouldn't stop hurting.

The cold at twenty-five thousand feet was like that, but Eagle Team wasn't at twenty-five thousand any longer, and the troopers were moving fast into increasingly warmer air. Sam saw four pinpoint light beacons to his right and slowly scanned for two more. One. No more. He dropped his right shoulder slightly and crabbed toward the lights just as they hit cloud cover.

He stopped his sideways movement and stabilized his body position. The clouds were thick with water, but also with warmth. The oxygen had his pupils dilating and he could see fairly well within the confines of the cloud; he couldn't see any of his teammates but he could see light. Since night jumping—HALO or otherwise—was one of the most psychologically adverse disciplines, any visibility was well appreciated. The oxygen increased one's night vision and for that reason the team would stay on O_2 until touchdown.

The clouds started thinning, and Sam spotted the first personnel marker, then another, and another. Four, five . . . and six. Somebody had been either above him or far off to his left. He keyed on the middle jumper and closed to within seventy-five horizontal meters, but stacked above by about a hundred. The jumpmaster had calculated all the wind drifts to the opening point and the forward throw created by the momentum of the plane. Ideally the middle man—the fourth "man" in this jump was Jennifer Olsen—in the formation should be centered on the target DZ, and the other jumpers would key on her. The TALON team just had to fly to the DZ which, as he'd found out many jumps ago, actually showed up where it was supposed to. Most of the time.

Each jumper carried a small self-powered laser light atop his head, pointing backward. The units were preset for burn time and would automatically extinguish when they reached their canopy release point. That was scheduled to pop at twenty-five hundred.

Sam looked sideways at his left wrist and checked his altimeter. Thirteen thousand. At twelve, they'd check azimuth and adjust. He looked out to his right wrist. They were on course, there'd be no shift.

His arms were getting tired holding his body stable and he toyed with the idea of doing a roll for a break, but this was a real-world mission, no time to screw around. He wondered why he hated jumping so much.

Ten thousand. Nine. Eight.

The team started to line up vertically, closing their dispersion to fifty meters. That was tight, and if you misjudged it you could end up with a face full of canopy. If you misjudged it badly enough—maybe you were a fraction off the other jumpers' release time—you and the jumper below would die before you knew what happened.

Seven. Six. Five.

Altimeter check nearly constant. Eyeballs snapping back and forth between extended wrist and the other jumpers in the formation. Quick peek at the compass.

Four. Three.

Pull the son of a bitch.

Bam!

The chute opening jerked the entire world to a stop. Every piece of equipment that had been fastened so tight that his body had been in a sort of Quasimodo position came loose. Sam looked up into the barely moonlit sky and checked his canopy. A-okay.

He looked around and counted. Got six, he thought. All

the other Eagle Team troopers were doing the same. Jen immediately started the approach glide. The DZ—picked from a three-week-old DEA flyby—should be within a klik's radius of their opening. The other six keyed behind her.

Jen led the downwind leg and spotted the two terrain features—a bald mountaintop with a river running east-west along its base—and adjusted the glide. At thirteen hundred feet she spotted the DZ and headed downwind toward it about a half-klik to its north. The sliver of moon and their oxygen-enhanced vision provided ample visibility. This wasn't a nasty night drop.

Sam could tell there was next to no wind from the lack of adjustments he had to make to the ram chute's movement; it was a piece of cake as night HALOs went.

The seven chutists sailed past the DZ, each looking at altimeter and the DZ. Not a soul around. The DZ was a deforested or overcultivated field surrounded by low bush then a treeline, but big enough to put two Ospreys into at the same time; a nearly perfect DZ, though in any wind conditions the treeline could become problematic.

Jen started a gentle ninety-degree turn back toward the DZ and into the wind—the base leg—and applied about 50-percent brake to the canopy. They all followed suit and the formation slowed appreciably, each jumper about twenty-five meters up and above the preceding one to avoid any turbulence caused by the ram air chutes.

At one hundred feet Jen released her combat pack on the twenty-five-foot line, laid on some more brake, and flared to a stumbling stand-up, dead center in the DZ. She quick-released her combat pack, collapsed the RAP, and released her XM-29. Travis, Jack, Hunter, Stan, Sarah, and Sam followed her in.

TALON Force Eagle Team was operational.

Chapter 7

September 17, 0700 hours
Mount Tchicharan, Haiti

With the entire team on the ground, the first order of business was sterilizing the DZ and gearing up. The seven worked at assigned tasks. After collapsing his RAP, and jacking a round into the XM-29, Jack moved with his entire kit to the north of the DZ. A clump of high grass with a thin tree growing out of it provided all the cover he needed. There he unpacked his combat bag, dug out his helmet, and powered up the Hyper Capacitor Belt. He flipped down the battle sensor device of the BSH and started scanning the sector 120 degrees to his front. The muzzle of the smart rifle followed every eye movement, tic, and blink. He was sweating heavily as he opened his insulated jump suit, but it was a welcome relief from the nearly paralyzing cold of the jump. Hunter Blake moved to the southwest and Sarah Greene to the southeast, where they both quietly mimicked Jack.

Sam took care of his RAP, then knelt low next to his combat pack and also powered up his HCB and donned his BSH. His immediate job was to acknowledge the team was down and operational.

"Aerie One?"

"Go," came the remarkably clear reply immediately. Aerie 1 was the command and control for the mission and was located in the bowels of the Pentagon back in Washington, D.C. It was quite possibly General Krauss on the other end of the earth-sat-earth transmission. Regardless of whether Krauss was actually on the line, he closely and personally monitored all insertions of TALON teams.

"B-One-Odin. In and clean," said Sam. Hardly a sound emanated thanks to the jaw-mounted biochip transmitter. All the team members could use the transmitters with varying degrees of audibility, but Sam was best at speaking without actually making any external sound. Regardless of who was speaking—and Jack had the hardest time keeping the noise down—anyone outside a six-foot diameter would be hard pressed to hear any of the TALON team communicating.

B-1-Odin was the team signifier for the insertion. It meant the team was in, and there had been no injuries. Once the team was saddled up and on the move, the signifier would change and then would continue to change on a daily and preplanned basis. Someone at HQ was on a Nordic kick and there was to be a lot of Valhalla Viking crap on this mission.

"Roger. Out," came the reply.

The actual time of the transmissions were less than a millisecond each due to the compression the communication software provided. Until Sam could figure out who was doing what with computers and *their* satellites, commo would be kept to the minimum. Something like this mission was a reason why pretechnology skills had to be maintained as well as the post-tech skills. Sam wasn't great with the former, but he didn't think anyone was better than he with the latter and anticipated no problem outfoxing the smart-ass running the operation inside Haiti.

Travis, Stan, and Jen moved to the north behind the big Marine, tapped him, and as soon as Sam joined them, the five moved about twenty-five meters into a thickish woodline. Jack said one word—"Moving"—and the two shadows of Sarah and Hunter rose from their position and slowly fell in with the others. This entailed walking backward and sideways, constantly covering the sectors of approach.

Quiet movement was an art form, and covert operations depended on that. In the jungle and woods there was only one sound that could rarely be explained away and that was the sound of metal on metal. In heavily bambooed mountains that sound could sometimes be mimicked, but to discern the difference was a survival skill. The best bet was to not make any metal-on-metal contact. And while other sounds could be explained away, "quiet" movement ruled. Generally foot movement was heel and toe, the heel placed slowly, the toe feeling through the boot for things that would crackle, snap, and give a location away. Hollywood interpretations of what all seven did for a living always provided much amusement. Small groups of commandos running about the jungle, hiding behind trees and rocks, never making noise was a laugher for anyone who'd ever actually done it. Noise control was the name of the game if you wanted to stay alive.

Of course, it would be hard to sustain any celluloid excitement if the facts were ever portrayed. In "Indian" territory—anyplace where the hostiles had the home field advantage—movement could quite often be as little as five hundred meters in an eight-hour day. Distance covered depended on the mission, the terrain, and the enemy concentration, but fast movement in covert ops only happened when it all hit the fan—and then you could never move fast enough.

The five not providing cover were the first to gear up. They divested themselves of the hot jump suits and donned their complete LOCS BDUs. Each person stopped as Hunter and Sarah closed on the location, then continued quietly gearing up.

Travis finished first, checked the time in his BSD, and looked at the others.

Until they could establish some kind of operational area for their prey, they'd rely as little as possible on the commo, though even the activation of the BSH was sending some sort of signal that could possibly be picked up. Until they knew the sophistication level of their bad guys, everything was going to be very touchy-feely—a true test of field expedience. Travis looked at his troops and nodded. Sarah, Hunter, and Jack started to get into their battle dress as Travis, Stan, and Jen stepped ten yards away. Sam followed Travis.

Travis and Sam settled to their knees side by side. Sam tapped Travis and made a shoulder shirking, one-hand out gesture and nearly hit the major with his smart rifle that automatically moved when he moved his left arm out.

Travis had taken a bit of time to get used to the brilliant little NSA draftee, but sometimes . . .

He gave the already contrite-looking Sam a hard look, then nodded his head in agreement. There wasn't anyone here, there didn't seem to be anyone coming, and he doubted anyone would. But "seem" and "doubted" weren't words that would keep you alive long. Until they could get to their target and get Sam set up, this was going to be handled as if they were inside a renegade Chinese republic with a nearly technologically equal foe. Complacence kills.

Travis barely detected Sarah's movement. Growing up in the mountains of Vermont was good training for quiet movement. That woman is good, he thought. Sam hadn't noticed at all. She made a circular motion with her left forefinger and the three quietly rose and headed deeper into the forest and uphill. The seven joined.

Travis nodded to Jack, who headed off on point. Regardless of his size, the big man could move oh-so quietly. He watched until Jack was almost out of vision, then nodded to Hunter and then Sarah. Sam was looking the wrong way and Travis tapped his arm with the XM-29's muzzle, took a deep breath, nodded to Jen and Stan and headed after Sarah. Sam stayed close. Stan walked tail.

Patrol movement was a well-thought-out choreography. The point man's job was to cover the front from roughly ten to two o'clock. The second would cover the left, third right. The team leader and commo man were in the middle and actually had no recon responsibility, but were left to eyeball wherever. The tailgunner covered where the team had come from and spent an inordinate amount of time walking backward, checking for broken twigs, replacing dislodged ground cover, and covering the left rear flank. Jen in this case would cover Stan as well as the right rear flank. The team, if working in a full complement, always walked in this order.

As well as the order of march being mandated, there were also skills—practiced and practiced and practiced—concerning every conceivable action that might occur in a covert-ops mission. Ambush from the left, right, front, or rear all had a certain structure dealing with how to handle them. In a right-side ambush it would be Sarah, Jen, and

Hunter who would charge the ambush as the remainder provided cover. Once into the initial line of ambushers, the rest would follow and leapfrog until through the attack. Or dead. You never back-pedaled from an ambush because good ambushes were usually booby-trapped or worse on the off side. It was better to deal directly with the ambushers and hope that the speed and violence of the reaction would carry you through it. Blowing through an ambush required serious and copious amounts of primitive heart-searing violence. Although TALON teams weren't *supposed* to get ambushed, just as with every other modifying word like "supposed," it had happened and would happen again.

"Boss?"

The voice came through Travis's BSH receiver and he snapped his head angrily in Sam's direction. They were supposed to stay off the air.

"It's okay. There's not a thing out there searching, intercepting, or anything. I've been scanning every and anything. Nothing. Zippo," said Sam quickly.

"Hold," said Travis to the entire team. Everyone froze and knelt. Travis killed the power in the LOCS and put his mouth to Sam's ear.

"How sure are you of this?" he whispered into the electronics expert's ear.

Sam remained on the air and the other soldiers heard him say, "One hundred and ten percent," then he went off the air and repeated it aloud to Travis.

Travis thought for a moment, then powered back up. "What kind of monitoring can you assure us?" he asked Sam.

"Real time? About ninety-five percent certainty. If anything comes up it might take me a second or two to know about it, but other than that—"

"Stan?" said Travis.

"Take the shot, boss. Our little tech weenie never misses," said Stan.

Sam smiled at the compliment.

Travis thought a moment, then agreed. "Okay everybody. On air. But lets keep it to a minimum until we get to first base."

Travis looked at Sam again and the little man gave him

an enthusiastic thumbs-up, part thanks and part agreement with his decision. He immediately went back to the face-up console, typed some instructions into the combat console mounted on his left wrist and continued monitoring com channels. The heads-up display would alert him to any attempt to intrude on the bandwidths they were using. It might miss a beat or two, but not much and not by more than that. Regardless, it would certainly not allow enough time for anyone to isolate their position.

"Let's move it out," said Travis. The team continued the slow move up an increasingly steeper hill.

Most of the ground cover in Haiti was either thin or had been so abused either by lumbering or by local people trying to eke out some meager crops that there was little thick vegetation. Erosion was a major problem and little grew or could be grown in the overworked soil. The hurricane had created landslides that had destroyed roads and washed away sides of mountains. They had inserted near Mount Tchicharan and were headed to its top because that was where the last satellite interference signal had originated. From there, Travis hoped, it would be a matter of tracking. Between the well-developed tracking skills of Jack DuBois and Stan Powczuk and the electronic-tracking capability of Sam Wong, he expected to be able to isolate the transmitter—and the person running it—fairly rapidly. Then it was a matter of finding and isolating this Louverture character and whatever men he commanded before he was able to create any more havoc. Time wasn't on the side of the Haitian people, so speed was of the essence.

Tchicharan was 1,037 meters high. To the team, which had worked in several mountain locales, this was a mere hill. Barrett checked the ATMP readout that would monitor fluid level. They had dehydrated quite a bit breathing oxygen and gearing up, but the river they'd guided in on originated on the side of the mountain and should provide an ample water source. Sarah would take care of ensuring the potability of the water.

"We're coming up on a track," said Jack.

"You and Hunter take a look," ordered Travis. The rest of the team knelt facing their respective areas of responsibility. "Anything Sam?" he asked.

"Dead as a doornail, boss. Whatever was there yesterday isn't sending now."

"Travis?"

"Go Hunter."

"Jack's moving out a bit farther. There's been some recent movement on the trail. Maybe ten or fifteen. Mostly males, possibly a couple of females. They're moving lighter than we are. Jack thinks the track is about six to eight hours old."

"Cover him up, Hunter. They might still . . ." started Travis.

"They were moving away, Travis."

"Damn!"

"Boss?"

"Go, Jack."

"They were definitely moving off. They started off in a hurry I think. It's downhill, but I think they were just booking."

"According to the topo, they should hook with a main trail that runs either out to the Dominican border via Cerca la Source or west to Cerca Carvajal and then out to Route 300," said Sam. His fingers danced on the keyboard without a look, calling info into the heads-up display. Sam was so used to having all manner of information in front of his eyes that he almost always saw the world as if through a large Plexiglas window dotted with a football coach's Xs and Os.

"Okay," said Travis. "Sam. How much further?"

"About four hundred meters."

"Jack. Feel like trail walking?"

"No sweat on this one boss."

"All right everybody. Hunter, keep it tight. Wait till Jen gives you the go. By the numbers people."

Trail walking was not an ideal operational decision. Sometimes it was used to intentionally draw an ambush, sometimes it was a quick way to catch up to a quarry and take them out. Other times it was simply asking for trouble. Travis trusted Jack's skill and it was the point man who would pay the price; if he didn't like what he was seeing he would call the walk and move back into the woods. You didn't trail walk without a damn good reason or as close to certainty as possible that the trail was cold.

Jennifer Olsen moved up within sight distance of Hunter. "Got you," she said.

Hunter and Jack, now separated by less that five meters, started moving. Jack threw up his BSD. He'd rely on his own two eyes for this.

The big man moved quietly and smoothly just off the slightly muddy track. His eyes scanned left, right, up, down. Searching. The XM-29 followed every move. In his time he'd seen booby traps in trees, on trails, in brush, on bodies, in innocuous pieces of wood. The BSD gave a slight tunnel vision effect after a while and Jack needed to see everything at once. Every anomaly, every color, and every shape with his own two eyes. He'd walked trails in a variety of terrains against a variety of enemies and was still alive and intended to stay that way. He didn't have a lot of respect for the men who'd used this trail. Yet. They didn't know anyone was hunting them, and he was quite sure—by the way they moved—no one had ever hunted them before. But even the rankest amateur and the dumbest guerilla in the world gets very smart when they *know* they are being hunted. That advantage still lay with TALON Force.

"Trav."

"Go, Stan."

"Me and Greene are a little bit down from where we intersected the trail. Buncha people took a break here. These guys are sloppy. Candy bar wrappers and cigarette butts everywhere."

"Okay. You and the doc close back up."

Twenty minutes had passed and Jack had covered half the distance to the hilltop.

"Sarah?"

"Yo."

"We got a river coming across the trail up here. Think we'll need water. There's a beautiful little fall here."

"Roger. Don't drink it. Word is there's no clean water on this island."

"Boss?"

"Go, Jack."

"The trail crosses here and wraps around a big boulder.

Then it hauls up about thirty meters. I think . . . wait a minute." Jack flipped down his BSD. "Yeah. We got a cave. The approach is about forty-five degrees and all open. There's enough cover for the team at the boulder. After that—"

"Okay," said Travis. "Hold until we group."

"Stan? Jen?"

"Trav?" came two voices.

"Jack is at three-fifty," interjected Sam. "Have 'em go off at thirty-five for a hundred then make the cut."

Travis outwardly hated when Sam anticipated his actions. Inwardly, he loved the fact that his team worked as a single entity.

"Who put you in charge, little man?" said Stan.

"Who you callin' little?" Sam snapped back.

They all heard Jennifer Olsen chuckle.

Travis shook his head. "Do it," he said to Stan and Jen. He nodded his head at Sam and they moved up the trail to the other three.

Stan and Jen closed on each other and circled to the east. They would—according to Sam—come to the cliff section out of the sight line of the cave and climb. One would maneuver above; one would close from the east to the cave's mouth. Both would be able to provide cover for the rest of the team without exposing themselves.

Another twenty minutes passed, and the two came into view.

"It's about thirty meters to your left at your ten o'clock," said Sam, checking their location on his heads-up display.

"Got it," said Jen.

The two maneuvered into position, Jen above the cave and Stan below. Jen unclipped a fragmentary grenade from her harness and laid it at her knee, as Stan settled his XM-29 in the crook of a rock aimed at the cave.

"Okay, Jacques," said Stan.

There is no worse a feeling in the world than exposing oneself to the possibility of fire. Jack DuBois looked at the rest of the team, leaned his helmet back against the rock, took a deep breath, and moved out toward the cave mouth.

"Clear, clear, clear . . ." Stan kept speaking, his eyes never leaving the cave entrance. Every gun that had a free lane of fire at the cave mouth was pointed at it, and while someone might get a shot off at Jack, they wouldn't get two off. If Jack DuBois, who was as fast as a cat, didn't get the drop on someone, they'd never see the next minute of their life.

It took Jack a long three minutes to maneuver to the cave mouth. As he pulled to its side, Stan came off hold, and Jen picked up her frag.

"C'mon, big man," said Sam. "Put your helmet on the ground in front. I'll handle the rest."

Travis could see Jack raise his head in recognition of what Sam planned. Jack should have thought of that, thought Travis.

Jack removed his BSH and placed it with the sensor down, looking directly into the cave mouth. A few key strokes and Sam was looking directly into the cave. A few more and the infrared made the darkness day. Stan moved down opposite Jack, as Sam said, "Clear, ladies and gentlemen."

Jack reclaimed his helmet, made sure the BSD was in place, looked at Stan, and the two dove into the cave.

Barrett and the rest of the team listened to their heartbeats.

"Clear," said Jack.

"Clear," said Stan.

Olsen re-rigged her frag.

"Okay," said Travis. "Stan, stay. Me and Sam are coming up. Sarah, you and Jack get water. Hunter, Jen cover the trail."

Travis and Sam moved up the hill.

0800 hours

"Well, what do we have?" Travis asked Sam.

"Gimme a second, boss."

The cave entrance belied its size. Though the cave's mouth barely allowed Jack and Stan entrance together, it opened into a fairly large cavern before disappearing back into the gloom. Stan walked back into the darkness and reported that the tunnel seemed to dead end after fifty feet.

"There's a crack back here that a serious caver might be able to penetrate. Want to get Sarah down into it?"

"No. It looks like we got what we need here."

The living area of the cave showed evidence of being used recently. There was a fire pit near the mouth and what looked like sleeping stations scattered all around. A small wooden box was placed next to a run-of-the-mill portable Sears Craftsman generator, which was at least twenty years old but in excellent shape.

Sam looked around the generator and made a "who knows?" gesture with his hand. "It's a power source. Can it do the job? Somebody's got some pretty sophisticated equipment on this here island, so this is plenty of juice. This is where the coordinates say the signal came from, and this is a power source. But there ain't nothing else that indicates what kind of equipment they're using. This'll do the job power wise, though."

Travis looked at the machine. "Stan, anything else of interest?"

"Some food supplies. Two old cases of U.S. Army MREs. Guess some quartermaster was making a little profit on the side. One case of 5.56 ball. Guess they're using 16s."

"Okay. Toss the ammo, dump the food. I'm gonna fry it," said Travis nodding his head at the generator. "Everybody wanna clear, please."

"Hang on a minute, Trav," said Stan, who appeared carrying an OD metal box of ammo. "Leave the damn food. Maybe it'll get 'em sick," he said as he scuttled out of the cave, followed by Sam.

Travis ordered the RF generator to arm and fire vocally. A pulse burst of radio frequency energy fried the electronic innards of the generator, followed by wisps of smoke drifting out of the machine toward the ceiling.

"We're clear," he said. He followed the two out of the cave and as he walked up to Sam, Sam's hand jerked to his keyboard. "Go Aerie One," he said. "Shit." A few beats later he said "Roger. Out."

"What's the story?" asked Travis.

"Sorry I didn't patch that guys," said Sam. "Well, apparently our friends have been busy. They locked down one of our comsats on the last pass, and a Red Cross relief plane just went into the runway at Port-au-Prince. Apparently it did a perfect instrument approach . . . right into the ground."

"Somebody doesn't want *anybody* helping anybody on this island," said Hunter.

"How sophisticated would that have to be?"

"A helluva lot less than stopping our comsats from talking," Hunter answered. "Feed it the wrong altitude, maybe lock the auto pilot and it's adios. If he's coming in at night on instruments, the altimeter's reading, say three hundred feet, but the plane is on the deck. Lousy way to go, 'cause you see it coming."

"Okay everybody, back to our last stop," said Travis. The team converged on the boulder where the assault on the cave had started, then fanned in a circle covering all points of the compass with Sam and Travis in the center.

"Your read on this?" Travis asked Sam.

"Mobile setup. No problem as long as there's enough juice. A bunch of car batteries could probably do it. Either that or they've got a couple of operators and stations. We know this last one didn't come from here. Aerie One should be able to tell us if the keystroking has a single signature or whatever. Right now I'd say they could be anywhere. As soon as Aerie One gets a fix they'll get back to us. Hard but not impossible with only one shot."

"Okay folks, what we have right now is a dozen or so Indians headed thataway about eight hours ago. Let's find these bastards. Same formation. Let's get rolling. Sam, as soon—"

"You'll get it all, boss, as soon as I do."

"Let's move."

As the team headed down the trail, Travis started weighing options and operational necessities. But he needed more info before he could plan the next move. This is like selling real estate, he thought. It's all about location, location, location. How the hell are we going to pin down this Louverture's location? Why this guy was doing what he was doing was another question, but Travis didn't feel a need to know the answer yet. Where the hell could this guy be? The why could probably only be answered after they found him.

Chapter 8

September 17, 1100 hours
Outside the town of Mirebalais, Haiti

"Are you sure this is the right way to be handling things?" asked Lily. "From what we've heard, there's been tremendous suffering in Port and—"

"Listen," snapped LePetit. "We've been over this before. We need to start with a valid, viable population and we need to be the ones in power when the relief comes. We're still about a day away from marshalling everyone to Port-au-Prince. If people die, so be it. We've got eight million peasants running around this damn country and if we're going to make this work, cutting down the population by a few hundred thousand—dammit, even a million—is going to help us when we move. They're starving and dying in the slums anyway. This is just going to bring the end sooner. Two, three days, Lily. Maybe a week on the outside and Haiti is m . . . ours. Then we can go about fixing things."

LePetit turned to the small window of the grass shack as he said these last words. Yeah, we'll fix things, he thought.

LePetit didn't think that Lily had any great misconception of what he planned to do, but he thought that her modern lifestyle and innate intelligence made her think she could control LePetit by virtue of her technological skills. Lily—somewhere in that beautiful head of hers—had the thought that she was influencing him. So be it. This was Haiti, and technology didn't mean shit on this island. For that matter, neither did the opinions of women. By the time she'd find out, she would either be in a position to reap the apparent benefits, or she could go the way of anyone who disagreed with LePetit. He wouldn't need her then. But he did need her now to keep the damn *merikens* and all the other do-gooders out of the way until he took the government down.

He'd been wondering when they'd react militarily. By now they obviously knew something was going on. But as long as he controlled the skies he was fairly confident that any military reaction would be by small units. He knew the Americans had the special-operations people who could get into the country. But then what? They'd never be able to triangulate locations of the transmissions as long as he kept moving. The assault on Port-au-Prince would be over before anyone knew what had happened. Then it would simply be a matter of passing the blame to the alter ego of Jean LePetit and assuming command, and the re-institution of order himself—Jean-Guy Louverture, Haiti's savior resurrected.

He was controlling his forces from this small mountain town a day or two's march from Port-au-Prince. His troops were emerging from hiding and moving to the rallying point near Menet, about twenty miles from the capital. From there it would be a quick move into the city by nightfall, take down what was left of the government, and assume command. Let the ships of the world move in, rally the people to bring in the supplies, feed the hungry, nurse the sick. He smiled out the window. A god like Louverture couldn't appear at a better time, he thought.

Lily'd been a bit skeptical of LePetit's plan at first. But the first boat had screamed onto the reef just outside the normal sea lane into Cap Haitien. The local people had a party by all accounts with the supplies. Then there was the relief plane. Lily hadn't liked doing that, but something had to be done for her beloved country and if this were the way, well, she'd deal with any moral questions at a later date. There'd been some military overflights, but as near as her equipment could tell, none had landed. She thought that eventually there would be troops—SEALs or Green Berets or the like—being dropped onto Haiti to hunt down the transmissions, but she and Jean-Guy didn't expect that for another couple of days. And by then they'd have the government.

I hope the Americans are as fooled as Jean says they are, she thought.

But even if the *merikens* did land on Haiti, Lily wasn't terribly worried. It was a big, mountainous island with thousands of spots that had rarely been trod upon by people. And the burst transmissions were impossible to detect. You had to triangulate to get a location, and they were never on-air long enough. Nor were they ever in the same place. Jean had planned things well. There were power sources scattered in caves and villages throughout the country. The radar unit—one she'd modified from some narcotrafficante's mule boat—was the size of a television receiver dish. Her computer equipment consisted of three laptops. The burst generator was the size of a cigar box, as was the satellite tracking/recording device. She carried all save the radar unit when they were on the move.

Her only difficulty came when breaking into the satellites. The codes varied daily, hourly, or in some cases by individual transmission depending on which satellite she used. She'd written her own software and continued to update it as NSA, CIA, or whatever other lettered organization tinkered to try and prevent her access. So far she'd been better at it than they had.

"Jean, I've got to get some rest. That march here just about wore me out."

"Be thankful you're not still walking," he said with a smile. "Get some sleep. Tonight we will be moving as long as it is dark. I'm going to take a little walk around and make sure everything is undisturbed."

"Be careful, Jean. I don't know how you remember where you place all those devices."

"Pretty one, you never forget where things are that keep you alive."

Chapter 9

September 17, 0827 hours
Outside the town of Mirebalais, Haiti

Jack DuBois followed the trail south to where they first picked it up. The going was always steadier and easier downhill, but the heat remained oppressive. He inspected every inch as he moved along.

"Travis?"

"What's up, Jack?"

"My terrain readout doesn't show this trail at all, so what do you want to do? Stay on it or head back to the DZ?"

"How's the track look?"

"These guys were moving. I figure, follow it and see what goes. We can move a little faster if we power up the LOCS. There's been no sign of booby traps, and I'm not picking up any sensor activity. I don't think this crowd will have any, no matter how advanced they are with their commo. If they're still using 16s, how well armed can they be?"

"All right, everybody. We'll pick up the pace a bit. Stealth on. Hunter, close a little tighter on Jack. Line of sight. Jen, Sarah, Stan, maintain your spacing."

Picking up the pace was a calculated risk that the LOCSs made worth taking. Jack was one of the best point men Travis had ever worked with and he was confident in Jack's ability and decision-making. If it seemed that the trail was heating up, Jack wouldn't take any unnecessary risks. He'd be off the trail and into the brush, meager as it was, in an instant.

Patrolling like this wasn't fun. Aside from the constant concentration on your surroundings, you couldn't let your mind wander. While the BSD could prove extremely helpful in open terrain such as encountered in deserts and mountains, jungle terrain could often negate its benefits. You needed to see more than subjectively and the BSD wouldn't always give you an accurate image. Sometimes a vine could resemble a tripwire; but sometime a tripwire could also resemble a vine. While the TALON troops relied heavily on their electronic equipment, they didn't do it at the expense of their natural battle talents. It was mandatory to be as good without the gear as with it, and Travis preached this importance constantly. The LOCS, BSH, BSD, and everything else were the cards that gave TALON Force the operational edge in virtually every action, and Travis wanted the men to think of it as an edge only. Relying on it completely was not a good thing no matter what the armorers and desk jockeys said. Your combat skills, raw and nontechnological, had to keep you alive in battle. Whether your weapon was a knife, stone, gun, or laser, combat skills got you back home.

Jungle patrolling was hot and quiet work—hot in this case since the LOCSs' cooling systems were turned off to conserve power. Nonetheless, combat pack shoulder straps dug into shoulders, feet were sweating and moving about even in their custom-made boots, and sweat poured from under their BSHs and ran into their eyes. Each trooper's ATMP activated some glucose concentrate and seeped it into their system as the sweat dumped more and more nutrients from their bodies. The BSHs enabled them to maintain a greater distance between each other. Though Sam could monitor all of their locations in respect to himself, Travis still liked to have a physical sense of who was where in case something went wrong.

That was another problem with patrolling and not getting any signs of imminent contact. The heat beat you, and then a sort of complacency set in. All of these men and women were the best the services had to offer, but human nature finds it hard to concentrate and keep adrenaline pumping when there is no apparent reason to do so. The point man was often the last to fade, but even he . . .

"Boss," said Sam. Travis turned to him. "I think it's time to flip the point," Sam said.

Damn, I hate when he reads my mind, thought Travis for the zillionth time.

"On my way," came Stan's voice.

"Holding," said Jack.

The patrol stopped and knelt.

"Water up, team," said Sarah. "Everybody check their glucose levels."

Stan came walking down the trail, his eyes still moving left to right. He gave Sam an elbow as he walked past, and the NSA man casually flipped him the bird. Travis shook his head tiredly.

"Passing," said Sarah Greene as Stan passed her.

"Passing," said Hunter Blake.

"Contact." Stan met with Jack.

"Everybody watered up?" asked Travis. When no answers came, he ordered them to move off.

Jack had stepped back off the trail and actually made himself look small, an amazing feat, aided by the LOCS. Travis finally spotted him and said, "Let Jen take the drag." That would put Jen as the tail gunner and give the big man's concentration a break.

Jack nodded at his CO.

Day had broken as the trail was winding out of the trees. Daylight came later under cover, but once they reached the edge of the woods, they found it in full bloom. A barely detectable breeze provided some cooling for a moment, but their movement downhill quickly brought back the full effect of the heat. Tropical work was not fun, thought Stan as he started off checking right, left, up, and down as he moved. But neither were cold weather ops, city ops, desert ops, hell, there never seemed to be good conditions when it came to combat ops no matter where they'd been.

He blew a quick burst of air at his nose and knocked some of the sweat into the air. It was working up into his nostrils now, his hands were wet and his LOCS looked like it had been swimming. I wonder if sweat can short-circuit this thing, he thought. He always had the same thought in tropical ops, and always got the same answer when he asked after every mission. No.

He realized his mind had started drifting, which was a

great way to get himself or his team killed. Got to get to business here. He called for a halt.

"I need to check some of these tracks."

"Roger."

After thirty seconds, he had several of the quarry firmly identified in his mind. There was Nike (a distinctive "N" on one print), Knock-knee (a bad pronator), Girl (smallest print), and Gorilla (a very large print). There was also one guy carrying the heaviest load, Packer. There were one or two others, but at least he had some of them fixed. It was truly amazing what you could tell from people's footprints. He'd once worked with one guy from New Jersey who could almost tell what you were carrying from footprints. It was an art form that developed over years of practice and one that came in handy on certain missions. Like this one.

"Rolling," he said.

"Roger."

Twenty minutes later Stan called a halt again. "We got a major intersection up here."

"Sarah, cover at the junction. Hunter, with her," ordered Travis.

"Boss, take a look at your topo. That should be right . . ." Sam made some keystrokes, ". . . there." The map appeared in Travis's BSD.

"Stan. Hunter. Got a map for you."

"Roger. Send it," said Hunter. "Travis?" Hunter called a few seconds later.

"Go."

"We're gonna mosey down a ways and see if we can pick up that second branch. This is kinda like a turnpike and our boys turned west on it. It's hard pack, so give us a few."

"We'll move up to the intersection," said Travis. "Let's go.

"Sarah?"

"Yes?"

"You need to move down to cover?"

"No, unless they get some folks walking out of the bush, I can cover from right here. It really *is* a big intersection. The main trail is about ten feet across."

"Roger."

Travis, Sam, and Jack converged on the trail intersection

over the next three minutes. Jen remained about twenty-five meters back up the original trail as a rearguard.

"Jack. Head east; see what's what as far as tracks go. Don't go far. Sam, cover him."

The two men started off while Sarah and Travis covered the intersection.

A minute later Jack reported in. "Nothing on this track since the storm blew through. Totally unused unless these mutts walk on air."

"That's 'cause they headed this way," came Stan's voice. "They took the branch and are headed south again. That'll get 'em toward Thomassique or a branch of the Guayamouq River."

"If they went by river . . ." Sam let that hang in the air.

Travis spoke. "Jen, up. Jack, Sam, Sarah, let's go. Stan, Hunter, hold at the turnoff. Sam, you gotta get me an update."

"Already on it."

The team headed off.

I hate when he does that, thought Travis.

The terrain opened further as the trail closed on the river. They'd been humping the boonies for an hour now. The sky was incredibly clear, bright, and hot. Daylight hours were rough for covert movement, but were essentially the only time to move in thick jungle. The odds of running into someone during night travel in triple canopy were just too stacked against you. But this mission was different on that account. Most of the terrain was open enough to allow excellent night travel; it was the day travel that was more dangerous in Haiti; if there had ever been triple canopy in Haiti, it was long before TALON Force ever existed.

There'd been little to worry about save tracking the group whose trail led Stan to believe that they were walking on home ground. When he and Jack re-exchanged on the point they'd conferred and agreed on that. The prey was spread out in no discernible order, and there were far too many scuffmarks and traces of their passage left around. They were moving much more casually and their tracks indicated they were much more close to something familiar.

Jack called a halt. "We got a turn in the trail and a lot of open air. Let me check it out."

"Roger," said Travis.

Jack walked slowly to where the trail disappeared around a jagged rock outcrop. He kept the rock on his shoulder and got down low. One thing too many people did when looking around blind spots was stay at normal height—the perfect height where someone looking in that direction would be focussed. You go low to take a peek and you increase tenfold your chances of not being observed.

Nothing. He pulled the quick release on his combat pack and left it behind the outcrop, then went to his belly and slithered forward.

Nothing. But the trail opened up and looked down a steep hillside to the river below. He trained his BSD on the valley. "We got a hut by a river. Five-three-five meters. No movement. No smoke. Nada."

"Any place we can observe?" asked Travis.

"Good a spot as any," answered Jack.

"Okay, we're moving up."

As the team closed up on Jack he spoke again.

"Hold it, hold it. We got a guy taking a stroll."

"Armed?"

"Pistol, I think. He ain't no farmer. Lost him in the bush. Come on up. Just stay tight to the cliff."

The team grouped in their usual defensive positions while Travis crawled to where Jack lay.

"It's about eleven o'clock," said the Marine.

"Got it," answered Travis. He looked for several beats. "Okay. No time for screwing around. Hunter, get a Dragonfly down there and into the hut. Let's see what we've got."

Hunter popped his rucksack, opened the top flap, and rooted around for a minute. He withdrew a palm-sized UAV, which looked like a kid's toy, and placed it on the ground in front of him, then sat back casually against the rock. He flipped down his BSD, grabbed a cigarette pack–sized control box with a small joystick centered in it, and pressed a button. Then the pusher prop on the Dragonfly spun to life. "Sarah, give it a lift, would ya?"

Sarah crawled to the 'Fly, lifted it, carefully avoiding the humming prop, and gently propelled it forward as if throwing a balsawood glider toy.

Blake held the control unit in his left hand and manipulated the joystick with a single finger on his right. He immediately received the bird's-eye view the 'Fly provided. He rolled the joystick and the UAV made an altitude-gaining circle before dropping down toward the hut below.

When Hunter first encountered the Unmanned Aerial Vehicles, he'd scoffed at them, but after the first few familiarization flights came to enjoy flying his "toys." As everything else in the team's equipment repertoire, everyone could fly a UAV, but Hunter was by far the most skilled.

Combined with the BSD image—and with his pilot's ability to block out all external stimuli—he found the UAVs easy to control, nearly as responsive as a fighter, and almost as much fun as traditional flying. When he flew the Dragonfly he liked to think of himself as an ant-sized pilot; that thought had come to him one day when he was watching perfectly formed half-inch waves roll ashore at a lake. He'd thought it would be "so cool" if he was small enough to surf the miniature barrels and after far too long staring at them, his thoughts had turned to the UAV. When he'd voiced that revelation to a few of the team, only Sarah had shown any understanding—he and Sarah definitely looked at life in a different way from the rest of the team.

Hunter expertly "flew" the craft down to the clearing where the hut was. "Give me a run up and down the river," said Travis. "Everybody else stay off the air," he added. The entire team liked watching the drones fly, especially when Hunter was the pilot.

Hunter flew across the clearing. The Dragonfly made only an indistinct humming sound. In confined quarters the noise was noticeable, but rarely alarming. At first you'd think it was an inordinately noisy bug, but it could be spotted by the eye. Nonetheless, no one knew what it was, and before anyone made a move to it, it maneuvered away and left. No one had ever swatted a Dragonfly yet, though there had been some attempts to do so.

Hunter flew the 'Fly around the outside of the hut and clearing, then banked it over to the river. He flew along the river. There were no people around, and they could see no movement. Just downstream was a small footbridge. The river was muddy and was running far below what had been the high water mark caused by the hurricane. He flew a minute down the near bank, did another roll and flew it up the far side, past their position. After about thirty seconds at twenty miles per hour, Blake noticed the watercourse steepening upriver as evidenced by increasing riffles of whitewater. He rolled the UAV back down the near bank, heading for the hut and clearing.

"Let's see if we can spot that stroller," said Travis.

Hunter circled the UAV in ever wider and slightly higher circles around the clearing and saw nothing.

"All right. What do we have in the hut?" asked Travis.

The UAV circled and climbed, and Hunter flew it back to the team's position before throttling the UAV down to a whisper and slowly power-gliding back toward the clearing.

On the first pass around the hut, Hunter had noted the window opening on the back. "Sam," he said. "Going in, need to video it."

Wong pressed some keys on his control pad, then said, "Rolling." He'd digitally tape the pass at real-time speed, then be able to roll it back for Travis at a viewable speed. When a building was large enough, the UAV could lap in it, but the hut looked to be about ten-by-twelve. Hunter would make as slow a pass-through as possible.

The Dragonfly glided down and Jack watched it disappear into the hut and fly out the rear. Travis and Hunter had been "aboard" it. Jack smiled. What a cool little toy.

Hunter powered on as the craft exited and flew it high before doing another classic combat roll and running it in the back window and out the front door again.

"Got it," said Sam. "Ready when you are, boss."

"Hold it," said Jack. "Here comes our stroller."

Neither Travis nor Hunter had seen anybody in the hut. Hunter thought he'd seen a radio of some sort on the right wall of the hut as the UAV had headed in.

"Jack, Stan," said Travis. "I want that guy in one piece."

Jack inched back from his observation point and he and Stan headed back the way the team had come before making their way down the slope into the woods headed for the clearing.

"Sam, give it to me. Hunter, bring it in."

As Hunter arced the craft around for an into-the-wind landing at his feet, Sam ran the tape for Travis. The hut had hammocks on one side, a small table, and, nestled against the wall, a radio set of indeterminate manufacture. But Travis couldn't see a mic or any kind of . . .

"It's a gah-damn ghetto blaster," said Sam. "An old . . . hmmm . . . Sanyo, looks like. Don't think he's jamming anything with that heap of junk."

Jack and Stan made their way as quietly as possible down the slope, not an easy task, since it was relatively steep and the ground's makeup was mud, clay, and loose shale or rock. They finally reached the bottom, split up, and headed in the direction of the hut through the tangled, stunted growth.

Above them, Hunter dusted off the UAV and repacked it, then donned his rucksack. He quietly made his way past Travis and went down the trail in the direction they'd been heading before. Sam moved up next to Travis, bellying the last few yards.

Neither could see the two men from here, and before Travis could speak, Sam did.

"Sitrep."

"Just getting to the clearing," said Stan.

"Check," said Jack in agreement.

"Got 'em," said Travis as he spotted the two.

"Stan," said Jack. "Why don't you hook around and see if you can spook the guy out or something. Some rocks on the hut or something. I wanna try something."

"Give it to me, Jack," said Travis.

"I'm gonna fire up my LOCS and fade in on this guy from the bushes talking Creole. If he freaks, then Stan can grab him from behind and I'll fade away. If he doesn't, then I'll pin him."

"Fine, but I want him alive. Give it a shot."

Jack knelt in position as Stan slowly made his way to the left around the clearing. With his LOCS on he stayed in fairly close, counting on the camouflage and the angle of the sun that left him mostly in shadow to avoid detection. The man had re-entered the hut and there was no sign of anyone else. The target was puttering around with something; Stan could hear metal clinking, and then the radio came to life with reggae music.

The thick brush petered out at the river and was replaced by stone with some sparse but thick shrubs. Stan made his way clump to clump and finally stopped when he could spot the back window opening at his two o'clock.

"Here goes," he said.

He picked up a fist-size rock and threw it toward the far front corner of the hut. It clattered onto rock. Overthrown.

"Nice pitch, Randy Johnson," said Jack. "Why don't you use a frag?"

The music continued and Stan hefted another rock at the hut. It hit a pile of thatch that had been placed on the tin roof as a patch. Ball two.

Jack chuckled. Stan fumed. "Get ready," he said.

"I *been* ready, boy," said Jack. Stan was real easy to rile, he thought, smiling.

Stan popped the quick release on his rucksack and gently lowered the pack to the ground, then placed his smart rifle carefully and firmly on it. He rolled his shoulders, preparing to throw a strike this time.

"What the hell is he doing?" Sam asked Travis. Both men could see Stan, but not Jack.

They watched Stan loft the rock and this time it came down with a bang on the tin roof, before rolling and clattering off. The radio snapped off. Stan ducked down, picked up his XM-29, and pulled down his BSD for target acquisition.

A face appeared in the back window, then disappeared. Stan started to move for the back of the hut as he heard Jack jabbering away in Creole.

None of the team could understand what either Jack or the individual were saying, but whatever it was, the man — as near as Travis and Sam could tell—was literally frozen in step about ten feet from the door of the hut. The man had his pistol in his hand but it was held somewhat listlessly by his side, and as Jack's voice got louder and deeper, they watched the pistol drop to the ground. Stan was at the side of the hut, and he could have gotten there along with a bagpipe band as far as the hut's former occupant was concerned.

Jack's voice seemed to start chanting, and his sonorous tones seemed to be lulling the man to sleep, until Stan smashed him in the back of the head with the butt of the XM-29.

"What the hell you do that for?" yelled Jack. "Jesus, Stan, the guy was practically ready to faint. Why'd ya hit him so hard!?"

Only Travis and Sam had seen Stan butt stroke the prisoner, but everyone had heard Jack's comments and could imagine what occurred

"Awright, awright," said Travis. "Everybody down to the hut. Stan, Jack. Tie him up and get him aside. Doc, get him awake"

"Sure," said Sarah. "Stan, would you mind waiting before blowing up the hut?"

"Travis, there's a path heading down to the hut up here," said Hunter.

"Roger. Everybody down there. Let's go, let's go."

When the team arrived they fanned out around the clearing.

Stan shook his head a bit red-faced. "Sorry, boss. Guess I got a little carried away there." Travis shook his head with a smile.

Jack DuBois snorted.

"Ahhhh. What the fuck. He ain't dead right?"

"No thanks to you," said Sarah as she entered the hut.

Travis made a "what happened?" gesture to Stan, who raised his eyebrows skyward in an "I dunno" response, then headed out the door. "Take the river side," Travis said to his number two's retreating back. Stan's hand waved up in the air without a glance backward in answer.

Jack remained in the hut with Travis and Sarah. He lifted the man, who was about two inches shorter than Stan Powczuk's five-seven, and about fifty pounds lighter, and plopped him in the hut's only chair. He popped his rucksack, went in a side pocket, and withdrew some six-hundred-mile-an-hour tape; the military version of all-purpose duct tape, so named because Air Force repair crews had often used it to seal windshields on planes and helicopters.

He ripped a foot-long strip and nodded at Sarah. She grabbed the man's hair and pulled his head off his chest, then held her hand up. She looked closely at the back of the man's scalp, then nodded and Jack wrapped the tape firmly over the man's eyes. So much for eyebrows, he thought as he patted the tape tight. He placed a smaller piece on the man's mouth, then did a couple of laps around his chest and the chair, then ripped another strip and fastened the man's legs to each chair leg.

Interrogation could be done several ways. Some techniques were very nasty and brutal but that didn't necessarily guarantee success. People in pain tended to tell you what you wanted to hear and the more unsophisticated the subject, the faster they babbled. In this case, with time ticking away, the team needed to know some very specific and very truthful information out of someone who was already scared out of his wits.

One of the more expedient and reliable ways was to start by totally immobilizing the detainee and then depriving him of as many senses as possible, preferably when he was unconscious. Jack had invoked some Vodoun words and spirit names he knew, and along with the specter of a huge, black, Creole-speaking image seeming to appear out of thin air, the man had been frightened almost into incoherence.

The man moaned. Sarah reached in the cargo pocket of her pants and withdrew what looked like a syringe barrel sans needle, and pressed it against the man's neck. There was a pressurized "pfft" sound and the man started to show further signs of consciousness.

"Nice laceration of the scalp, concussed naturally," she said. "That'll wake him up. Do we want to . . ."

"Let me try first," said Jack.

As soon as the man's head jerked in response to the adrenaline shot, Jack started speaking softly into his ear. The man winced at the first words and kept jerking his head away each time Jack said something. The jerking decreased in intensity each time. He tried to speak several times, and Jack finally took out his knife, flipped it butt out and rapped the man on the knee painfully. The man remained quiet for the rest of the time Jack spoke.

In a nonchemical interrogation of this sort, judicious use

of pain accompanied the isolation and sensory deprivation. It rarely required undue amounts, just multidirectional; a sharp rap on the head, a bang on the knee, a forearm-tingling shot to an elbow. The idea was to keep the person completely off-balance and unaware of when or where he was being struck. The physical aspect also had no rhyme or reason to it; its purpose was simply further disorientation and a simple and fast method of proving the interrogator's dominance over the subject. It wasn't fun, and none of the team liked doing it, but it was effective.

Sarah had chemicals that would make the subject talk, but—as she had seen before—they weren't as fast acting as what Jack was going to do. Besides, she wasn't keen on jamming the guy full of a combination truth serum/hallucinogen/opiate after the shot on the head Stan had given him. The skull is a marvelously thick and hardy part of the skeleton, and she was quite often surprised at the amount of force it actually took for a blow to render someone unconscious for any appreciable length of time.

Jack kept speaking gently and no longer hit the man. The man listened more intently and no longer tried to speak through the tape. Then the interrogation stopped. Jack nodded his head at the doorway and he, Sarah, and Tarvis very quietly left the hut. They could see the man from the doorway. The man squirmed trying to look, trying to listen, trying to hear but getting nothing. It was one of the most disconcerting elements of the interrogation because of the abrupt nothingness of it.

"Let 'im sit a couple of minutes and then I'll wring him out," said Jack. "This guy's gonna fold on the double."

The three stood watching the man through the doorway, and finally Travis looked exasperatedly at Jack. "Awright, boss," said the big man.

Jack reentered the hut quietly and leaned over to address the prisoner, who seemed to jump out of his skin when he spoke.

Jack uttered a few words, touched the man's head gently once (causing another convulsive wince), and then quickly tore the mouth tape off. The prisoner started speaking—Travis and Sarah couldn't make it out, but the man was definitely pleading—when Jack spoke quietly. The man's mouth shut immediately.

Jack questioned the prisoner for several minutes, then stood up. He replaced the tape on his mouth and left the hut.

"And?" asked Travis.

"The guy is scared shitless, boss. Doesn't know what or who I am, all I know is he figures it's undead stuff come back to him for something. He pretty much was just trying to say saint's names and stuff. He's also definitely part of this Louverture's group, militia, gang, whatever. So what else we want out of him?"

"When the rest of his crew left, was Louverture with them? Where they were headed, what he's doing here, what Louverture intends, is there a com center, where, what—?"

"Boss?" came Sam Wong's voice.

"Go."

"Okay, here's the skinny. We can fix four beacons so far. The one we just left, one twenty kliks south of Port de Paix, one on Gonave Island, which is just offshore of Port-au-Prince and pretty much controls the shipping lane into it, and one—that fired about two hours ago and is why they haven't got back to us 'til now—from about sixty kliks south of here near a place called Menet."

Dammit, thought Travis. This was a waste of time. Sixty kliks. That's an all day hump.

"Roger."

"Jack, find out if these suckers were headed for Menet. That's down near Port-au-Prince. I must—repeat, must—know whether this Louverture was headed there. Now. No more screwing around."

"Got it boss." Jack quietly headed back into the hut.

"Sarah. Two choices here. We kill him, or you guarantee me he doesn't move for at least forty-eight hours. Your call."

"I can shoot him up and then slap a patch on him that'll keep him sleeping like a baby until next week, no problem," she answered. Sarah Greene wasn't above killing in the line of duty, but as a doctor she couldn't abide killing for noncombat reasons. She'd come up with the patch idea early on when she'd joined TALON Force and found out what the team's jobs were like. The patch was a simple modification of motion sickness and nicotine patches—only Sarah's seeped an endorphin-based opiate into the body over a longer period of time. The man would awake several days later, very hungry, very thirsty, and *very* confused. But alive.

Travis and Sarah heard Jack speaking to the prisoner, and now—with the tape off his mouth—he was a torrent of Creole. Jack finally yelled at the man—regardless of language skills, it was obvious he was telling him to shut up—and then disgustedly replaced the tape on his mouth mid-sentence. He came out of the hut.

"Talky bastard, eh boss?" said Jack, shaking his head. "Here's the scoop. He's a foot soldier more or less in the MPP. The Mouvman Peyizan Papay. Near as I can recall, it was a big peasant movement back in the 1990s that was sort of responsible for getting Aristide into power. Anyway, Louverture—yeah, he was with this group—resurrected them about five years ago. He says there are thousands, but I'm pretty sure he's talking out his ass on that. He's here to hustle some others coming in from the boonies on to Port-au-Prince chop-chop. He doesn't know how exactly, but he says they're gonna run the island from here on. Gotta figure he's going after the government. Oh. Hey, Sammy. You'll be interested in this one. The person with all the computers and stuff—is a young Haitian female. Our boy here calls her a witch, a *mambo.* She brought the hurricane down on Haiti on behalf of Louverture, according to Chatty Kathy in there. Sam, little buddy, I think you got competition," said the Marine, thinking of how serious Sam Wong was looking at this moment.

Jack turned to Travis, no levity apparent. "Want me to do this guy?"

Travis shook his head. "Sarah's gonna give him a nice long nap."

"Boss, if he's gonna meet up with some more of his guys we can't leave him here, even with Sarah's knock-out patches. If you put him in the bushes, something'll kill him anyway, just slower. Slow death, fast death, boss," said Jack.

"Shit. I hate this kinda stuff," said Travis, shaking his

head. He thought for a second. The mission has priority. He turned to the muscular Marine. "Make it quick. Sarah, c'mere."

Jack disappeared into the hut as Sarah walked over to Travis. "We can't take the chance, Doc," he said to her pointedly.

"Ah dammit," said Sarah. She offered no more argument regardless of her personal feelings. When TALON Force went somewhere, they went to war. And this was a war where the stakes were the lives of thousands of people and perhaps the fate of an entire country. She didn't have to like the team leader's decision but she would not dispute it. She knew the rules before she signed on.

Jack exited the hut a second later, unscrewing a silencer from his 9mm Baretta. "Sorry, Doc," he said as he passed her.

"Stan, I want this place mined."

"No problem. These guys are sloppy. I'll do the hootch, the trail in. Jen, c'mon with me for cover."

"Everyone else back to the trail," said Travis

Chapter 10

September 17, 1800 hours
Outside the town of Menet, Haiti

LePetit's MPP had slowly filtered into a staging area near the town of Menet and was spread around the southern section of the town in an arc covering some five hundred meters west to east. The entire force hadn't assembled yet—LePetit figured he was short about fifty-odd men—but that wouldn't affect his plans. His five senior "officers" were all here and that was all he really needed to worry about.

LePetit also had all twenty of his Tigers. Jean-Guy had hand picked these men and had come up with the name in lieu of using the infamous Leopard Commando name of old Papa Doc's regime. These twenty men formed a personal bodyguard of sorts, though LePetit never felt he needed one. They'd also spent the most time training in several facets of warfare that would come in handy as LePetit pushed onto the capital.

Four of the Tiger Force were on their way to the main airport at Port-au-Prince, and four others for the airport outside Cap Haitien. Their job was to mine the airfields in case the runways had to be blown. LePetit learned a technique from an old book by Bernard Fall about the Viet Minh and French in Indochina. Every airport had drainage aqueducts; the Tigers would simply mine them from below. He didn't want the runways blown—he would want the foreign aid as soon as he took over—but he wanted them ready to blow should the Americans or other helpful foreigners figure out just how Lily was mucking up their electronics and decide that troops were the answer to Haiti's current problem. He thought it would only be a matter of time before they'd be able to circumvent Lily's skills . . . no matter how good she thought she was. It behooved a good military leader to be ready for all contingencies.

Six of the Tigers had been taught underwater combat. The necessary diving skills had been obtained through a Cap Haitien resort's dive program. Faced with economic pressure by the Haitian government, the resort owners had come up with a plan to put locals in other than menial service jobs. While socially admirable, it was simply the most expedient method of offsetting the profits the obscene luxury of the all-inclusive resort represented in a country of such incredible poverty. LePetit used their guilt to create a very good weapon.

The six Tigers had learned well and put in the hours working at the resort at varying levels, all of which mandated a large amount of diving. Now it would pay off.

Jean-Guy found it amazingly simple—he was actually somewhat astounded by the ease—to purchase U.S. military field manuals on the arcane field of underwater combat to further supplement his men's novice skills. The hard part had been designing the mines and explosives that would work underwater, but by and large Lily had figured out most of the electronic problems.

Three of the Tigers, along with three troops to act as boatmen and security, were headed for Port-au-Prince's harbor. The other three with their support troops should have reached Cap Haitien last night. What was left of both harbors' land-side infrastructure was to be mined for destruction, and several ships in both harbors, located in key unloading areas, were to be readied for sinking. Like the airports, if everything went according to plan, Jean-Guy preferred the waterfront intact.

The remaining six Tigers would stay with Jean-Guy for the assault on Port-au-Prince.

The MPP on hand numbered, at LePetit's last count, 375 well-armed individuals. Like any guerilla-style force, their numbers were ephemeral. The years of building the force and by necessity keeping it spread throughout the countryside in smaller units gave everyone—including his own troops—the impression of a much larger force.

Jean-Guy thought the number of fighters plenty enough for his plans—especially if one now considered the havoc created by the hurricane. Managing a larger force—mostly due to the paucity of communication he'd started with—would have meant losing the tight control he had over the men. As it was, he'd managed to "visit" every group at least once a month as he made his rounds of the interior.

Another reason for Jean-Guy's decision to limit the size of his force was that he also ascribed—courtesy of his father's journals—to Fidel's maxim that he had begun "a revolution with eighty-two men," and if he had to do it again he'd "do it with ten or fifteen men of absolute faith."

The MPP certainly had absolute faith. Not in any cause necessarily. Jean-Guy didn't think many of the men *had* a cause other than taking care of themselves. But they did have absolute faith and belief, along with fear and respect, in Jean-Guy—spirit, savior, and soon-to-be ruler of this country.

One of the largest logistical problems Jean-Guy had faced in the early days of re-creating the MPP was arming his troops. He hadn't wanted rag-tag armament; it was hard to take seriously a guerilla force armed with bolt-action rifles, scatter guns, and assorted civilian-style weaponry. He hadn't been able to arm all the men at the same time, but over a period of three years he'd been successful. He tried to keep the sore point of a guerilla operation—ammunition—as similar as possible however.

It had started mercurially enough when he'd obtained twenty-five U.S. Colt Commando "CAR-15s" for himself and the Tigers from the Colombians. These sliding-stock, short-barreled versions of the M-16, while certainly old, handled quite like a machine pistol and fired the widely available NATO 5.56 round to the tune of twenty rounds in a second and a half.

Most of the police in the hinterlands were armed or had armories of the U.S. M-16. While the gun design itself was also old, it was in service globally and was an excellent weapon for forces that traveled light. The MPP over the past year had liberated some two hundred of them. Rather than drawing attention by taking out entire police stations, Jean-Guy had instituted his own bread-for-guns program; the poor-as-the-populace policemen were more than happy to do a bit of trading and swapping and none of the transactions left records that indicated the guns had "disappeared" from service.

Lucky timing, Jean-Guy's reputation, and an enterprising young dock worker had netted another coup for the MPP: a fifty-gun "aid" shipment of French FA-MAS assault rifles. The MASs were destined for what constituted a police force in Haiti, admittedly one that had gotten more professional over the past decade. But these rifles had conveniently "fallen off the truck." The MAS shot the standard 5.56 NATO round and was just slightly longer than the CAR-15; it also had the benefit of a three-shot-burst selector along with the usual auto and semi-auto modes. LePetit had worked hard to instill in his men the needlessness for long auto burst fire, and many were fairly decent in fire discipline. The three shot abetted it well nonetheless.

The only weapons of his father's caches that he deemed usable were shotguns. His father had stashed several crates of 12-gauge guns—mostly pump action—of various lineages. One of the nice things about the pump guns was the ease with which ammunition could be obtained. Twelve-gauge ammo in its many forms was available nearly anywhere there was subsistence hunting; in Haiti that meant everywhere. Fifty of the MPP were armed with shotguns and would spearhead any house-to-house work in the city.

The remaining hundred-or-so of his troops carried older model AK-47s. The Russians had long ago gone to the lighter 5.54mm version of the Kalishnikov, but the 7.62x39 AKs—always available for hard cash back in the Cold War days—were as plentiful and easily obtainable as 16s nowadays. Ammunition would be problematic as the years went on, but for now LePetit was loaded with the stuff. After all, that bastion of ancient economics, Cuba, was only fifty miles away, and one boatload of guns in exchange for one stolen boatload of cocaine had seemed to be quite the deal to the Cuban militia head that'd dealt with Jean-Guy's representative.

The Cuban had been barely able to contain himself at

the amount of cocaine the MPP man had offered, but Jean-Guy cared little; who it had belonged to was fish food, and better to have greed as the motivating factor in what he was doing rather that political interest from Cubans, who still seemed not to understand the world had passed them by.

The Cuban simply thought it was some "stupid" Haitians cheating themselves, but the way things were looking in Cuba these days, perhaps the *soldato* would rue that thought. Who knew? Maybe Castro's old philosophy could be used in Cuba again, only this time by LePetit.

Well, first things first.

Because the AK was such an extremely reliable weapon and would fire under practically any condition whether cleaned or not, the more poorly disciplined troops of the MPP had them. They also went to those who demonstrated a lack of grasping the concept of keeping their weapons clean—the single drawback of the fast-firing 5.56s.

The remainder of each MPP man's weaponry consisted of two M-26 "baseball" fragmentary grenades per man. Many of the men carried pistols—the most common, the venerable .45 caliber 1911 Colt—some of which were in a condition that made Jean-Guy wince whenever they were fired. A few had managed to obtain 9mm Barettas as well, and there were the usual assortment of Smith and Wesson, Colt, and Ruger revolvers. Nearly every man carried a machete or bush knife as well.

Jean-Guy had considered trying to obtain some light-crewed machine guns. He probably could have gotten his hands on some old *meriken* M-60s and even some M-249s (the drug runners were remarkably well armed). He'd also considered obtaining a few mortars of the 81mm size, but opted against it. First off, surprise was completely on his side. Secondly, ammunition and training for both would have been problematic, and third, he wasn't intending on going to war with anyone.

If Lily—both the hurricane and the woman—hadn't come along, perhaps he'd have changed his mind about initiating the final stages of the long-nurtured plan. No, if this action was going to require heavy weapons—which it might have without the opportunity the Lilys presented him with—he would have reconsidered the entire idea and simply opted to take care of himself for the next few years. He would have had the capability to live much along the lines the elites and the narcos did presently, but . . . well, he who hesitates is lost, thought LePetit.

Thirty of the MPP had infiltrated into Port-au-Prince already. "Infiltrated" was perhaps too strong a word. They'd gone into town, hidden their weapons, and made the rounds of the city, spreading the word. They'd brought food and money and passed it out liberally along with the message that "Louverture is coming." Louverture would save the people, and no one would stop him. He would materialize in various forms where and when he chose. He, not the foreigners, would feed their children.

Most of the city's residents had migrated there from the mountains and were ripe for the message. And the ghost figure of LePetit/Louverture was not unknown to them. LePetit kept the message as simple as possible. He would do good for them.

There was no point in confusing people—especially now—with messages about democracy or politics. That would quickly evolve by itself. For now, assuaging a hungry belly was the surest means of gaining power. While he knew there would have to be some bloodshed, the entire concept was based on the idea that opening the supply lines in his name would ingratiate the populace to him. Oh, certainly not the elites—and therefore the bloodshed—but the millions of peasants would swear by the name of Louverture.

The thirty scouts had brought the message to the people and by all accounts it had already started spreading. His men started the graffiti campaign—"Louverture will help" and "Louverture will feed you"—but many others had picked it up according to his men's reports. There were variations on the theme already appearing on walls, even as the people dug themselves out from the destruction caused by Lily.

Word of mouth was the fastest means of communication in Haiti before the hurricane. With nearly the entire communications infrastructure destroyed, it was the only efficient means now, and the word spread through the impoverished city like lightning.

LePetit's communications lines were short; most information was passed among the MPP by the direct word of runners. This was another plus in managing the small force he'd chosen. There were ten field radios—old U.S.-made PRC-25s—which had been obtained courtesy of the gendarmeries. Five were with the troops in the field—the four Tiger groups and the man leading the city "disinformation" group each had one, and two were at relay points in the north of the country to transmit messages to and from the two groups in Cap Haitien. Lily had rigged a clear plastic kite antenna to monitor all of them, though Jean-Guy had cautioned all the radio operators to stay off the air except for arrival sitreps and completion of mission sitreps. Threatening them to limit airtime—at the behest of keeping their tongues in their mouths—had worked well.

Jean-Guy checked his watch: six P.M. It was time to move.

"Lily, start packing it up. I want you to go with Geffrard and five of his men. Stay where the small Thai restaurant by Rue des Casernes and Rue de la Reunion was."

Lily looked up at LePetit and then returned to her laptop screen.

He called over his shoulder to two runners patiently sitting outside on a log, who entered the hut immediately. "Get me Geffrard, Ti Rouge, and El Sikki," he said to the first. "Tell them to get their men ready to move, and that I want to see them this minute."

He shook his head and called to the runner in disgust before he was out the door. "Tell them to get their men ready," he said slowly to the young man, "but tell Geffrard, Ti Rouge, and El Sikki I want them here now. Not the whole troop. Understand boy?"

The young man nodded and ran out of the hut. He turned to another runner. "The same thing for you. Get me Ti Bobo and LeBlanc and tell them the same. Hurry." This runner also bolted out of the orange glow of the gaslantern lit hut and faded into the dark as if the devil himself was chasing him.

He turned to Lily, who was still crouched over her laptop. "Lily," he barked, "I told you to get ready to move."

She looked at him coldly. "There's someone out there," she said.

"What do you mean?"

"Well, unless there's a microwave tower in a twenty-mile radius of us that hasn't been destroyed—"

"There isn't," snapped LePetit.

"Then someone on the ground is sending microbursts to a satellite from somewhere near us. It's rolling across the frequencies, and it's a new bird, not the ones I need. Do you have somebody else working for you I should know about?"

"No. But it's somebody we both should know about. Now. What are they saying?"

"That's going to take a lot of time to figure out," said Lily.

"Dammit, we don't . . . Who could be sending it?" asked LePetit quietly.

"This is very sophisticated stuff, beyond what I'm doing. *Nobody's* that good on this island."

"Somebody is now," said LePetit.

Chapter 11

September 17, 1900 hours
Outside the town of Mirebalais, Haiti

As the team waited for Stan and Jen to return, Travis stood alone and planned his next move. He was looking at a sixty-klik forced march, of which the last ten or so would have to be done much slower. It would take even his troopers eight hours. Tactically unacceptable. The team had to "four-F" the enemy—find 'em, fix 'em, fuck 'em, forget 'em—and do it now. Travis looked at his watch. Nineteen hundred hours already. The MPP would probably make their move tonight. Possibly tomorrow night, but it seemed more likely they'd go with the first darkness.

He looked down the slope at the hooch where the dead MPP man lay and let his mind wander. What would he do if he was in Louverture's place?

Well, Louverture had left for Menet sometime in the last eight hours or so. That's a long march and a rest might be in order. Send scouts into the city to recon . . . what? He flipped down the BSD and called up the map overlay. He's got a 13.5-klik hump into the city from Menet; make it fifteen all together. I'd need to know troop strength, location, and approach routes. Or I'd wait in Port-au-Prince at the . . .

"Sam. Give me a blow up of the capital. Identify the government buildings, military, police, television stations. Hell, anything a rebel force'll need to control the government."

"Coming up, boss."

A street map of Port-au-Prince appeared in the BSD and

Travis studied it carefully. South of town was a big cemetery and across a canal was the Sylvio Cater Stadium. Good enough staging areas and both were a straight run down Guilloux Avenue from the national palace. Of course he'd have to circle south of town to get his force in there unobserved.

Unobserved. Hmmm, thought Travis. Does he even have to worry about that now?

The cemetery makes the most sense, but there's the canal to worry about. There're bridges on both sides, but still that's a bottleneck. Even if he hooks out the side and up Ambroise to the palace, he's still got a bridge to cross. The stadium. That's a walled-in killing zone. I wouldn't marshal my forces there. Think about it, Travis, he said to himself. This guy's got this far unobserved and undiscovered, and we only find out about him when he's actually starting to make his move. This guy is no dummy.

Okay. So. The National Fort on the northeast of town . . . there's Notre Dame Cathedral a couple of blocks north of the palace . . . what if he doesn't want the palace?

Wait a minute, thought Travis. This is still a banana republic. The guy has to take the seat of power. The television and radio ops are down. He's got to physically take the government.

I have two choices. Stop him before he makes it to the city—if it's not too late already—or take him hard when he hits the palace. Travis's face showed he'd made a decision, and Sam, as always, was a step ahead, courtesy of watching his boss so closely.

"Why don't we go clear and say the hell with what this guy hears and . . ." started Sam.

"Sam." Travis held up a hand in the techie's direction. He'd make the decision. "Here's what I want you to do. Can you get to a sat that isn't one they're intercepting?"

Sam looked at his boss. "Hey, Hunter, what's the ceiling on those Dragonflies?"

"By itself I can give you maybe fifteen hundred feet. Do you need to carry anything?"

"Lemme think," said Sam. He turned to Travis. "If I can place a small relay on the 'Fly, I can . . ." He hit some keys on the console and seemed to look into space as images loaded down into the BSD. "I can possibly hit one of the South American units clean. Yeah, if I can get a thousand feet up . . . lemme check the terrain south of here." More fast fingers on the wrist console. "Yeah, all downhill from here. I can get a clear shot at something way south of here."

"How much will it weigh?" asked Hunter.

"Ounces," said Sam. "Say six."

"I can play with some updrafts and thermals. I'll get you fifteen no matter what. Guaranteed," said Hunter.

"Okay. Here's what we want," said Travis. "I want two V-22 Ospreys here now. What's the flight time from Edwards?"

"I ordered some up for Guantanamo about two hours ago, boss. They should be there in about thirty minutes."

"Nice going, Sam. Don't do it again without letting me know," said Travis. "What's it carrying?"

"Two arsenal boxes set up for antipersonnel, a Predator, and a couple of cruise missiles on the outriders. That's about all it'll load once we're in it anyway," said Sam.

"When can we have the Ospreys?"

"Figure two hours tops."

"Okay. Get 'em here ASAP. Next, get Aerie One . . ."

"Valhalla now, boss. I told you there was a Viking kick going on."

"Whatever. Get one of the C-117s out of Pope rolling. I want a Wildcat and a Hummer ready to come into Delmas. I want two RIBs ready for airdrop. I want drop boxes with resupply for the XM-29s, dive gear for Jack, Sarah, and Stan—figure shallow water ops—three or four NLGs, and I want—"

"Hey, get me some old claymore mines, too, will ya Wing-Wang?" came Stan's voice. "I got enough of these antipersonnel poppers, but I want something that'll bring some damn on somebody."

"You the man, Stan," came Jack's deep voice. "Let's kick us some serious ass."

"Get him some claymores if they're handy," said Travis, shaking his head at his number two's exuberance.

"Why don't we just nuke 'em, Stan?" asked Sarah.

"Hey," said Jen. "Leave him alone. He's all excited after

setting those mines. You'd think he was having sex or something. You're a scary dude, Powczuk."

Powczuk just grinned through his beard.

"Knock it off everybody," said Travis. "You get all this, Sam?"

"Yeah. I'll fix up a relay and we'll get this little message off in zero-five. Hunter, get that toy of yours—"

"Ready when you are Short Round," interrupted Hunter, to Travis's satisfaction.

"I want to know when the 117s're ready to lift and I want to know time on station. Hunter, when can you take control of the Predator?"

"Without any interference factor? Pretty much from Guantanamo. But if this MPP broad can screw around with the signals, better off flying from here, where Sam's got some control of the frequency variations. If you need it, and there's only one, Trav, we better play it safe."

"Okay. Normal security out until the Ospreys get in. Anybody shows up armed, take 'em down. No screwin' around. I wanna see bodies folks, we're through talking. I don't want *anyone* walking away. Jen, Stan. You two take the rear so nobody steps on your stuff. Sarah, you're with me down by the hut watching the river. Jack, you cover the front. Sam, as soon as you—"

"You'll get it as soon as I do, boss."

"Let's get this show on the road," said Travis. No sooner had the words left his mouth than one of Stan Powczuk's mines ignited. "Sonuvabitch!" yelled Travis as he took off running after Stan and Jen. "Sarah, down to the river."

The noise of the explosion had dissipated and finally some small arms fire started crackling. Travis ran up-trail and spotted Stan lying on the left side of the road. For a heart-stopping moment Travis thought . . . then Stan turned his head back at him.

"They musta missed the one I set up-trail. They're in the bush here"—he pointed to his left—"shooting at nothing that moves."

"Anybody get a count?"

"No, man," said Stan, "we barely turned the corner when it went."

A submachine gun sprayed out an entire magazine. Jen

lay on the right of the road ahead of Stan and heard two rounds go over her head. "Sounds like AKs," she said. The hours the team had spent lying on a rifle range with instructors shooting a variety of weapons over their heads paid off.

Special-ops troops were aided by knowing the weaponry of their adversary. A multitude of different weapons would generally mean a not too well-armed foe, whereas if everyone was similarly armed it could mean a trained force. Multiple weapons also became confusing and could trick you into thinking there were more of your adversary than there actually were. Then again, none of this meant a damn thing if they had you pinned down with accurate fire. But it helped to know every little bit in combat.

What Travis, Stan, and Jen did know was that an indeterminate number of people in front of them seemed to be armed with AK-47s and weren't acquiring targets worth a damn. Full magazine burns were the sign of Beirut street fighters—the kind who stuck a gun around a corner and pulled the trigger. Not exactly effective fire. These guys were also shooting high. The terrain—they were downhill of the three TALON troops—was partly the cause of this, but with the combination of shooting at nothing, full-magazine fire, and high rounds, the conclusion was they weren't facing very skilled troops. But unskilled personnel on their home grounds had killed many a special-ops soldier. A bullet, after all was said and done, didn't think. It just killed.

Another mine went off, and Jen saw part of a body thrown in the air along with the black column of dirt, dust, and smoke. The fire intensity picked up.

"Sounds like ten or a dozen, eh?" said Stan.

"I'll go with that," said Jen.

"Jen, can you high arc a grenade down in front of them and get them moving back up here?" asked Travis.

Olsen looked into the sky. "That's gonna be almost straight up in the air, Travis. Tricky if it drifts."

"Hey, Blondie. Can you or can't you?" challenged Stan.

"Or what? You gonna throw seven grenades this time?" She started to roll onto her back, then realized she still had her pack on. She popped the quick release, then scrunched forward and rolled almost flat on her back. She brought the XM-29 to her shoulder, adjusted her position, looked across the road, moved the muzzle of the smart rifle a hair, and popped off a 20mm grenade round. The round made a hollow sound, like a bang on a six-inch piece of PVC piping with a crowbar. *Bwonk.*

Travis and Stan watched Jen as she followed the round. Sometimes you could track a 20mm slug by eye, but you had to be behind the shooter and watching it from the get-go. They watched Jen, who kept her eye on the round as she lowered the smart rifle.

"Annnnd . . . oh-ho-ho. Perfect," she said as she watched the round drop. There was a hollow but rough-edge "crump" and the firing started anew, this time in the direction of the round and the hut. "God, I'm good."

Two men burst out of the grass and indiscriminately sprayed fire up and down the trail. One headed directly toward Travis and Stan, never even noticing Jen. The other headed in the opposite direction. Jen shot him twice in the back, and the man collapsed in a heap.

The other soldier ran past carrying the AK with two hands. He stopped when Travis stepped away from the rocks. His eyes were wide, and he seemed to be fumbling with his ammo pouches. Travis shot him once in the heart.

"Get some frags in there, we ain't got ti—"

"Here they come," said Jen.

Six men burst from the grass. Three carried AKs at the ready, one was dragging a wounded comrade, and one held only a machete.

The three TALON troops muttered the same words at the same time. "Aw shit!"

The firing was over as fast as the words.

"Jeezus," said Stan. "That almost made me feel bad. Do these guys have *any* idea what they're doing?"

Travis shook his head disgustedly as Jen went to the six men and moved each carefully with her foot. "Dead as doornails, Trav," she said after a moment.

"Okay. Round in the head. Let's get those bodies into the bush. Stan, find out why the up-trail didn't go off, dammit, then wire up the trail again."

Jen was looking back at Travis and Stan, unholstering her 9mm, when a shot rang out. The bullet took her in the head and she went down as if hit with a sledgehammer.

"Fuck!" yelled Stan as he charged into the grass, Travis hot on his heels. Another burst, shorter and more controlled sang through the grass.

"Okay, at least one guy knows what he's doing. Go left, I'm right, five and hold," snapped Travis. Both men split up and dived into the grass five meters before freezing.

Patience was a virtue, as any hunter knows, and whether the game was deer, lion, or man, that was fact. Whoever blinked first would lose. Travis and Stan fired up their LOCSs and stood quietly, listening. Their prey did the same, but without the advantage of the LOCS.

Sarah's voice came over the com system. "I can see you on infrared, Travis. But I can't see Stan. If one of you isn't on the trail, somebody else is. He's about five to ten meters off you, between you and the hut."

Travis looked downhill and could make out the top of the hut. "Got it. Stan, I'm gonna make noise wide. You take him." Travis started down the hill in an arc away from the other soldier making some noise, but not an undue amount; just enough to draw the other man's attention. If the enemy soldier fell for it and concentrated on Travis's movement, Stan would be able to take him out. Stan could move real quiet anywhere.

Travis stopped walking, started again, then stopped. This guy wasn't too bad. No indiscriminate fire. Ah jeez, I hope he doesn't have frags, thought Travis glancing skyward.

Bup. Bup. The barely discernible sound of two XM-29 rounds canceled Barrett's last thought and any future thoughts the MPP trooper had intended on having.

"Got him, Trav," came Stan's voice.

"Nice and quick, Stan. That guy was better than the other bunch. You head down and take over from Sarah. Forget the trail and wire the hooch. Doc, up here with Jen."

Travis ran back up the hill—why was the distance covered after a firefight always so much longer than that same distance at the beginning of the contact?—and scrambled over to Jen. She was lying on the trail and at first glance emitted that peculiar nothingness that dead bodies always did—appearing as just a lump of viscous fluid held together by a semitaut outer covering.

Head shots were not a good thing, but he hadn't seen the typical blood-bone-brain spray pattern when she'd been hit, so hopefully . . .

Jennifer moaned. "What the fuck happened?" she mumbled loudly.

"I'll tell you this, babe, if that BSH *was* a soft hat, you're partying days'd be over now. Lie still 'til the doc gets here."

Travis knelt beside her and placed his hand gently on Jen Olsen's shoulder. His eyes kept scanning the trail and the brush, the XM-29 following wherever they looked.

Chapter 12

September 17, 2200 hours
Outside the town of Menet, Haiti

"*Mon Dieu.* What you mean you can't tell what they're saying, woman?" said Jean-Guy quietly.

"For the hundredth time, Jean-Guy. Whoever is transmitting this stuff from our island is using a similar but more sophisticated system than mine. The frequencies rotate automatically and at random. And the last burst wasn't even directed along the satellites I've been able to access. Whoever it is that's sending isn't from this little paradise," Lily finished haughtily.

Jean-Guy paced to and fro in the hut, deep in thought. So the *merikens*—it had to be a *commando* or *les paras* of the damn Yankees—had sent someone down. And much faster than he'd thought. He had thought to have at least five days to take the reins of control and announce his new "savior" government, complete with popular support. But now . . . now it looked like someone was here and that someone seemed better equipped than the military unit that the foreigners had sent to Haiti before this.

"Do you get any sense of where they are? What they are saying?" he asked quietly.

"The last signal originated to our west. But that could be anywhere in a straight line between here and Santiago. My guess would be closer—"

"Your guess?!"

"—than farther insofar as the strength of the signals, but signal strength isn't a very good indicator on microburst transmissions."

"Could it be Dominicans? *Traffique diplomatique?*"

"Could it be?" said Lily. "Sure, but it's not Dominican diplomatic traffic. It has to be American. Electronically, these little keyboards and boxes I've designed are so far ahead of anything any of the local governments have, that it has to be either a U.S. military or CIA station encoding. I doubt it's normal traffic," she added. "Someone has been trying to find our locations. They've been trying it from the satellites I've been accessing, and they've probably isolated a half-dozen or so locations we've sent from, but this one is probing along the same lines as the burst transmissions. If it *was* Dominicans, Jean-Guy, the transmission direction would be out of Santo Domingo, not Santiago or San Francisco. No. Someone's on to us. Or at least is trying to get on to us. Someone is definitely looking for us, that's for sure. And I don't think it's to pat us on the back. Do you?"

"Spare me, *mon cher.*"

"Jean-Guy, we've got to—"

"Hush. Let me think."

LePetit strode out of the hut and look up into the night sky. So. With all her computer expertise, all her assurances of being able to outfox the Americans, they've still managed to put someone on our trail. He spun back into the doorway of the hut.

"I don't suppose you've got any idea how many there are, do you?" he asked Lily.

The pout on her pretty face was all the answer LePetit required. "*Bon,*" he acknowledged. "Tell me this then. Is there any way you can tell me anything exact—anything certain—about *mes amies*? Anything?"

"What I suggest we do is—"

"Woman, I don't need your suggestions," said Jean-Guy with a hint of menace heretofore unheard by Lily. "What I do need is for you to tell me something of value. Anything. How far away are they, how many of them, which direction they're headed, what kind of soldiers they are. Anything at all. You've told me how good you are with your little magic computer systems, now make them do something that will truly help me for a change. And do it now."

Lily's eyes widened at Jean-Guy's tone, but her surprise

was overcome by the challenge, and she whirled angrily back to the laptops and started typing intently.

So that is the modern Haitian woman, eh? thought LePetit. This woman has been helpful so far, but I wonder just how valuable she really is.

LePetit dismissed Lily from his mind. He had to make a decision now. Could this force in the hills be merely a technical team sent to Haiti to discover the source of the jamming? A possibility. They would have some kind of protection but it would be for defense only. Was it worth sending someone out to look? Yes, but where? If this woman could just give him a decent locale perhaps a dozen or so handpicked soldiers could find them. But a location "west" of here was relatively valueless.

LePetit laughed quietly to himself. So this is what it has been like to fight against me, he thought. A spirit force, rumor, maybe here, maybe there. No wonder I've been so successful. And now these . . . whoever they are . . . have turned the tables somewhat. He turned to speak to one of the waiting runners when he saw five men walking toward the hut. His commanders.

Geffrard was as thin as LePetit, but not as tall. He'd learned some of his military skills courtesy of the trainers who had established the new Haitian National Police back in the days of Haiti's second democratically elected president, Rene Preval. He'd also ended his association with the HNP about that time due to his exuberance while serving in the CIMO, the department's crowd control unit. Geffrard's interpretation of the word "control" was quite at odds with the dictionary's definition and he'd found himself cashiered.

Ti Rouge was a bandit, plain and simple. Short and nearly as wide as tall, his face bore an African jungle tribesman's amount of scars, his smile displayed a conscientious lack of dentistry, and his broken nose gave his otherwise completely unattractive face a somewhat baffled look, and was his only softening feature. Though not the most formally educated man, he consistently demonstrated his Ph.D. skills in pure cunning.

El Sikki was almost as studious looking as LePetit and actually had graduated secondary school. He'd worked for a bank in Cap Haitien, but had ended this career under a cloud of suspicion as to the whereabouts of some elderly patrons' money. The suspicion had not been provable—though it had been correct—and El Sikki had taken to the hills when a particularly honest HNP detective had come around for the second time to have a look at the part-Arabic teller. El Sikki had joined up with LePetit about three months later and had been with him for over a year.

Ti Bobo was a street tough. A medium-sized man with an incredible build (honed on the docks of Cap Haitien and Port-au-Prince), he was a human Cuisinart with a knife as well as the twelve-inch baling hook he carried on his belt. He'd used the hook on several occasions—none of the recipients had survived, though their deaths had been rather long and painful—and led his men by a reputation reinforced by the hook.

LeBlanc was the only real oddity in LePetit's command. As educated as Jean-Guy, he was intelligent, schooled, trilingual, quiet to the point of taciturnity, and vicious for no apparent reason—often. Jean-Guy trusted him with any complicated assignments and never turned his back on him when they were alone. When Jean-Guy finally took power he would make LeBlanc his chief of police, he thought. Or have him executed immediately by whoever *was* appointed chief of police.

LePetit looked at the men thoughtfully. If it was a *meriken groupement de commandos* out searching for him, they would have to be removed and LeBlanc was the man. However, if they proved to be only a rumor or were a radio team, using LeBlanc would be a waste. He would need him in the final hours in Port-au-Prince. And there was the problem. If there were to be final hours . . .

"Bobo. That man, your lieutenant, Jeune? How good is he?"

Bobo thought for a while before answering. "Pierre Jeune? He do what I tell him. And he fight hard."

"*Bon.* I want you to pick a dozen men and put Jeune in charge. Perhaps one more good man to assist him as well. You know the two trails that lead out of the mountains into Menet?"

"Below the river crossing east of Poste Rouge?" asked Bobo.

"Yes. I want ambushes set on both of them. Six men each. Have Jeune take the main trail, and put the other in charge of the little one north of the crossing. But make sure they are all good fighters."

"Has something happened we should know about?" asked LeBlanc. His voice drew surprised looks from all the men.

LePetit looked at his dangerous captain and thought carefully before speaking. "Nothing has happened, but it is always better to be prepared. There is a possibility someone has intercepted our signals and if they have I would rather not have them behind us unless we know about them."

"How many?" asked Bobo.

"We don't know if anyone is coming. Jeune's job is to make sure that if anyone does come they only get as far as there and no farther."

LeBlanc methodically lit a cigarette and watched as LePetit spoke. None of the others said a word.

When no one else ventured any comment, Bobo said simply, "It will be done."

"The rest of you, get your men ready to move. We need to be hidden in the city by first light. Tomorrow night we take the government. LeBlanc, I want you and your men in the catacombs of Cathedrale Ste. Trinite. I will join you there. Geffrard, the Place de Heros de L'independance has become a refugee camp. Take your men in quietly this evening. Do it in four and five man groups and set up around the outskirts near the Musee du Peuple Haitien along Rue Oswald Durand. Let no one see your weapons. Go in like spirits and make camp quietly opposite the Palais National. El Sikki, I want most of your men between the post office and city hall, but place fifty to control the entrance to the piers. Ti Rouge, the area around Dessalines Barracks is por vous. No one comes out of there alive, understood?

"I want everyone in place by morning. Have your men bring enough food to get through the day, but some of you must look like refugees, so be careful how much you bring. Do not look like a guerilla force going in to take over the government! You must look like the people in need of help. And do not get involved with any officials no matter the cost. If one of your men so much as smells what food someone else has or refuses to move when a policeman orders or causes any kind of disturbance, when this is over I promise you I will have him buried alive. No one must know we are there. Those of you out among the people, say nothing of Louverture unless others bring it up, and then only that he will come. Keep your weapons hidden from everyone as best you can. If an official does see your weapon you may kill him, but without guns. It must be done quietly. Do all understand me?" LePetit looked in each man's face. Each nodded in reply as their eyes met.

"Make sure all your watches have the same time as mine. It is twenty-two-fifty-five now." The men all checked their wrist watches. Ti Rouge made a hissing noise and struggled to undo the watchstrap. He handed it to Geffrard, who reset the time for him.

"At eighteen-fifteen tomorrow night," continued LePetit, "LeBlanc and I will leave the cathedral and attack the national palace. El Sikki, you will send twenty-five men into the post office. Kill the postmaster and no one else. Send twenty into city hall. Kill any guards and take the mayor, but do not kill him. Anyone who offers resistance, kill them. You will send twenty men to guard the road at the north pier and twenty to the main pier. I want no one in or out, understood? You must strike these places fast but quietly. Don't run up shooting no matter what you hear coming from the national palace. Get as close as possible before pulling the trigger. When your targets are down stop shooting them. We don't want it to sound as if *la guerre* has started.

"Ti Rouge. Surround the barracks first, then send grenades in. It will help if you can get your best shooters on the roofs surrounding Dessalines. Make sure you have cover. If you can force an entrance immediately, do so. If they are able to stop you—and if you do this quietly and fast they should not—take cover, but let no one out of that place alive.

"Bobo, the airport is yours. No one leaves, no one goes in. Four of the Tigers will meet you—I want you to go to the control tower; you, not your men. Take the tower, but destroy none of the equipment. Make sure your men do not mistake the Tigers for enemy. There are still UN troops garrisoned outside the airport. Keep them in their compounds, they are lightly armed. If any attempt to break out, try and take their machine guns if they have them, but take no risks. If they decide to fight, kill them and do not worry about the vehicles or guns.

"Geffrard. I want your men assembled and ready to take the palace at eighteen hundred. It will take us fifteen minutes to reach the palace from the cathedral. Wait for us to go in first. When you hear our first shots, you wait fifteen minutes before going forward with your men. I don't care who you kill or what you do—and this is for all of you—this is not to be a riot of wanton destruction. Kill who has to be killed, but if I see one window broken that did not have to be I will want to know who and why. Tell your men: Any man who disobeys will join the undead by the hand of Louverture. Tomorrow we will have to be running a government as if we have been all along. I want nothing more destroyed than this hurricane has already done. Geffrard, your men will take care of the grounds around the palace once we have taken the government and disposed of those who will not be with us."

Four of the men chattered in agreement. LeBlanc looked through the smoke rising into his eyes in the still tropical air at LePetit and merely nodded. The five men faded into the darkness.

"LeBlanc," called Jean-Guy. The quiet man stopped and turned. "We need to plan the assault on the palace before we meet at the cathedral."

LeBlanc nodded and slowly returned to Jean-Guy.

"Is there a problem, *mon ami*?" asked LePetit.

LeBlanc looked LePetit directly in the eyes. Several beats passed, but Jean-Guy maintained the eye contact, staring more intently into the other's eyes.

Though LeBlanc was as cosmopolitan a man as one would find in Haiti, there was a deep core of his being that still reacted to the darker side of Vodoun. It had been ingrained in him—for that matter in all of them—from infancy, and no amount of modern thought or training could totally erase the knowledge—and fear—imparted as a child. The feeling was like that of anyone who has ever whistled as he walked past a graveyard late at night, or strolled down a dark alley way in an unknown town. A twinge of old memory, a slight raising of hair on the neck and a sense that one is 99 percent sure everything is all right but . . . LeBlanc broke the ocular stalemate.

"No Jean-Guy. I do wonder about this need to protect our rear," he added.

"It is nothing. At least not yet. And Bobo's men will ensure it stays that way," said Jean-Guy. He looked into the man's face. This man would not follow so blindly as the others. "The woman"—he inclined his head toward the hut—"thinks someone is trying to eavesdrop on what she is doing. She is trying to discover exactly where or who it is as we speak. That is why I sent the men back to watch the trail. If anyone is there—and we do not know that it is more than a signal somewhere between here and the border—they will have to come that way if they are following us."

"Merikens." It was a statement, not a question.

"If there is anyone, it could only be them. Perhaps a *petit commando*. The *merikens* have many different ones of those. But we needn't worry. Certainly it is nothing large enough to stop us now."

LeBlanc looked back at his leader then nodded his head once, somewhat grudgingly.

LePetit moved to place his arm around the other man and felt him flinch, albeit ever so slightly. Good. "To more important business."

"Aside from the actual takedown of the president, his staff, and the national police, the key to our success lies in surprise and silence. We cannot have this turn into a pitched street battle. I don't want our men running the streets, shooting, looting, and raping. By morning's light all must look normal. After we make sure the leadership is dead or in cells—I want anyone who is willing to go with us taken back to the cathedral and held in the cells below until we see whether they are truly with us—we will send most of the men to the ports. We will need to get Bobo's men to Cap Haitien as soon as possible after everything has settled down. I need you—personally—to commandeer some vehicles and make sure any civilian pilots staying in

Petiouville are rounded up and ready to fly. As for attacking the palace itself . . ."

With LeBlanc settled and the plans for taking the national palace ready, LePetit rubbed his hands over his face, digging his fingers well into his eye sockets. He rolled his head around loosening his neck and shoulder muscles, then turned back to the hut. It is ready, he thought, and now it must be done. There is but one more thing. The Americans.

He straightened himself and walked into the hut.

Entering quietly, he pulled out a chair and sat and watched Lily as she continued working the computers. "Anything?"

So intent was the woman, and so quiet was Jean-Guy's entrance, that she jumped when he spoke. "Perhaps," she said. "Give me more time."

"Time is something we have little of, dear Lily. You have nothing?"

"Yes, I have something, just wait a minute . . . I think."

Chapter 13

September 18, 0100 hours
Outside the town of Mirebalais, Haiti

"About gah-damn time," said Sam Wong. "Boss, I got a download. Looks like they finally woke up back at command."

"What do we have Sam?"

"A shit load. Take a seat, this is gonna be long. Apparently they've been running and re-running tapes over at NSA and back at TALON HQ and have finally come up with some answers on who's doing what to whom. There have been about a dozen interferences and probes on the eyes in the sky. All from different locales. Either the operators are moving fast—in other words they have access to air transport, which seems unlikely—or there are multiple operators. Or, and this is where my money goes, they have remote-site transmitters here and there. Nobody can tell which it is, only that the signals have been coming from different sending sites or areas over the past three days. From what they're telling me, I'd go with a single operative and multiple sending sites. Whoever's doing this is good and there just aren't that many of us out there.

"Which brings me to the who. There's an excellent chance it's a woman named Lily Rebuffat."

"How the hell did they come up with that?" said Travis incredulously.

"She's a Haitian computer geek—I ran into her back at Comdex a few years back. Beautiful woman, but not very approachable. I tried, but I'm not Jack or Hunter. Anyway, she's a Haitian national, educated in the States, came up with a shit load of very sophisticated hardware and software developments all through her high school and college career and—"

"Jesus, Sam, you should marry the broad," came Stan's voice over the com.

"Hey little buddy. You marry a Haitian broad and you become part of the tribe," said Jack DuBois. "A bunch of little black Wongs running all over the place." He laughed heartily.

"Awright, awright," said Travis. "Everybody pay attention to what they're doing and just listen."

"Thanks, boss," said Sam. "Anyway, seems she sold everything she owned in the States and disappeared. Fibbies show her leaving on an ALM flight for Port-au-Prince about nine months ago and there's been no sign of her since. NSA says they were trying to recruit her, for God sakes, and she's vanished, sooo . . . I'll tell you, boss. If she's the one, she's good, and she could easily pull it off."

"Interesting," said Travis, "but it does nothing for us. So we've got a good tech up against us. Does that help you any, Sam?"

"Well. Yeah, I guess. At least I know there's something out there looking for me. Kinda like cyber chess, or hide-and-seek if you get my meaning."

"Good for you. Glad you're finally having fun," said Travis sarcastically. "What else do they have? Give me something I need to know, Sam."

"Okay. We've got definite radio transmissions—FM band stuff—from just north of Menet to both Cap Haitien and Port-au-Prince. Apparently someone's been sent to wire the harbor at Cap Haitien. According to NSA, it's probably happening as we speak. There's also been several commos between Port-au-Prince and Menet, as well as some traffic out of the airport. The burst decode comes out sounding like they're also wiring the runway at Delmas. The commos out of Port-au-Prince are quick and don't make much sense, but are apparently sitreps of some kind. This info is all at least twelve hours old, and there hasn't been much since then that they can tell. They're still going through tapes of the shutdowns and incursions. Maybe they'll come up with more, but for now that's what we've got."

"Nothing about anything happening in Port-au-Prince or Cap Haitien?" asked Travis.

"No noise out of our embassy. The Marines are on full alert but report the street scene as normal. That's current info, by the way. Neither the DEA nor the CIA hear anything on the street. Apparently they're all hot to trot because NSA is asking questions about Haiti and they practically can't even find the damn island on the map."

"Was that in the report?"

"I know who's sending this, sir. Just some interservice rivalry."

"What about our transport?" asked Travis.

"Ospreys inbound in zero-zero-twenty. The big bird'll be ready to drop gear in about an hour thirty. Your call on time and place. She can stay on station just about forever if you want her to."

"Okay everyone. I want to be ready to move in zero-ten minutes. Stan, get the LZ ready. Sarah, go with him."

What we have here is one very fluid situation, thought Travis. Command decision time. Primary responsibility is to find the main force and stop them, that's a given.

"Sam. There's no idea on the size of the force?"

"This doesn't sound like your typical military ops, boss. Not a lot of traffic and not a lot of call signs. Just the three different transmissions. They're playing this close to the vest."

"We need to keep the airport open as well as the ports," Travis said, thinking out loud. The ports at Cap Haitien were closer to the States than Port-au-Prince, but the majority of the populace was located in the capital. The seat of government's in Port-au-Prince so that's got to be where the enemy's obvious efforts will be concentrated. Cap Haitien is a gimme for now.

"Sam, give me the street map of the capital again," said Travis. "Jack. What did the prisoner say about estimated strength?"

"He said thousands, boss, but I don't buy that. Even as piss-poor as the intelligence coming out of here has been, there's no way you keep a couple of thousand troops hidden and unknown. You gotta feed them, arm them. Hell, on this island feeding them would be a chore and somebody would have known something. There would have to be a trace and—"

"Hold it. Sam, see if there's been anything—and I mean anything—that might indicate a large underground operation. Have base hit up everyone and anyone. INS, DEA, CIA, whoever. Ask about a Cuban connection too. Now."

"Roger."

"Go ahead, Jack."

"Well, Trav, I just don't see it. If there is a large force, they've got to be piss-poorly armed, and just as hungry as the populace. It doesn't make any sense. If this guy's as smart as he seems—"

"And to pull this off so far, let's assume he *is* very smart," interrupted Travis.

"—then he kept his force relatively small. Say under five hundred men scattered about the countryside. He could arm them well without drawing a lot of attention, and if they were splintered into, say five or six cells, they could feed off the economy without drawing a lot of attention. I'd go for a small group. Maybe as few as two hundred, but certainly no more than five. And certainly no 'thousands.' "

"Any disagreements, people?"

"Well, even if it is five hundred, that's a lot of people to stop with seven of us," said Jen. "And my head still hurts," she added just to make sure everyone still remembered.

Jen thought she heard someone mutter something about "time of the month." It had to be Stan.

"Stan. The LZ?"

"Ready to mark on your call."

"Ospreys—Ghostriders Four and Five—are ten out," said Sam.

"Ghostrider Four, this is B-One-Odin."

"Ghostrider Four. Go Odin."

"I need a side scan VR about sixty kliks south of here. Subtle. Over."

"Roger, Odin. Give me the coordinates. I can do about five minutes fuel time. Over."

"Sam, numbers on Menet."

"Roger, boss. Downloading to you, Ghostrider."

"Odin. Ghostrider. Got 'em. Over."

"Ghostrider, I want a thermal imaging. Gimme a big

loop and tell me if you've got anything between Menet and the capital. Over."

"Roger, Odin. Vehicle, personnel, cows, what? Over."

"Personnel. Over."

"Odin, I'll be back to you in five. Out."

"Okay. Sam, you and Hunter get that Dragonfly in, then get down to the LZ. Sam, as soon as—"

"You got it, boss."

As the team converged on the LZ Stan and Sarah had prepped, Travis continued to weigh the team's options. Priority one was stopping an attack on the established government. Priority two was keeping the airfield open. If the Eagle Team could stop the coup attempt before it got rolling and keep the strip at Delmas opened, they would have the "luxury" of having the time to track down the leader of the coup afterward. Travis wondered who Louverture was and how he'd gotten the entire plot to this level. No dumb ass here, he thought. That also begged another question. What did this guy even look like? Well, he'd worry about that afterward.

The team maintained a perimeter around the LZ. The field was as large as their original drop zone had been and would easily handle both Ospreys at the same time.

"Sitreps," said Travis.

"North is fine," said Jen.

"South side looking good," said Jack.

"East is okay. There's one tall tree that they want to watch on approach," noted Sarah.

"Fine on the west," said Stan. "Sam's heading in."

"On the way, boss," came Sam's voice.

"Hunter, call the ball on approach," said Travis.

"Roger, Travis."

"Sam . . ."

"Zero five out," said Sam. "Thermal imaging is downloading. I think it'll be easier to read from a hard copy."

"B-One-Odin. Ghostrider Four. Light me up. How's the ground wind?"

Hunter de-powered the wrist-mounted RF generator, pointed his arm to the southwestern sky, and fired. Hunter Blake had come up with using the RF generator as a marker beacon—on its low-power setting—the first day he'd been introduced to the RF unit. The technique had been incorporated as SOP in the TALON arsenal ever since.

"Negative ground wind, Ghostrider. Best approach east to west, you have a bit of a gust there. There's a big tree blocking the egress," said Hunter.

"Roger, Odin. We're inbound."

As the first Osprey appeared over the treeline, it slowed to tilt-wing mode. The second banked high and wide around the LZ on its wingtip.

As Blake listened to the pilots chattering back and forth, the first V-22 completed its transition to full vertical flight and somewhat gracefully touched down on the LZ, then turned and rolled back to the LZ's eastern side and readied for launch. As soon as it cleared, the second went into approach and touched down where its sister ship had, then rolled to the LZ's northern side, facing toward the first ship ready to roll. Both VTOLs powered down, but kept their blades turning and throttles on. With their stealth propulsion on, the blades' aerodynamics made a loud swishing sound, but the engine roar was negligible.

"Odin, you want a printout of the VR?" asked Ghostrider Four. "It's not great so I don't think you'll get that good detail on the BSD screens."

"Coming in," said Travis. "Stan, I want you and Jack in one bird. You get Delmas. Ghostrider, I need to know your loads. We're splitting the team."

"Shit, Travis," said Stan. "We're much more effective as a unit."

"I know, I know, but that's the only way to handle this. I want you and Jack to make sure that airfield stays intact. You'll get a recon going in but it's going to require ground work. Sam, get them a schematic of the runway. I want to know where all the drainage systems are. That's where they'll have to hit to interdict. Stan, Jack. Find them and stop them."

"Roger, Trav."

"Done deal, boss," said Jack DuBois. "Hey, Stan. We get to get down and dirty."

"Fucking lovely," answered Stan Powczuk.

Chapter 14

September 18, 0430 hours
Delmas International Airport, Haiti

"Holy shit! You ever seen a mess like that in your life?"

"Yeah, twice," answered Jack. "Once in Kosovo, and once in a movie with Christopher Walken about some mercenary rebellion in Africa back in the nineteen-sixties."

"Oh yeah, man," agreed Stan. "What the hell was the name of it? It was pretty good. Shakespeare. Yeah, *The Dogs of War*."

"Cry Havoc," intoned Jack in his deepest voice, "and let loose the dogs of war. What was that? *Richard the Third* or something?"

"No, I think—"

"Uh guys, enough with English lit and movie reviews. Whattaya want to do here," interrupted the voice of Captain Ian Scarr, aka Ghostrider Five.

"Sorry, Cap," said Jack.

"Give us an infrared scan around the perimeter on flyby, then we'll do another on thermal. Let's see who's out there," Stan said.

"Roger," said the Osprey pilot as he banked the V-22 on a wide circle around Haiti's international airport.

Delmas Airport could be mistaken for either an airplane graveyard, a rather bad internment camp, or a defunct industrial park. On a good day. Surrounded by barbed wire, with tall grass growing seemingly everywhere, the airstrip brought to mind a lazy Pacific atoll fueling station that had lain unused since oil replaced coal as a propellant. One side of the arrival buildings was crowded with enough different elderly airplanes to make a Rhinebeck plane restorer giddy. There were DC-3s, 4s, and 6s of Caribbean airlines long gone in the drink, dubious lineage short hoppers and seaplanes, helicopter bodies here and there, and a virtual "history of aviation" coffee table book's worth of the hulks and hulls of small private planes.

No, on a good day Delmas was not the most attractive airport in the Caribbean. Not by a long shot.

The hurricane had added to Delmas's "did anybody win this war?" ambiance. One of the two control towers was still standing, but the beacon mounted on it lay at its foot atop a pile of rubble. Wherever Stan and Jen looked, courtesy of the night vision aspect of their BSHs, they saw jumbled and blown down hangars. Windows on the arivals building were gone, fencing was down and the main control tower was—if in any kind of operation at all—certainly sans electricity. There was not a soul to be seen moving about, and it looked as if people had taken up residence in the airplane hulks.

"How the hell they gonna tell if this place *is* blown up?" wondered the Ghostrider pilot.

"Lets take a look at the runways," said Stan. "As long as they're intact, some Pathfinders can get this place back in ops in a couple of hours."

"Yeah," snorted Jack. "As long as they bring some engineers and bulldozers along with them."

The Osprey flew near stall speed in slow orbits around the airfield. The runways were intact.

"Let's do the thermal run," said Stan. "Run us along the wire, let's see what's hiding in the grass."

"Instead of patching through your BSHs, why don't one of you guys sit in the two spot and use our helmet," offered Scarr. "You'll get a better image." He turned to his copilot. "Bill, switch seats with one of them."

Jack nodded at Stan to take the front seat, and the pilot leveled the Osprey off while they made the exchange. While the image transfers to the BSHs were fine on a ground-level basis searching at close range and not covering such a large area, the height from the aircraft caused the image—especially a thermal one—to show practically nothing but masses of black spotted with the ocassional varying intensities of the red of targets. Too much information had to be absorbed and the BSH wasn't set up for it.

"I take it we're looking for people," said Scarr, once Stan had the copilot's helmet on and was seated and plugged into the Osprey's ops system.

"You got it."

"Okay, I'm gonna fine tune this for people-size images," said Scarr. "It'll discount little critters, hotspots from old fires, whatever bigger animals are around, etcetera. If you see bright red concentrations, you got people. Oh. And don't touch anything up here unless I tell you to."

Jack looked at the copilot who had joined him in the troop carrying compartment and had donned Stan's BSH. The flyboy was grinning away. The man turned to Jack and said something that the big Marine couldn't hear. Looked like he said, "This thing is pretty neat." Jack gave him a thumbs-up and the copilot went to fiddling with the BSH visor array. Now if we could just drill some holes in your head, thought Jack, you'd be a happy camper just like us.

Scarr banked the Osprey and ran it down one length of the perimeter and up another. On the third pass, Stan yelled, "Mark it" into the mini-mic.

"Jesus, commander, you fucking blew my eardrums. Lighten up, that mic's as sensitive as the stuff you have," said Scarr.

"Sorry. Did you get a fix?"

"It's reading. What did you see?" asked the pilot.

"Some bright stuff in . . ."

"Hold on. Bill, come up here and feed this back to him and get a translation."

The copilot squirmed between Stan and Scarr and pressed several button on the console to the right of the throttle controls. He jabbed his index finger forcefully at the console screen directly in front of Stan indicating he should look there. The plane's run up, one hundred yards prior to Stan's call to mark it and three hundred after, ran in a loop on the screen.

"See the white button midway down the right side of the screen?" asked Scarr. "When you see what you want, punch it and we'll get numbers. After it grabs the numbers, hold the button down and use your other finger to punch the button directly next to it. That'll tell you what you're seeing, because believe me buddy, you ain't gonna know."

As the digital image rolled, Stan saw what looked to be several jagged red blobs. He pushed the button as instructed, and a PPS number appeared on the screen. He held the button down and fingered the other. The display read "3/98.6+/-.9."

"What the hell is that?" said Stan with a laugh.

"What's it say?" asked Scarr.

"Three, slash, niner-eight point six, plus, slash, minus, point niner."

"You got what we like to call three humanoid types down there good buddy," chuckled Scarr. "Or at least three something's pumping out good ol' ninety-eight point six Farenheit heat. Plus or minus a degree or so."

"Okay. Those could be our boys. Get us out of here for a while."

As the Osprey angled up and headed west toward the mountains behind Delmas, Stan and the copilot contorted past each other, exchanged equipment, and re-took their original positions.

"Okay, thermal says we got three people in the deep grass about a hundred meters off the east-west runway," Stan said to Jack.

"Does it match up with any of the drainage tunnels?"

"Gonna check that now. Hey, Scarr, can you overlay that image or match up the location with that schematic of the runways we gave you?"

"Already done, sir," said the copilot. "Looks like your mark is off one of the main drainage tunnels, 'cause about midway across the strip, it intersects with four tunnels coming in from the north and south. Kinda looks like one of them Jewish Christmas candle thingees," added the copilot.

"That's a *menorah*, Wolensky," said Scarr. "And Jewish Christmas don't make any sense a'tall. You really gotta get out more, Lieutenant."

"How close can you put us down without them hearing us coming in?" asked Stan.

"I can put down on the southwest end of the runway and they shouldn't notice a damn thing. You'll have about a klik walk up to the target area, but you can do most of it along the runway then cut back into the woods when you get close."

Stan looked at his teammate, who nodded and said, "Let's do it," to the Osprey's pilot.

Stan and Jack conferred with each other as the V-22 turned back to Delmas and made its approach.

"We'll move down on the runway about five hundred meters, then hook through the wire and come up behind them," said Stan.

"How do we know how many? I mean, there's three there, but I'd be leaving some security if I was under the airfield. Wouldn't you?"

"Yeah, well, let's try and take one of them alive. At least temproarily," said Stan. "You do that voodoo that you do so well and we'll find out just who's who and where the fuck anybody else is."

As the Osprey's wings rotated into vertical lift mode, Jack looked at Stan and said, "Sounds like we got us a plan, man."

"C-One-Odin. Ghostrider Five. Com check, over," came the pilot's voice over the TALON frequency.

"Ten by," answered Jack. "What're your plans Ghostrider?"

"We're heading back toward Gitmo. We're a tad low on go juice. You want us on station?"

Jack looked at Stan, who shook his head. "No, but we will need an extraction in a while and we'll have to link back with A-One at some point."

"Already arranged. Listen for us on the net. We'll be back in about nine-zero loaded for bear."

"Nice doing business with you," said Jack as the crew chief slid the troop carrier door open and the Osprey thumped down. Stan flipped down the BSH's visor, took one look out the door and jumped out of the craft, followed by the big Marine. They activated their LOCSs and moved into the grass, vanishing from the crew chief's sight. The crew chief slid the door shut and told Scarr to take the Osprey back to the sky.

The two Eagle teammates waited until the Osprey had cleared the ground then headed east along the runway. While not running, they were moving faster than they normally would have on a typical combat patrol. What they had seen so far of their adversary had filled them with a sense that their foe was not of the best caliber, nor were they numerous. In this case they also were more willing to trust in the thermal-imaging run than they would have in a hotter AO. They were not complacent, but were more concerned with speed at the moment. Stan walked the point with Jack trailing. Both men's eyes—aided by the night vision devices—scanned all around, though Jack spent little time covering their rear.

Two-man patrols were not unheard of in special ops, but it could give the enemy an advantage of sorts. With two men you simply couldn't visually cover all the ground needed to ensure security, no matter how hard you tried. Not if you expected to move any faster than a well-meaning snail. However, those who had partaken in this size patrolling considered the benefits to well offset the detriments. You and your partner operated on the same mental wavelength (Stan and Jack had done this several times before) so all communication was reduced to the very basics. Speed, stealth, and surprise were also on your side; who, afterall, in their right mind would enter hostile territory with only two men? Jack and Stan were confident in what they were doing and considered the risk necessary to the mission.

Stan stopped at what he considered five hundred meters (he was off by ten) and Jack followed suit. He looked around, turned to his partner, and nodded to the bush. Both men melted into the higher jungle grass bordering the runway. As the tall grass closed behind them, Jack heard Stan call a stop.

"Wire."

Jack moved up next to Stan and held the strands of barbed wire as Stan cut them. Each clip sounded loud to the two men, but what noise there was—and the noise they made was never as loud as it sounded—was swallowed up by the thick, high grass.

"There better only be a few of these fuckers," grumbled Stan.

The wire strands separated. Each man held a piece as he passed it and didn't let go until the other grabbed it from him. Barbed wire—in this case razor wire—was as old as the hills as a defensive weapon, but it had survived every modern invention of warfare and still would grab and tangle you no matter how sophisticated your weaponry. It was always a pain in the ass—literally and figuratively—to maneuver through and had to be done carefully.

They cleared the wire field and moved deeper into the grass.

"Shit," said Stan after moving ten meters. "More wire."

"What is this, a fuckin' war zone?" said Jack.

They went through the cut, bend, hand off routine and continued moving through the grass, finally leaving any vestiges of wire behind them. Before the grass gave way to a reasonably thick wooded area they had to ford a six-foot deep and ten-foot wide drainage channel.

"You smell that?" said Stan, referring to the odor emanating from the stagnant water and who-knew-what in the ditch. The muck came knee high.

"No. I'm dead," answered Jack.

Both men's minds suddenly turned to the possibility that they would soon be crawling in the same substance if they had to make their way under the runways and disarm any explosive devices.

Using hands and feet they quietly slid and clambered up the far side of the ditch. They stopped next to each other at the ditch's top—only their heads showing—and looked down the cleared area to where they thought their prey was. Beyond a twenty-foot cleared trail was a fairly thick stand of trees and brush. They looked up and down the ersatz trail, saw nothing, and quietly crossed into the woods. The two turned east and angled away from the runway while moving parallel with it.

After about three hundred meters of ear and eye straining movement, Jack saw Stan come to a halt and raise his hand. He pointed to his nose then made a chopping motion with his hand to his ten o'clock. Jack smelled it as well. Cigarette smoke floating downwind. Someone was smoking on an ambush, one of the biggest no-nos in the litany of combat dos and don'ts. The two men moved slowly upwind toward their quarry.

Four men, not three, were carefully ensconced on the

far side of the drainage ditch. They were observing noise discipline it seemed—certainly neither Stan nor Jack could hear them speaking—and were relatively well camouflaged. There was a radio operator whose backpack-type radio was carefully propped with its antenna well hidden in the reeds and three others sitting in a semicircle. One was watching the woods where Stan and Jack stood but incredibly was still smoking a cigarette. He had it well cupped to avoid any telltale ash glow, but you just couldn't discount the manurelike smell of the French-made Gitane cigarettes. Jack would have recognized that smell anywhere.

Stan spoke carefully. "There were only three on the readout. I wonder if one of these shitheads was under the runways."

Jack studied the four men intently. "Can't tell if they're wet and I don't see anything that looks like a firing device either. Can't see if there's any wiring heading off to the strip either." He heard Stan sigh.

"Okay. Let's figure the radioman ain't the explosives guy and neither are the other two sitting down."

"The one with the cigarette," said Jack. "There's our EOD man."

"Shit. If they did go in already, we gotta know where this stuff is. Especially if it's on a timer."

"Nah. They ain't using a timer, I'll bet. One of them has a firing device of some kind," said Jack. "Probably radio controlled. Hell, if they can beat our satellites, they can come up with a remote igniter."

"Possible," said Stan. "So . . ."

"So let's waste the three sitting down. Try not to hit the radio. And let's take Smoker alive. He sees me appearing out of the bush all of a sudden, he'll get to talking real quick."

"Okay," agreed Stan. "You gotta make sure he's down though, Jack. I'm gonna move down a bit for a better angle on the others. Go on my shot."

Jack leaned against a tree and steadied the XM-29 on Smoker's left shoulder. The first round should pretty well ruin that joint and spin him to his left. He'd go for a very painful hip shot as the man went down.

Jack heard Stan's smart rifle fire and saw the radioman's

head explode just as the soldier who had been lying down went into a well-controlled cough paroxysm. Jack fired, saw Smoker spin, dropped his sight, and popped another round into the man's lower back.

Stan shot the second soldier between the eyes, but the cougher had recovered immediately, spun behind his pack, and squeezed off a magazine in a well-disciplined arc as he wiggled back into the grass trying to draw his pack with him.

"Gahdammit," Jack heard Stan curse as his XM-29 kicked dirt around the man who now had rolled onto his back, quickly reloaded, and was returning burst fire in Stan's direction.

Jack bolted east through the woods, then practically dove into the drainage ditch. "Keep him there Stan," Jack said. "I'm gonna flank him."

Stan was carefully popping rounds at the soldier, who had all but disappeared into the grass. Guy's good, thought Stan. While the XM-29 was flash supressed and silenced, the target could see the gun's discharge, especially at night. It wasn't much, but if the enemy was good, it was enough. His man was using—it sounded like a very fast, light round, maybe an MAS. It really ripped through that first magazine and had lit up his position like a flare. Stan had fired off ten rounds and slid about a dozen feet away before taking the man under fire again. The enemy soldier returned fire in short three-round bursts and had also moved to a different position before firing.

"Jack, watch this guy. He's good," said Stan.

"Not anymo— Sonuvabitch!"

Stan heard the man scream in pain, then cut loose with several bursts in Jack's direction. Stan saw the muzzle flash, aimed lower, and skipped two rounds in. The man yelled out in pain again, and then his voice abruptly cut off.

"Got him," said Jack breathing heavily.

Stan stood and headed across the drainage ditch, his eye on the wounded smoker who was moaning and yelling at the edge of the ditch. "Keep your eyes on Smoker, pal," said Stan as he disappeared into the ditch.

"Don't worry about him," said Jack.

"What happened with the other guy?" asked Stan as he crawled up the ditch's far side.

"That damn barbed wire again. Just as I go to cap the guy I get tangled and start to go down. I get off one fucking round, and he's on me like stink on shit. Wait until you see this guy. FN-MAS, full camouflage, subdued sergeant stripes, looks like a West German Alpine ruck, good boots, the whole bit. Same with the others. You clear?"

"Yeah, I'm up," answered Stan. "This is the same crew that we took in the mountains? I don't *think* so. Things suddenly ain't looking real good, my friend."

"I'm thinking the same thing. Let me have a little chat with our well-kitted-out Gitane-smoking buddy here. We need to find out a damn sight more than whether or not the runways are rigged to blow."

Chapter 15

September 18, 0500 hours
Outside the town of Menet, Haiti

"Dammit, dammit, dammit," cried Lily, pounding the handmade wooden table in frustration. "What in God's name is—"

"What's going on?" asked Jean-Guy as he buckled a web belt and holster around his waist. "Have you been able to find out anything at all about our visitors?"

Lily spun around to face LePetit. "This isn't so funny anymore, Jean-Guy. There's someone out there and they have aircraft now."

"What!" yelled LePetit. Lowering his voice he growled at Lily. "*Merde.* What the fuck do you mean they have aircraft? Who? Where?"

"I can't tell exactly . . ."

Jean-Guy's hand went immediately to the Glock 9mm on his hip. He spun on his heel as he realized it and turned from the young woman before she noticed the look on his face. Calm yourself, he thought. You may still need her and she's certainly no good to you dead. He slowly and deliberately took a deep breath before turning back to face Lily's now wide-eyed countenance. Fear showed there for the first time. Good, thought Jean-Guy. Perhaps she now realizes this is all quite for real.

"What exactly *do* you have, Lily?" he asked in a gentler tone.

The young woman was obviously flustered by Jean-Guy's mood swing. "These . . . people to our west are real. I think what they have been doing is trying to track us through our jamming transmissions, brief though they've been. I also believe that—probably the NSA—has been able to find out something about us. The satellites I've been accessing are being queried at length. While they won't be able to backtrack through them, I'm relatively sure they'll be able to get some idea of locations on us." She saw Jean-Guy's eyes widen and hurriedly continued. "They won't be exact locations. We've been too quick and moved often enough. Plus, with the remote transmitters they'll only be able to get vicinity locations. Of that I'm fairly sure."

"Fairly sure," noted Jean-Guy, "is not sure enough when my life is at stake. Nor when yours is, *cher*."

"I understand that. But there is no way, not in the limited amount of time they've had, that they can get any closer to us than generalities. They are not going to pinpoint transmissions. I'll bet my life on that."

"You already have," noted Jean-Guy, "especially if American military are involved."

"A poor choice of words, Jean-Guy," apologized Lily.

"What about aircraft?"

"Again, I am not one hundred percent sure, but I am willing to bet that at least two and possibly three stealth aircraft have landed about thirty miles to our north. I'm accessing the American satellites, but even they have a hard time picking up their own aircraft. That's why I think they are stealth-technology planes. There also has been an interpolation of satellite data and microburst communication coming from a satellite heretofore unused that leads me to believe that aircraft have landed. They've certainly flown in or near us at sometime in the past hour. Have any of your . . ."

"No one has seen anything. And even if they were looking at the skies, what would they have seen? Nothing. But what would the planes have been able to see of us? That is the question."

"Jean-Guy, the sensor technology for real-time photography, thermal, infrared, and seismic imagery is all portable enough to be flown in planes. They can see anything and everything if they know where to look and what they are looking for. The question is do the Americans have stealth technology in aircraft that can land in mountain terrain? I know they have the high-altitude fighters and bombers so the technology is there but are you aware of any—"

"I'm not privy to what *les Americains* have and don't have," he snapped. "What do you mean they have to know what they are looking for?"

"Unless they're mapping the entire country—and even with satellites and aircraft that would takes months, not to mention the interpretation time—they would have to be looking in specific areas to find anything. These aircraft have flown in within the past hour or two. None have been directly over us, though I suppose they would be able to side scan away from their flight paths—"

"Side scan?"

"It would make sense that if the military has developed a system to peer into enemy positions it would have to be able to accomplish that from locations away from the exact place they'd like to look. The sensors would detect out to the sides as well as directly below. I know the satellites are unidirectional and every time they've tried to photograph on their passes I've stopped it."

"You *think* you've stopped it every time," snapped Jean-Guy.

"Of that I'm certain," replied Lily adamantly.

"Finally you are certain of something."

"Jean-Guy," said Lily, ignoring the last remark. "Let us assume they have such aircraft. With three, four, no more than six landings—and the takeoffs might very well be accounting for the numbers. I can't get the computers to have the satellites discern the difference, and I've thwarted all attempts to turn the satellites off when I want them on and vice versa—how many men could they have landed? You have nearly five hundred with you; we are poised to take control of the country in less than eighteen hours. What possible effect can a dozen, two dozen men have on your plans? We are almost there, we know that they are behind us. Intelligence is the key, and now we have it."

Jean-Guy stared at Lily for what seemed to the young woman to be an interminable amount of time. He turned slowly and walked to the hut's doorway, cocked his elbow, and leaned on it looking out into the night without saying a word. Lily waited, nervously casting quick looks at her computer consoles.

It is quite easy for this one to think that her little bit of knowledge means anything, thought Jean-Guy, but she's not a fighter. I have stayed alive this long by always controlling my environment. Nothing went on, nothing happened unless it happened how I decreed it. There may be a kernel of truth in what she says. How many men could they have set down? For that matter, since they apparently don't even know we exist why would they send combat troops? What does disturb me is that they have somehow decided to mount their operation from the interior rather than from Port-au-Prince. And that makes me nervous. Why start in the mountains unless they know something?

Jean-Guy shook his head and continued staring out into the darkness. On the other hand, if they are located in the hills, there is only one or two ways they can get down to Port-au-Prince by foot, and that at least is protected. He turned to Lily.

"I do not like the idea that your information is so limited. Especially with all you have told me you can do with your little computers. But you may be right. How many men could they have landed? Lily, I ask you this: Is there any way you can keep track of whether or not there are more of these aircraft?"

Lily thought for several seconds. "They leave a signature of nothing, if you understand my meaning, and that in itself is signature of something. Perhaps if I have access to strong radar . . . say the system at Delmas . . . I can tell you what is there by what isn't."

Jean-Guy thought long and hard, his eyes never leaving Lily, the long stare making her uncomfortable. He'd thought he would keep her with him during the attack, but of what value would she be? Perhaps it would be better if she could keep track of the Americans or whoever was behind him. He called to the runners outside the hut.

"Tell Petard and the remaining Tigers to get ready to move. When you come back, you and your friend will help the woman carry her equipment and meet with Bobo's men on the road to Delmas. Understood?" Both young men bobbed their heads in understanding.

"Listen to me and listen well," LePetit said to Lily. "You and your equipment will go with Bobo to the airport. I do not think there is any power there. Tell Bobo to either get the emergency generators working or confiscate generators . . . whatever he has to do to get you what you need. If Bobo doesn't understand what you need, look for the Tigers. Four of them will meet him at the airport. Show Sejourne—he is the leader—this." LePetit removed a necklace and placed it over Lily's head. "He will know it is from me and will get you whatever you want, no matter."

Lily reversed the silver medal, a stylized silver cross that all the Tigers wore, and looked at it. "Do not fail me," said LePetit. "I must know anything that happens back there."

"I promise, Jean-Guy, no matter what goes on, I will find out and be the one to tell you. I will see you at the national palace tomorrow."

"I hope you will, my dear. Regardless of where, however, I will see you tomorrow. Now this time, break down your gear and move out of here. I want to hear when you have met Bobo. I do not like surprises and it is most important to the entire plan at this stage that there be none. We are too close and I do not wish to lose all now."

Chapter 16

September 18, 0515 hours
Outside the town of Mirebalais, Haiti

"Where to, Major?" asked the pilot of Ghostrider Four.

"What's your name, Lieutenant?" asked Travis over the Osprey's intercom.

"First Lieutenant Gus Miller, sir. You can call me Goose."

"Okay Goose, here's the deal. Can you put us on top of a building, probably one with a lot of antennas and flag poles and stuff, in the middle of a blacked-out city?"

"Hell, sir, I'll take you wherever you wanna go. If you got the numbers, I'll put you on it. If there's a lot of crap sticking up though, you might wanna consider rapping in. There's a limit to what I can do with this bird. It ain't a Blackhawk."

"Okay. I'm not certain exactly what's there, so rig it up. You got rap gear?"

"Yes sir. Enough for six and there ain't but five of you."

"Go to it.

"Sarah, Hunter. Get those equipment containers out. I want everyone loaded for bear. Double ammo loads, at least four XM-11 robot sensors per man, grenades and have the arsenal boxes rigged and ready to drop. Goose, how long to rig for rappel?"

"Chief, how long to rig?" said the pilot to the crew chief.

"Gimme twenty minutes, sir," he answered, as he looked at Travis standing outside the Osprey.

"Twenty minutes, Major."

Travis gave the pilot a thumbs-up.

"Sam, anything from Jack and Stan?"

"Ghostrider Five just made the drop. He's headed back to Gitmo for re-fuel and will be back on station in nine-zero. He said Stan got thermal tracking on three individuals right outside the field perimeter near the drainage system entrance of the east-west runway and he and Jack were heading to interdict. Want me to get in touch?"

"Leave them be for now. They'll let us know what's what. What about C and C?"

"They're analyzing Four's thermal run. They said to give them thirty minutes."

"You tell them I want it in fifteen, not thirty. It's my ass hanging—"

"Uh, boss, General Krauss already relayed your message. They just said they'll have it in five."

Travis and Sam grinned at each other. "Damn right they will," said Travis.

"Listen up, folks," Travis announced. "We're going into the national palace. It's in the middle of downtown Port-au-Prince. We're going to try and have our embassy people alert the Haitians, but let's consider everyone hostile until we know what the hell is going on. Let's try and avoid killing any friendlies, but don't take any chances. Once we neutralize the palace . . . well, we'll figure that out after we get there. Sam, get the message to our people and tell them to alert the Haitians. Make sure the palace people know we're considering it a combat insertion and to make sure their people are clear on intent or we'll take them down. Now all we gotta do is find out numbers and locations and we can maybe stop this whole mess before it takes off."

The five team members went about re-packing their gear as the Osprey's crew chief continued rigging the plane's interior.

Each of the five rappel ropes—11mm black, kernmantle ropes—were locking-caribiner rigged to flush-mount rings recessed in the troop area bay around a door that would slide back into the plane's fuselage. Unlike on most helicopter raps, where the soldiers would stand on the helicopter skids before dropping, coming out of the Osprey mandated an almost free fall initial jump through the inner door to clear the fuselage. The strength and power of the Osprey's downdraft with its props in hover position negated the possibility of coming out the side doors. The interior bay door was the design method chosen to deal with this peculiarity. It made for a scary initial move, and the rappeller's brake hand had better have a serious grip on the brake line or it was a free fall to the ground. The team would go out one by one in nearly as rapid succession as a static line parachute drop. Since each man would go out backward, the fact they were carrying full combat rucksacks prevented multiple exits. Like many of the maneuvers the Eagle Team performed, it was all about timing, and they'd done it often enough that it was down to balletlike precision.

The ropes wouldn't be deployed until they could ascertain whether they were needed. If the Osprey could get into a hover within ten feet of the roof, they'd free jump. Higher than that—and it would be Travis's call. The possibility of twisted and broken ankles made it too risky otherwise. If the Osprey couldn't get close enough, it would hover higher and allow for a fifty-foot rappel instead. The ground commander called the shot regardless.

"C and C coming in," said Sam. Travis stood next to the little commo expert and waited impatiently.

"Boss, C and C wants to speak direct."

"Patch it."

"A-One-Odin, go." Travis listened as the voice of General Krauss came over the com as if he was standing next to him.

"You've been rather busy, I see, Travis."

"Yes sir. It's been, er, interesting, General."

"Here's the story," said Krauss. "The thermal has picked up a wide movement of men in Port-au-Prince. Roughly five separate hundred-man groupings. From the direction of movement we've established from the one flyby it would appear that all are headed for the center of the city, though one looks like it might be headed for the airport."

"Lovely, sir," said Barrett.

"We're trying to figure out how to deal with the Haitians. We don't know if this has inside support and are rather loath to tip your hand," said the general. "Plus, when we mentioned that you were going to take the palace it seems to have set off quite a bit of consternation at the White House amongst the State Department types. Attack on sovereign territory, and all that."

"Sir, I'm not risking my people, and we're trying to save *these* people!"

"Relax, Travis. You do what you have to and let me worry about the attaché case crowd. It would be nice if you could keep the, ahem, collateral damage to a minimum, but I think you'll have to introduce yourselves to the locals rather than have us do it. Unless you're sure of the security aspect of it. Your choice."

"Is there anyone in direct contact with President Antoine, or does it all have to go through diplomatic corps?" asked Barrett.

"We're efforting that, as they say on the Hill, but as of this moment . . ."

"Then leave it alone, sir. We'll take care of it from this end. And we'll try to minimize the collateral damage but I am definitely *not* promising anything."

"Understood. A wiser, if riskier method I think, but at least it will keep the lace panties in State dry. What they don't know won't hurt them," said Krauss.

"Roger, sir."

"Do you have an ETA on the festivities, Travis?" asked Krauss.

"No, sir. We're going in now. We've been playing this by the seat of our pants so far. We need to get into the city ASAP. We figure they'll make the move today or tonight. By the way. Any make on the head of this ops? This guy seems to know what he's doing."

"Nothing more than what you got in your briefing, I'm sorry to say. I'm sure people will be paying a bit more attention from here on in, but for now, there's nothing. We're still trying."

"Roger, sir."

"Anything else, Travis?"

"Well, it wouldn't hurt to scramble another team or two just in case this doesn't go. The odds are pretty long on the face of it, though the troops we've encountered so far haven't been the best."

"We'll have two teams at Gitmo in six hours. You say the word."

"Roger, sir. That's it from this end," said Travis.

"God speed, Travis," said the general. "Out."

"Anything worthwhile?" asked Jen Olsen.

"Everybody listen up. We have about a five-hundred-strong force moving on the capital in five groups. We're going into the national palace to introduce ourselves to the locals. The rules of engagement are as follows: everyone is fair game. The good guys don't know we're coming, but neither do the bad guys. We'll try to avoid contact until we make it to the presidential suite and inform the president of who we are and what we're doing. But nobody takes any chances."

"And what *are* we doing, Travis?" asked Hunter Blake.

Travis shook his head. "That, people, remains to be seen."

"Want me to find out what Stan and Jack are up to?" asked Sam.

"Just tell them they may have a light company's worth of bad guys headed their way. Everybody rigged and ready?"

A chorus of "yes, sirs" answered Travis.

"Ghostrider Four, this is A-One-Odin. Com check. You about ready, son?"

"If y'all get your harnesses from Sergeant McCarthy there, we're ready to roll," said the pilot.

The five TALON troopers walked over to the Osprey as Goose Miller wound the engines up. They climbed into their waist harnesses, double looped the buckles, put on their packs, and climbed aboard.

"Ready to rock," said the pilot.

"Let's hit it."

The crew chief slid the door shut and the Osprey slowly clawed its way into the sky.

* * *

0535 hours
On board Ghostrider Four en route to the Palais Nacional, Port-au-Prince, Haiti

"Dammit!" spat Travis.

"What's up, boss?" asked Sam.

"How fast can you get a download of the floor plan of the palace?" he barked. The other three troops looked at Travis in surprise. Mistakes will kill you, and the major had made one.

"About as fast as you can drop your visor. I asked for one from C and C the first time you mentioned the place. Took them a little while to dig it up, but it came in not long after the Delmas plans did. Sorry I didn't mention it before," said Sam.

For once Travis wasn't annoyed by the commo man's precognition vis-à-vis his own thought patterns. *I wonder if any of the other team leaders have developed this kind of relationship with their IMS,* he thought.

"Good man," he said gruffly. "Sorry people. Shit happens. Won't happen again."

A chorus of "no sweats" answered Travis's frank admission.

"Loading down," said Sam. "You get a frontal first. Place kinda looks like a mini White House in front, but it's got two more cupolas on either end. Not real big."

Travis flipped down his BSH's monocle-like visor and looked at the hologram picture. "Rotate it," he said. The views changed to cover every side.

"Lots of open space around it. Good fields of fire," he noted. "Let's see the roof."

"Nothing of the roof, boss," said Sam. "From what I see, the place looks kind of flat on top but I think a rap'll be in order. Don't think there's enough room to risk the Osprey. Unless you want to go in the front door. I don't recommend that. We didn't bring any cake."

"We're going in from the top down. Let me see the floor plan top to bottom."

"Third floor coming up."

"Do we know where the president's or prime minister's quarters are?"

"No, but the executive level is the top floor."

"Get C and C and see if anyone knows whether the president's in residence, and let everyone have a look at this," said Travis.

"Roger."

Travis pondered the floor plan. Four sets of stairs led to the roof level; two right about in the middle of the building behind the dome and one each on the wings. "Talk to me, people," said Travis.

"Have Ghostrider make a slow pass east to west," said Hunter Blake. "Two at the first door, two in the middle, and one at the end."

"It'll make for an easier rap, Travis," said Sarah Greene. "The last drop is a single and the Osprey can get the hell out real fast."

"If there're any guards on the grounds they'll see us, but it'll take time to get up to us. We can get to the third floor before anyone can react," said Jen.

"Okay," Travis said. "Third floor."

"Well, if I was the president, I'd want a view. Figure offices in the front, quarters in the rear," said Jen.

"Probably centrally located," agreed Hunter.

"Both the president and prime minister are at the palace, sir," interrupted Sam. "State says that the embassy has been doing all communications direct to the palace. The Big Boss says that don't mean dick and he won't guarantee it means they're really there. He also wants to know if you want the embassy to attempt notification."

Travis thought for a second. "Can't risk it, Sam. We go in hot as planned."

"Roger."

"Goose, we need a slow drift along the length of the palace east to west or west to east, your call. As quietly as possible. We're rapping down," said Travis. "How's your fuel?"

"I can give you this but then I gotta haul ass for Gitmo and juice or me and my men are looking at a long swim. I'll give you the drift, but if you want it real slow, it ain't gonna be real quiet. Not at rooftop level. I'll do what I can though."

"People, I want shape charges on the door. We blow them all at once. Order of drop: Hunter and Jen, me and Sam. Sarah you're on your own. Sarah calls the doors. Once we're inside, Hunter and Jen converge on the middle. Me and Sam'll check the executive offices. Sarah, you hold that end of the building; we'll be pushing anyone that runs toward you. No chances people, but let's maintain fire control. And for God sakes, let's avoid killing the president and prime minister if they're there!"

Jennifer Olsen laughed first. "That'd be nice. 'We're here to save your country.' Whack. Oops."

Everyone laughed, but Travis added, "Yeah. But let's make sure that *doesn't* happen. If it goes bad, people, we rendezvous on the roof. Goose, I want two of the rappel ropes left on the roof along with the arsenal boxes."

"Sarge, you got that?" said the pilot.

"They'll be coming down behind you," answered the crew chief.

"Make sure we're not on them," said Sarah. The crew chief's helmeted head made an upward nod.

"We're zero-five out, Major," said Goose.

Travis gave the order to rig up. The rappel ropes were bight-threaded through a metallic figure-eight lock-carabinered to each trooper's waist harness. Their XM-29s were strapped to their combat packs and all wore black leather-and-Kevlar gloves; the initial quick drop through the floor created enough speed and rope friction that leather gloves alone wouldn't be able to hold the braking line.

The crew chief looked at Travis, who pointed out the order of the rappel, then stood. He pointed to Hunter and held up one finger, then to Jen and held up two. They both nodded. He repeated the gestures for Travis and Sam and finally for Sarah, then spoke into the Osprey com system. The carrier bay lights went to infrared, the belly door slid open, and the noise and wind roared in. Each Eagle Team member flipped down his or her BSH visor. Hunter and Jen dangled their legs out into the night sky. Everyone stared intently at the crew chief.

Travis saw the green light shine on the crew chief's visor

and missed Hunter's drop through the floor. He saw Jen go, saw the crew chief point his finger at him, and he dropped out into the night sky, slapped the brake end of the rope that had whipped through his hand unbelievably fast tight against his hip, then released and felt his feet hit the roof. Sam was standing next to him before he was able to release the figure-eight from the harness.

The Osprey continued its drift along the roof. As Travis saw Sarah undoing the rope on the other end of the palace's roof, the plane disappeared over the city and out to sea.

The five rushed the doors, a small cigarette pack–size device in hand. They slapped the small sticky packages of C-6 plastique to the door locks and waited for Sarah's okay.

"Go," said Sarah.

Everyone pushed a button on the explosive charge and spun back along the side of the stairwells for cover. WAP! WAP! WAP! WAP! Four not-so-muffled explosions, not quite simultaneous, blew the locking mechanism out of the doors—Sarah's had actually blown the door completely off—and the five poured into the building.

No one encountered anyone on the stairs, and the building itself was eerily quiet and dark. Travis had expected some sort of alarm sounds and emergency lighting, but nothing echoed or shone. Travis reached a doorway at the end of the staircase and tried the ornate knob. The knob turned and the latch released. Travis leaned back against the wall, took a deep breath, then opened the door and spun into the hallway in a full crouch. He slammed his back against the door and looked both ways. Nothing.

"In," he said, and was answered the same by four other voices.

As Travis straightened up and carefully perused the corridor Sarah Greene's voice came on the net. "Uh, Travis?"

"Go."

"I got two ladies and five gentlemen down here who, er, say they're the president and prime minister and would like to know what the hell is going on."

"Oh, Jesus," said Travis. "I'll be right there.

"Sam. There are two staircases there. No one in 'til I

say so. Hunter, Jen. Get back here with Sam. Leave your end clear."

Travis walked down the corridor, heading for Sarah and her "hostages," his head swivelling at every door and hallway, his XM-29 at the ready.

"Boss? Sarah?" radioed Sam Wong.

"Go," said Travis.

"Want a picture of the two gentlemen?"

"That *would* be nice. Hold it until I get to Sarah."

As Barrett rounded a corner in the hall, he came upon seven individuals clad in various stages of dress lined up with their faces against the wall. Sarah Greene stood in an alcove covering all of them yet remaining out of any possible line of fire.

Man, there's probably gonna be some State Department shit over this, thought Travis.

"Nice job, Sarah," he said.

"Nothing to it, Travis. They were moving out of here on the double. Never saw me. The three big ones were armed. They saw the error in their ways."

Travis cleared his throat and spoke aloud, making the two women jump and causing all five men to turn their heads toward the noise.

"Sarah," said Travis, still speaking aloud. "Could you move the two ladies away?"

Greene tapped the left-most women on the ribs with the muzzle of her XM-29 and pushed her toward the other. Both moved down the wall.

"Thank you, ladies," said Travis. "Does everyone speak English here?" he asked. A man with thinning hair showing traces of gray along the sides, turned slowly. "Sir, we don't want to do anything foolish now," said Travis in warning.

"I am President Robert Antoine. I demand to—"

"Hold it a second, sir." said Travis. "Sam, give me the president," he said reverting back to the TALON com system.

The man who had turned from the wall watched Travis's face—and the XM-29s muzzle—with a look of puzzlement. The soldier's mouth had moved and he seemed to be speaking to someone, but . . .

Travis looked at the download, then at the person who'd

identified himself as President Antoine. To the president it seemed as if Travis had suddenly gone into a trance and was staring into space.

Travis checked the download on the visor again, then looked at the man standing at the wall. He switched the smart rifle to his left hand, lowered it to his side, muzzle down but finger still on the trigger, snapped to attention, and saluted the now agape president of the Republic of Haiti.

"Greetings from the United States government, sir," said Travis in a heavier-than-his-usual Texas twang. "My name is Major Travis Barrett and this is Captain Sarah Greene." Sarah—not quite as stunned as the Haitian president at Travis's performance, but nearly so—kept her XM-29 trained on the seven civilians. "We're American soldiers, sir, and *you* have a rather large problem."

Travis's statement and President Antoine's look of surprise were enhanced by the sounds of gunfire.

"Whatta ya got?" said Travis.

"Some guys trying to force entry," said Jen. Fire could be heard through the corridor as well as over the com system. In the confines of the hallways it provided a weird echo effect in the TALON com receiver. "We got 'em held right now with cover fire, but if they start thinking it's gonna have to get hostile in here."

"Sir," said Travis to the president. "Is there any way you can call your men off? Nobody's been hurt so far and we'd like to keep it that way."

The president looked at Travis and then at his four companions.

"Sir, honest to God, we're here to help. I'll explain everything, but we have to stop this before your men get hurt."

The president noticed that Travis didn't consider the option of his own men getting hurt. He made a decision he hoped he wouldn't regret. He turned to the largest of the three bodyguards. "Tell them to stop, that everything is all right for now," he said.

The bodyguard looked at the president but did not move. "They could easily have killed us all by now," said the president. "Go."

The three bodyguards looked at each other, then one backed off the wall.

"Hey," said Sarah, "you may want this." She flipped the man the mini-Uzi she had taken from him earlier. The guard caught it, nodded to Sarah, and turned to go when Travis placed a hand on the man's chest.

"Everybody okay down there?" he asked of his three men. A series of rapid single-shot fire answered.

"Yeah, no problem, Trav," came Hunter's calm reply. "They're still trying to figure something out. Lot of yelling back and forth going on though. They may be making a move soon."

"Okay, you got one rather large gentleman headed your way. It's the president's bodyguard. He should be able to calm things down. Jen, Sam, Hunter. He's carrying. Mini-Uzi . . ." he looked at Sarah, who held up three fingers, ". . . with three mags. Should be okay. Somebody watch him."

"Roger, boss," said Hunter.

"Major," said the president. "To whom are you speaking? You are speaking to someone, are you not?"

"Sir, can we go someplace where we all can speak? Your staff is welcome to join us."

The president nodded his head. "May I introduce Prime Minister Duvalle. These are our wives, Madame Antoine, Madame Duvalle. My guards are Marc and Joseph," he said indicating the two remaining bodyguards. "Erique is the one meeting with your men."

Travis tried not to smile as Sarah's voice came over the com system. "Jesus, this guy's hard core. We could have been here to axe him. What the hell's with all the formalities?" Travis nodded to each person as the introductions were made.

Travis fell in behind the president as he strode down the corridor. "It's called statesmanship, Sarah, statesmanship."

President Antoine escorted the entire group into his office. "You'll have to excuse the lack of lighting," he said. "I am afraid the hurricane has dealt my country quite a severe blow, and we have not been excluded from it. It seems the gasoline supplies for our emergency generators were not what we thought."

Travis noticed the president throw a hard look at his prime minister. "Sir, that's part of the reason—the hurricane that is—why we're here. But it's really only part of the problem. I'll explain all this in a second, sir. I need to get my men settled first."

The president's eyebrow raised as he looked at Sarah Greene and heard Travis's "men" remark. "Of course," he said. "You do have the guns."

Travis shook his head. "Believe me, sir, it isn't like it looks." He turned to Sarah. "Doc, check everyone out. Make sure they're wide eyed and bushy tailed."

"Yes, sir," she said as she left the office.

Barrett turned his back on the president and started speaking to the rest of the team.

"Are we clear?"

"Yeah," said Hunter. "The big boy seems to have calmed them down. Even a little laughing going on. I'll be damned if I can understand anything though."

"I'll tell you this," said Jen. "It ain't French. I wish Black Jack was here."

"Everybody get some rations and water, but keep everyone off the floor. If the big guy wants back in the office let him. Sam, you guard the door to the president's office. Jen, I want you in here. Sarah, Hunter, close the perimeter up on the office, but keep the hallways in sight clear. I don't want anyone up here until we get things settled. Sam, get me a sitrep from Stan and Jack and then get C and C ready to do some explaining. If they've got someone who's personal friends with President Antoine it'd be a good idea to get him on the horn. Anything new on the communication problem?"

"Been off the air for a while, and our satellites are recycling," said Sam.

"Okay. Get me readiness reports on air support and the big bird."

"The big bird's doing laps around the island at about twenty thou. Ready when you are."

Travis turned to the president and prime minister. The president's face seemed to be saying, "I've got a hundred questions and all the time in the world." Well, we'll have to change that, thought Travis, as the door opened.

"Lieutenant Jennifer Olsen," he said to the assemblage. "Lieutenant, this is President Antoine, Prime Minister Duvalle, and their wives.

"Sir," said Travis to the president, "I'd like the lieutenant to go with your wife. She's going to need to borrow some clothing and things. Lieutenant, I'm going to need a street recon and I need you to get to the embassy as well. Leave what gear you don't need here."

"Got it, Trav. Ladies?" The president nodded to his wife, and the first lady escorted Jennifer through a side door and out of the office.

"Major," said the president. "I think we've been most understanding up to now. Would you care to explain just what is going on?"

"Sir, there's a coup d'etat about to go down. We think either in the next few hours or later tonight. Either way, there's a guerilla force headed into town—hell, they may be here already—and near as we can figure, the only reason you send five hundred organized men into a capital city is because you want to take it over."

"Preposterous!" yelled the prime minister. "Our only problem is that no one has seen fit to send us aid after this devastating storm. It has been three days now and not a single ship, plane, or anything has arrived. Our people are dying, and—"

"Sir," said Travis. "We don't have a whole lot of time here. The reason no ships or planes have come in is because someone is controlling all communication and maritime and aerial navigation into this country. That's why we were sent here. To find out who and stop them."

"And *we* are *who*?" asked the president.

"We're a special-operations force. We do jobs like this."

"But how have you landed enough men and material in my country to battle an insurrection when you say these guerillas control everything?"

"Boss?" called Sam over the com system.

"Just a second, sir," Travis said to the president. "Go, Sam."

"Sitrep from Jack and Stan. Good news and bad news. The airport is secure as far as they can tell. And check this out. Apparently Jack stumbled upon some cavalry. A squad of Gurkhas of all things that were doing some jungle training with the Belize Defense Force, decided to take their R and R as a group in Haiti—go figure. They were supposed to leave but got held up by the hurricane. They're camped out with the UN advisors out at Delmas. Jack says they're armed and rip roaring ready to go. The bad news? Jack and Stan have done a recon and think a group of our boys are heading in. They also said that the group that was trying to blow the runways was considerably better armed and considerably more professional than the crew we encountered in the mountains."

"Let's hope it's, at best, a mix. Regardless, we play the hand we're dealt. Get this info to C and C and get me operational command and all the damn details on these Gurkhas. Gurkhas." Travis laughed, shaking his head. "Only in Amer . . . uh, Haiti."

"Roger, boss. I thought you'd be happy with that one. Oh. The Ospreys are en route. Stan says they can get them into Delmas, but he's still trying to locate some AvGas. By the way, General Krauss is standing by. Says he has someone President Antoine should be willing to listen to. Our president. I've got an external plug-in set for the BSH so he'll be able to use one of our rigs to speak with him."

"Get the Ospreys in and get in here and set the president up."

Travis whirled around to President Antoine, feeling lighter than he had in the past twenty-four hours. "Sir, I've got someone who'd like to speak with you. He'll explain pretty much everything."

President Antoine handed Travis back his BSH and sat hunched over at the desk looking at the American officer.

"I am not sure whether to be appreciative, horrified, afraid, or . . ." His voice trailed off as he stared at Travis. "What can we do to help? What can we do to avoid any more death?"

"Well, sir, I don't think there's anything we can do about more death," Travis said ruefully. "If these people are making a move on the government, we'll stop them. As for help, well, the only thing I can say is listen, give me what

I ask for, and we'll do our best to make this come out all right. For you *and* for your people."

The door to the president's quarters opened and the two men turned as Madame Antoine walked in accompanied by what appeared to be a servant. Travis turned to continue speaking to the president but noticed a look of puzzlement on his face as he looked at his first lady. Travis looked closer, then realized what he was seeing.

"Damn, Jen! If Jack could see you now," laughed Travis. Next to Madame Antoine stood a stooped, elderly, Haitian woman who looked as if she was having trouble walking.

"You'll have to thank Madame Antoine for the makeup and sartorial tips," said Jen, straightening up. The president's wife beamed a smile.

"This young woman is quite extraordinary," she said. "If I had not seen her enter my lavatory, I would never have known it was she who returned. Are all your 'men' so adaptable, Major?"

"Not quite, ma'am," said Trvais smiling. "But the lieutenant here is one of the best at what she does."

"I should think so." She turned to her husband. "From my brief conversation with the young lieutenant, I think we are in good hands, Robert. If you need me, I shall be in my quarters." She turned to Jen. "Be careful, my dear. You have a long life ahead of you if you do nothing foolish."

"My wife thinks she can foresee the future," apologized the president as Madame Antoine left the room.

"I got people that think that too, sir," said Travis. "Excuse me," he said as he placed his arm around Jen's shoulders and spoke to her. "I need you to get to the embassy and tell the Marines what's going on. Tell the guard you want to talk to the gunny who broke up the ambush last month. I also need a street recon. Around the palace mostly, but let me know if you see anybody moving in anywhere. It's almost daybreak and in that get up you shouldn't have any problems. Use a scooter or a bicycle or something. What're you armed with?"

"Got a 9mil in the blouse, an XM-73 pistol in this bag. Got my Gerber strapped to my forearm."

"Right now you ain't exactly the most attractive babe I've seen but you are the best armed. Be careful." Travis looked at his watch. "It's zero-six-fifteen. You got three hours. If the shit hits the fan, get back to the embassy and stay there until they can get some other teams in. Let those embassy types—including any spooks that might be there—know what's going on if we don't make it."

"Damn, Trav."

"Don't worry. Just be careful out there. See you in three hours."

"That is a very brave young woman," said the president.

"And tough," added Travis. "Sir, how well armed are the folks in the palace?"

"Mostly just—what do you military people call them?—small arms. After disbanding the military, we've relied on the HNP for security. The men in the building are some of the best we've got."

"Can you trust them, sir? We don't know whether this Louverture has infiltrated men in or what. And speaking of trust, may I ask where the prime minister's gone to?"

"Prime Minister Duvalle and I may not see eye to eye on everything, but I *do* trust him. He is checking the security arrangements in the palace. As for that security. There are but twenty men, Major, and I know most by face. This storm has had many leave their posts to help their families as well as maintain some semblance of order in the city. It has been especially tough on the people in the Soleil district."

"Well, sir, I need you and the prime minister to get your people ready for a shooting war. But they can't let anything look like they're suspecting something. I need them on full alert, and ready to batten down the hatches when the dance starts. We'll be up on the roof setting up a few surprises."

"That I can have done."

"And, sir. Perhaps you and the prime minister might want to think about evacuating the palace—quietly—for our embassy."

"We won't leave the palace. We are the democratically elected heads of Haiti. The people have chosen us. When all is said and done, it is our responsibility to stay here and stop any who dare try to turn us back to the horror that was the days of the Duvaliers and their ilk. We will stay."

"Sir, I understand how you feel, but I can't guarantee your safety."

"Major. Your president assures me of your expertise and ability. He assures me as soon as this day is over the relief supplies will flow. He assures me that he believes in the will of the Haitian people to stay on the path of democracy. I have faith that you can stop this Louverture imposter and keep Haiti free, and help us in this time of great need."

"Yes, sir," said Travis. Ohhh, great, he thought as he saluted President Antoine and headed out the door. He stopped with his hand on the door handle. "Er, sir? Our president *did* tell you that we—me and my team that is—were never here, right?"

"He mentioned that, Major. Which is another reason I cannot leave." President Antoine gave Travis a rather large smile. "Someone has to save this country," he said.

Travis looked at the president, shook his head, and smiled. "Very good, sir."

Chapter 17

September 18, 0637 hours
Palais Nacional, Port-au-Prince, Haiti

Travis assembled Eagle Team on the roof of the palace. The sky to the east was finally showing the red of early morning and the team could hear the city awakening. Dogs barked, roosters crowed, and there was the ever-present hum that a city emits as it wakes for another day. They heard the *rap-blaht* of an unmuffled scooter as it made its way down Guilloux Avenue on the west side of the palace. He spread the three remaining members of the team to each compass point on the top of the building. A haze of wood smoke—endemic to third world countries—hung over the city. Travis took the south side overlooking the parklike front lawn of the palace and activated the BSM's binocular mode.

There was little activity immediately in front of the palace, but he could see what appeared to be literally thousands of refugees in makeshift tents, lean-tos, and cardboard shacks out past the palace's fence line.

"Sitrep, folks," said Travis.

"What a mess," said Sarah. "People, tarps, fires. Hey, there's one of those tap-taps."

"What the hell is a tap-tap?" asked Sam. "Same on the east side, boss."

"A tap-tap is one of those real colorful buses," answered Hunter.

"They're colorful all right, but obviously they've never heard of emission testing here," added Sarah.

"Be that as it may, things are the same on this side,"

said Hunter. "Refugees, fires, and one massive tent camp. Lot of structural damage to the buildings too. These folks got their asses kicked by that storm."

"No organized concentrations?" asked Travis.

"Ha," snorted Sam. "Looks like one giant concentration to me. As Jack would say, 'What a cluster fuck!' "

"Except for the fact that there appears to be about a zillion civilians out there," noted Sarah, "this is an ideal killing zone for the arsenal boxes."

"Same here," said Hunter.

"Ditto," said Sam.

"We got two up here, right?" said Travis.

"I say the east side is a sure bet," said Hunter.

"Ditto on the north," said Sarah.

"My side's mostly buildings except for that big ol' mausoleum or whatever it is," said Sam. "Across from that the shops are all busted up. Great hiding places. The arsenal boxes are loaded with antipersonnel clusters. If they come from this side you're gonna need some fire power. The boxes won't be as effective."

"I have nothing but trees and open park. Lot of people," said Sarah.

"I got that, um"—Hunter checked his map on his BSH—"Place de Heroes," he pronounced decidedly un-Frenchlike, "and some wide-open spaces. Ditto on the people."

"Okay. Let's say they ain't coming in the front door. We set up the boxes to cover the north and east sides in close."

"Why don't we have the Osprey bring in some more?" asked Sam.

"I don't want anyone to know we're here, or know that they're there. Better we keep a low profile and take these bastards. I don't want to come back down here again."

"Sam, program the boxes for in-close remote fire. Any thoughts on how we get some sensors out there?"

"Do I ever," said Hunter Blake. "I was kinda roaming around the palace this morning and guess what? They got a Chinese dude in charge of the lawn and shrubs and stuff." Hunter laughed. "Since you all look the same to us, Sam, I think you should get to water the shrubs and stuff and drop the MSs right out in full view of the bad guys."

"Fuck you, flyboy," said Sam, as the others laughed.

"Sorry, Sam," said Travis, "but if the Nordic Ms. Olsen can play a Haitian woman, I think you can be the Chinese gardener. You're getting good at the menial labor jobs anyway . . . you were Jack's Filipino houseboy on the Iran ops, weren't you? Looks like you're tailor-made for this covert ops. Where was the guy, Hunter?" asked Travis.

"Where you keep the hired help. He's got a little apartment in the basement."

"Probably isn't even Chinese," grumbled Sam. "Probably a Korean or Japanese."

"Head on down there and get dressed. I want the Motion Sensors set for minimum range. Get them out about fifty yards, no more. Doesn't look like there's much plant life beyond that. Before you go, check all the coverage angles from here and plan accordingly. I think it'll come from the north or east, but make sure there're no coverage gaps on any side. Do we have enough MSs?"

"If everybody took their load, we should have five each. That's twenty. More than enough," answered Sam.

"It'll be you and Sarah up here. Me and Hunter will be down on the first floor until we see how things develop. Give us all direct commo until you get back. Make your survey and then get going. We'll cover you while you're out there in case, then I want everybody to rest some. Could be a long day. Or a longer night."

Sam checked out in front of him once more, then moved to each position and reconnoitered the fields of fire. In fifteen minutes he was satisfied and left the roof. "Any of you guys mention this to Stan, I'll get you for it," he said as he disappeared into the building.

"By the way," said Travis. "You heard anything from Stan or Jack? Or anything on the communications intercept?" He could hear Sam's footsteps echoing as he walked down the stairs.

"Nada on both. The bad guy's commo's been off the air. Do you want me to—"

"I want you to put the MSs out," said Travis.

"Roger, boss," said Sam resignedly.

Travis turned around and sat with his back leaning against his combat pack. "Stan. Jack. Sitrep," he said.

"Hey, Trav," said Stan. "How goes it?"

"Getting there. What's with the airport?"

"Explosives neutralized. Immediate field is secure and no sign of bad guys. We're trying to crank up the emergency generators, but there's no juice around. Put a tanker on the top of the list."

"Is it secure enough to start moving some equipment?" asked Travis.

"I wouldn't start with the big bird," said Stan, "but yeah, we can start moving stuff in. Maybe that'll shake these guys out of the woodwork."

"What's with the Gurkhas?"

"Man, I would not mind going into battle with these guys."

"On their side," added Jack.

"Tough cookies. When we asked them for help—and they all speak the King's English, which is very weird—you'd a thought we were promising them a million rupees or pounds or whatever."

"Do they realize I have operational control?"

"They didn't seem to care, but their sergeant, Amblam, said your code words were right, so him and the rest of his boys of the Tenth Princess Mary's Own Gurkha Rifles are happy to be with us."

"I do like the Brit's way of naming units," said Travis. "What about bad guys?"

"A few of the Gurkhas are getting dressed in mufti, as Amblam calls it—Limey for civvies—and going out for a recon. If there's anybody out there, they'll find 'em. As soon as they get back we'll give you a heads up."

"Okay. I don't want to open the strip until we know there're no heavy weapons around. Last thing we need is a tanker taking a mortar or rocket hit. Tell them to keep their eyes out for that kind of stuff. How well armed are they?"

"Light weapons. SR-88s. They said there's a good amount of 5.56 ammo in the UN compound, so shouldn't be a problem. Plus they got those damn knives."

"Kukris," said Jack. "They do like their kukris. If it comes to close-in stuff, I don't think we got to worry a whole lot even if the bad guys're all as good as the guys we took out. The only thing they're taking on the recon are their kukris. Amblam said they wanna 'fit in.' His words."

"Like to meet these guys," said Travis.

"If we ever get to Aldershot, England, we got an invite," said Stan. "And apparently one of the privates has a sister back in Nepal that he's dying for Black Jack to meet. So we're covered east or west."

"If you can make sure the bad guys don't have any heavy weapons, go ahead and get some Pathfinders in and get Delmas back in ops. Maybe if they see the airport working, they'll step up the timetable and we can get this thing over with."

"Roger, Trav. Talk at you later."

"Out."

Chapter 18

September 18, 1045 hours
Cathedrale Ste. Trinite, Port-au-Prince, Haiti

Jean-Guy walked amongst the men, most of whom were asleep or trying to sleep in the dampness of the catacombs below the cathedral. They had completed the infiltration well before sunup and had only had to overcome a night watchman and one priest. Both were dead. There had been hundreds of people on the grounds and in the pews of the eighteenth-century cathedral, but none had paid much attention to the coming of the MPP men. If any had wondered at the fact that men were entering the cathedral but not exiting, they certainly didn't express an opinion or question who they were. Most were refugees from the hills and were tired, hungry, thirsty, and seeking sustenance of any form after the storm had driven them from their farms, villages, or towns.

LePetit was pondering the Americans. He'd heard nothing from Lily, but that didn't worry him yet. There were no signs of any American soldiers in town and the skies had been quiet toward Delmas, so the airport was still closed. He knew that the first place troops would come in would be the airport. El Sikki reported that the port, about ten blocks west of the cathedral, was as deathly still as it had been since the hurricane. The Tigers up in Cap Haitien reported the same. Even if the Americans were able to stop Lily's interference with their navigation, by the time they landed men by ships either in Port-au-Prince or Cap Haitien it would be too late. The only one to greet them would be emissaries of President Louverture.

No, no matter what was going on up in the mountains, Lily's computers had worked their magic and given him the time to complete this audacious plan. Soon, it would be over and he would open the ports and airport to all the people who wished to help Haiti. By then his only problem would be bodies and disease, but bulldozers can take care of bodies, and as for disease, well, it wouldn't affect him. The fewer the people, the easier to manage, he thought.

He was lost deep in thought when he felt a presence just behind him. His natural instinct was to turn immediately, but he knew who it was. "LeBlanc, may I help you?" he asked calmly.

That he did not turn yet knew who was standing behind nonplussed LeBlanc for a minute. LeBlanc did not subscribe to Vodoun, but deep within his Haitian soul there was still a spark, and though intellectually he knew LePetit was merely a man, his words caused a spark of wonder to shoot within his brain. He stepped out of dimness and walked in front of LePetit.

"Have you heard anything from the woman?" he asked.

"Nothing," said Jean-Guy. "Soon, perhaps."

"It does not worry you?"

"No. And you?"

LeBlanc mulled over LePetit's assuredness. The man had been correct in all he said would happen so far. And he had been able to control the seas and skies as he had promised. "I just ask," said LeBlanc.

LePetit merely nodded at his lieutenant and slowly walked away.

LeBlanc watched him fade into the catacombs. A good place for the spirit of Louverture to walk, he thought.

Jean-Guy found Petard and his remaining Tigers. "Take two men and go up to the steeple with the radio and contact Bobo," said LePetit.

Petard shot a surprised look at his commander. "We hide no more. Use the radio and ask him if he is ready to take the airport. And tell him I want to hear word of the woman. Then contact El Sikki, Ti Rouge, and Geffrard. Ask them if all is well and tell them from now on I want word from them every thirty minutes. When you are done report back to me, but leave men with the radio. We will rotate them every four hours. Go."

Petard kicked two of the sleeping Tigers in the soles of their boots and told them to follow him. They grumbled as they awoke, saw LePetit standing nearby, quieted immediately, and hurried to follow Petard.

My presence alone is such discipline, thought LePetit contentedly. *Now we must wait. Simply wait until evening and the country is mine.*

Chapter 19

September 18, 1046 hours
Delmas International Airport arrivals building, Haiti

"My men and I are ready, Commander," said the Eton-educated Regimental Sergeant Major Jangbu Amblam to Stan Powczuk.

"How many you taking, Amblam?" asked Jack DuBois. "And please, will you call him Stan?"

"Yes, Captain . . . um, Jack. Just three men. You know, dear fellow, it's quite hard to deal just with Christian names where we come from. The officer corps in the British Army is quite rigid and all that. I'd say you two would have some sincere difficulties."

"Well, back at base and with people we don't know and stuff like that it gets a lot more formal. A lot of saluting and stuff," agreed Jack. "But we're out here in the boonies—"

"The boonies? Ah yes. The camp."

"Right. The camp. Anyway, military formality just seems to get in the way sort of."

"Y'know, Amblam, where DuBois comes from *every*-body calls him 'sir,' " said Stan.

"That's a joke, Amblam, don't listen to him," said Jack.

"You sure just the four of you is a good idea?" asked Stan.

"We're quite used to small ops," said the Gurkha. "And dressed the way we are I don't believe we'll have any trouble passing for locals. Of course if anyone starts speaking French or Creole we might have a problem, but we'll just do our very best to avoid any interpersonal contact."

Stan smiled and muttered the same thing he'd been saying since he and Jack had run into the Gurkhas. "You guys are something else."

"So you've said, Stan," smiled the sergeant. "Well, we're off for a yomp. Give us, oh, say two hours, and we'll be back with the information you need."

"Watch your ass," said Stan.

The Gurkha laughed after digesting the colloquialism. "Your American slang is quite colorful," he said.

The four men were dressed in ragged pants and shorts, one wore sandals, one shoes, and two were barefoot. They had T-shirts or shirts they'd scrounged from a rag bin in one of the hangars and were wearing four different shaped and colored caps. They looked like your everyday, ragtag assemblage of street scroungers, and Stan and Jack wouldn't have let them clean their cars' windshields had they encountered them on an American road. Quite a difference from the strat troopers they actually were.

"You just like those guys 'cause they're as tough as you. And shorter," said Jack smiling.

Stan gave the big Marine the international hand sign expressing strong disagreement. "They are shorter," he said. "But they might be tougher. I ain't interested in finding out. You?"

"Fuck no," said Jack. "Those boys impress the hell out of me." "Impress" was one of the highest accolades Jack DuBois gave anyone.

"That boy back at the airstrip hung in there too. Different from that bunch in the mountains," said Stan.

"Yeah. Too bad I hit him that high. I really thought I had his hip. Hell, he even might have lived," said Jack dryly.

"You're getting rusty, pal," said Stan grinning. "I'm just glad we didn't have to go crawling in the drainage tunnels looking for the explosives."

"We?" said Jack. "You got a mouse in your pocket white boy? You're the EOD man. I wasn't going in there."

"Wonder why they hadn't planted them yet?"

"I wonder why that old C-4 didn't go up—and me along with it—while you were shooting the hell out of his pack."

"Luck of the draw," said Stan.

"Well, those ol' boys sure ran out of luck," noted Jack.

"No shit. Well, I guess we wait for the Gurkhas to get

back," said Stan. "I'm gonna check the entrance road, make sure the claymores and MSs are set up. I'm glad your little Oriental buddy got those claymores for me. They *will* come in handy. Then what say we water and feed up? Could be a long day."

"Or night," said Jack. "I'll check the service road. Meet you back here in three-zero. Wouldn't mind some arsenal boxes, though."

"You watch what I do with four claymores," said Stan smiling.

Two hours later, almost to the second, Amblam and his three men returned and found Stan and Jack sitting in the shade cast by the storm-destroyed landing tower. The two men stood up as the four Gurkhas approached. Amblam shot a command out in Nepalese, which was totally indecipherable to either Stan or Jack, and the three other men headed back to their squad mates.

"That was most interesting," said Amblam. "There are a fair amount of people camped out there. Many I would say are civilians, but not all. Have you a map of the airport?"

"Not a paper one," said Stan. "There's one on the wall in the departure hall, though."

The three men walked to the terminal and crunched along the broken glass and wind-blown detritus of its interior as Amblam described the foray.

He and his men had simply strolled along the road, checking drainage ditches or any likely target for usable garbage. "We looked like right charwomen, I'd say," he said, drawing smiling headshakes from the two Americans. The Gurkhas had split up so as not to draw attention and meandered over several kilometers of road front and woodline and fields. All had drawn the same conclusion. There *were* people out there, and many were actual refugees.

"I'd say it's the clever ones who've been through this type of situation prior. They'll expect the first relief supplies to come in by air, and I'd dare say they'd be correct," said the sergeant. "But there are others out there, and I don't think relief supplies are their objective."

The Gurkhas had encountered small groups of men sitting around campfires, obviously idling the time away.

"They looked rather healthy compared to their fellow countrymen," noted Amblam. "While all of the civilians were of mixed sex, with children running here and there, elderly, and whatnot, these chaps were hard-looking. All male and waiting for something other than the first Red Cross flight. You'll have to forgive our counts, but it would have been a bit dicey to get more accurate as close as we were to them."

"How close *were* you guys?" asked Stan.

"Oh, we walked right in amongst them," said Amblam nonchalantly. "A few rocks were thrown, and quite a few dirty glances, but other than that they pretty much ignored us."

"What do you figure on numbers?" asked Stan.

"A low of eighty-five, ninety; a high of one-fifteen, twenty," answered the sergeant major.

The three arrived at the painted aerial view of the airport. A large crack ran down the middle of the glass covering the painting. Amblam pointed out to Jack and Stan where the men they'd seen were most heavily concentrated: an area less than a half kilometer from the main gate.

"Oh and one curious thing. I saw the most stunning young Haitian woman right in the midst of one little grouping of these fellows. Actually, she was with this one group that seemed to be in charge of this beastly looking gorilla. That is to say g-o-r, not g-u-e-r. The gent had a face only the proverbial mother could love, and I daresay she swooned when she gave birth."

Stan slapped Jack in his rock-hard midsection with the back of his hand. "Bingo," he said.

"Am I missing something?" said Amblam.

"Not any more, Sergeant Major," said Jack. "We think that 'stunning young Haitian woman' just might be one of the keys to this entire mess."

"Well, if that's the case, I'd say perhaps we should invite the young lady for tea," said the Gurkha.

"Not a bad idea," said Jack. "What about weaponry?"

"Can't say definitively. We didn't actually see any, though I'd wager that's what was under the small blanket-covered piles that every group had," said Amblam. "If they have heavy weapons I doubt it's anything more than a few light machine guns; perhaps a few old L7A2s, M-60s, or the like. At best some 60mm knee mortars, but certainly nothing bigger. Could they have RPGs or LAWs? Possibly. I don't mean to be facetious, but they just didn't look the types to me. Seemed like hit-and-run chaps."

"Hmmph. That's a gamble," said Stan. "We need to get planes in here and I don't know if I want to chance rocket fire. Hell, I don't wanna chance rocket fire on *us*. I gotta think about that."

"I've to get back to my men. I assume we can look forward to some strenuous activity in the coming hours?"

"Yeah, I think that's a safe assumption," said Jack. To Stan he said, "Let's get in touch with the boss."

Chapter 20

September 18, 0946 hours
Palais Nacional, Port-au-Prince, Haiti

"Major, sir." President Antoine's large bodyguard approached Travis.

"Erique, right?" said Travis.

"Yes, sir. There's an old Haitian woman at the front gate of the palace. Our men won't let her in, but she seems to know that you are here, so my men thought they'd ask me. Is there anyone—"

"Damn," said Travis. "Yes, Erique. Have your men let her in and bring her to me immediately. Erique?"

"Sir?"

"Have your men push her around a bit, but don't hurt her. Make it look like they're taking her into custody."

"Yes, sir."

When the bodyguard left, Hunter looked at Travis. "Jen?"

"Yeah. Wait until you get a look at her."

"I was hoping maybe you had a Haitian intelligence asset out on the street and were holding out on us," said Hunter, " 'cause it sure as shit seems like nobody else does."

"Well, I do. Just doesn't happen to be a local."

The two men headed to the front doors of the palace. They heard the doors slam open, and then the yelling started. Travis and Hunter arrived to the sight of two dumbfounded HNP men and the equally stunned bodyguard being harangued by a decidedly not old Jennifer Olsen.

"I got the idea," she yelled, "now get your goddamn hands off of me or I'll bite your throats out."

"Better let her go, Erique," said Travis. "She's one of mine."

The slight twinge of fear on the mens' faces at the no-longer-old crone's outburst was now mixed with puzzlement and finally a smile. The two HNP shook their heads and talked boisterously to each other as they headed back to their post. Erique approached Jen, who had ripped off her wig. "My pardon, madame, but the major . . ."

"Yeah, yeah. Don't worry." She turned to Travis. "I risk life and limb and that's the greeting I get, Trav?"

"Had to make it look real in case anybody was watching. You think just any old bag can get in to see the president?"

Jen shook her head resignedly. "Sitrep first or after?"

"First," said Travis.

"What the hell are you grinning at, Hunter?" she snapped.

Hunter tried answering but could do nothing but laugh. He turned to say something to Travis, but ended up still laughing, waved his hand, and headed to the stairs shaking his head.

"C'mon, lets go find some place to sit down," said Travis.

The two walked into an anteroom off the large foyer and sat. Jen stretched her long legs out and rolled her neck around. "Damn, I'm all cramped up from that act."

"So what do we have out there in cosmopolitan Port-au-Prince?"

"Man, these people have it rough. I know it was supposed to be bad anyway, but now . . . I've seen more dead bodies today than I've seen in some of the actions we've been in. That hurricane did some major damage and what the storm didn't do it looks like lack of food and drinking water is going to finish. The people are in some dire straits, I'll tell you that."

Travis didn't speak.

"I left here walking and gimped around the park or whatever it is on the east side of the palace. Plenty of *campesinos* or whatever the hell they call them on this island, but our boys are over there. Small groups of men just sitting around. Seems like the real civilians are families, know what I mean? You've got women, kids, mothers, fathers, grandparents, the whole bit. They all look a little shell-shocked. These other guys are waiting. Period. Just waiting. Didn't see any weaponry, but they all have a bad look to them. You wouldn't head down an alley if these guys were standing there. Near as I can tell seventy-five, maybe a bit more."

Travis said nothing except, "Go on."

"I boosted a bicycle from some hut up north of here, rode up past that old cathedral, and then out toward the waterfront. There're some bad boys over that way as well. Same setup, couldn't really tell numbers. They weren't as consolidated as the group in the park. Probably hunkered down in what passes for housing. I rode down by the piers. There seemed to be about two dozen who've sort of taken up residence. They look like they are already controlling the flow into the docks. Still in fours and five, but you can see they're all together. Same attitude as the ones in the park. I ditched the bike over there and moseyed along, checking things out. I'll tell you, Travis, I still can't get over the pure poverty and despair on the people's faces."

"Did you get to the embassy?"

"Yeah, that's on Harry Truman Street. That's the road that runs along the waterfront. Finally got one of those young stud guards to get me the gunny. I had to question the kid's gender, genus, and suggest several things—some of which were new to him—that were anatomically impossible before he'd finally listen, but he finally went and got him. Think I woke the gunny up. He was in a shit mood too, but I gave him the poop. Told them to arm up for a *putsch.* He wanted to know if he could help, and I told him he'd damn well better make sure the American Embassy stayed American. He said something about 'damn Iranians' and 'nothing's happening on my watch' and that's when I think he came up with the idea to have one of the guards kick me in the ass. Just in case anyone was watching, I'm sure." She smiled at Travis and gave him her best come-hither look. "Intelligent minds do think alike, Trav."

"Nice try, Jen," said Travis, smiling. "Anything else?"

"I dumped the bike, 'borrowed' a Vespa and drove around some more. Looks like more of the same crew up near the post office. Same deal. Groups standing around, but not a lot of them. Hard to tell the count. There may be more around, but if there are I didn't see them. The biggest consolidated bunch I saw were in the park right next door."

"No problems?"

"After that Marine kicked my ass, anybody who messed with me was a dead man," she answered rather seriously.

"Okay," said Travis. "Go get rigged up, chow down, and then get up on the roof with Sam and Sarah."

"How about an update here?" she said as she stood to go.

"We marked the guys in the park and we think we've got more on the north."

"Shit, I missed them completely," she said.

"No worries. Arsenal boxes will cover those angles. We've got MSs out all around. Why don't you ask Sam how the gardening's been? Stan and Jack have the airport covered. They got the sapper team before they planted the charges. The bad guys Sam and Jack took care of were a little more hard core than the ones up in the hills. We'll see how that plays out down here. Our guys also have reinforcements with them out at Delmas. A squad of Gurkhas."

"Jesus. Where the hell did they come from?"

"Long story. Anyway, they're good out there. We still don't know who Louverture is, but we know where a lot of his men are. We're in wait and see mode, but I'm trying to figure out something to give things a push. Go get rigged. Good job, Jen. Definitely one for the Oscars," he added, referring to her makeup job.

Jen nodded and began to head for the presidential quarters. "We're gonna pull this off aren't we?" she said before leaving.

"Could be, Jen. Could be."

When Jen left, Travis placed his BSH on and headed up the stairs to the roof.

"Hunter. How's it looking?"

"Same-o, same-o."

"Sarah, Sam?"

"All quiet, Travis," said Sarah.

"Ditto, boss," said Sam. "Stan and Jack called in. They want to powwow."

"I want to wait until Jennifer gets up there," said Travis.

"Tell Stan and Jack I'll be back to them in ten. Anything from C and C?"

"No interference for the last couple of hours. They're ready to start sending transport. Just waiting on your say-so," said Sam.

"Roger."

Travis walked up the stairs slowly, mulling over a plan of action. Up until now all the moves had been on Louverture's side and time schedule. Perhaps it was time to seize the initiative and see if they could flush their quarry out. He reached the entrance to the roof and looked out from the doorway at Sam and Sarah. Both had found some small spots of shade on their respective sides and were sitting quietly with their backs against the low wall. He heard footsteps enter the stairwell and turned to see Jen coming up. She gave Travis the thumbs-up, and he nodded to her.

"Stay low. We don't want any profile yet." Sarah and Sam looked to the doorway when he spoke. Both Travis and Jen crouched low. He pointed Jen to the unwatched west side and scuttled over to where Sam sat. When he settled down next to the IMS man he looked to Sarah. She shook her head.

"Stan, Jack. You guys up?" asked Travis. There was a brief moment of silence.

"Go, Trav," said Stan.

"I want to push these bastards and see if they go for it," said Travis.

"One-Odin."

Travis looked at Sam. "You said to keep you on the net. It's Lorelei now."

Travis's eyebrows raised. Who thinks up these operational names? he wondered. "Lorelei. One-Odin. Go."

"Message from C and C. 'FM communications all over the band. Central is north of the palace inside one kilometer. No jamming. Interpreter working. Advise.' Repeat—"

"Lorelei, I got it. I'll get back to you. Out. Sam, put us back on internal commo."

"Roger."

Chapter 21

September 18, 1400 hours
Outside Delmas International Airport, Haiti

Bobo's radio operator walked over to him and spoke softly in his ear. He nodded his head at the man then tapped Lily on the arm. "Louverture wishes to speak with you."

"He's here?" she said in complete surprise.

"On the radio."

"No!" she snapped. "He mustn't use the radio yet."

Bobo just looked at her and pointed to the radio operator.

Lily jumped up and pushed the radioman along. Bobo followed. She trailed the radioman into the tall grass, nearly losing him in its thickness. The broad blades left paper-cut-like slices on her forearms and she started to roll down her sleeves when they reached a small clearing. The old military radio was set up leaning against a tree, its ten-foot collapsible antenna undetectable against the trunk. The operator spoke in Creole, then handed the telephonelike headset to Lily. She keyed the switch on the handset's side and spoke.

"What are you doing?" she hissed in English. "I'm not operational. Anyone could be listening. Do you want to lose everything?"

There was a long period of silence. The radio operator grabbed the handset from her and held it in front of her face. "You must press to talk, let go to receive. We are *Erinle*. Louverture is *Ogun*. Say who you are and who you are calling first. Then speak. And say 'over' when you are done," he said as if lecturing a child.

"I know that," she snapped, although she'd never actually spoken on the radio before. She calmed herself before speaking again.

"Ogun. This is Erinle. Why are we using the radio?" she asked with less stridency. She turned and sneered at the radio operator and said, "Over."

"You learn well," said LePetit, eschewing the operational necessities of radio communication. "It makes little difference now. All is in place. They can do nothing." He added "over" as an afterthought.

"You do realize that we're not in control of the satellites right now." There was no response, and the radioman tapped her fingers that had released the transmit bar on the handset. She pressed it again. "Over," she said.

LePetit's voice changed when he spoke. The venom Lily had heard in the hut when his hand went to his pistol came across the airwaves loud and clear. *"Pourquoi?* Over."

"Because I have no power source until we take the tower," she said angrily. She let go of the transmit bar belatedly. The radioman shook his head and sat back against the tree.

No response came to Lily's statement. Finally the headset crackled to life. LePetit's voice was again measured and controlled. He asked for Bobo and no more. She handed Bobo the handset and walked back into the grass, heading for her equipment.

"Sam, are they downloading the intercepts to you?" asked Travis.

"Two seconds and they can do it," answered Sam.

"Get them. Jack, you ready to translate?"

"Let it fly, Trav. They're keeping a copy, right?"

"Yeah. We're taped at C and C," said Sam.

"How ya doing, little buddy?" asked Jack.

"Tell you all about it when I see you," said Sam. "Here goes. You'll get about a two-second gap in between 'overs,'" explained Sam. "Not the best in technique, but they're working it. They also keep trying to get Cap Haitien, but there's no answer. Distance problem I'd say."

Everyone listened to the Haitian Creole patois and said nothing as the signal from C and C repeated whatever had been eavesdropped. After nearly three minutes of listening, Jack came on the air.

"Stop it there. I've got enough. Here's the story. Everybody's calling a station named Ogun. So that's our Louverture, probably. Ogun's some kind of spirit or god or something. All the call signs they're using are Vodoun gods I think, but there's a couple I don't recognize. They're also using what sounds like first names or *noms de guerre* or something. Anyway, someone named Bobo is here at the airport. Ogun wants to know if he can take the airport now. They also confirmed that the lady the Gurkhas spotted is the one we want. Ogun said to make sure Yemanja, which is a female spirit, got what she needed."

"I'll go get the Gurkhas," said Stan, who left Jack immediately.

"Or he said to give her what she wanted. Or what she was supposed to get. Maybe they're gonna whack her," said Jack. "Shee-it man, you can't tell some of this lingo without facial expressions sometimes.

"Ogun called Agwe station and asked how long it would be to clear the piers. So there's a group on the waterfront," continued Jack. "Let's see. He called three other stations. Sam run it back and do it again."

"Boss, they have a Creole interpreter at base. He says he can do the translation pretty much in real time."

"Jack," said Travis. "Get things ready. We'll handle the mail from here. We'll give you a shout if anything goes down as far as your position is concerned. Let us know immediately if they make a move. Sam, have them do the translation and give us a synopsis and load that down to us. I want it yesterday.

"Here's the plan. If they make a move on Delmas now, we'll see how they react here. If they plan on keeping this to a night ops in town, we'll force the issue." He turned to Jen. "You think you can pick a group of them from here?"

"They're pretty noticeable. I'd say so."

"Damn. Wish I had a PS-G1 or a PM," said Travis. "Okay. Take a look, get range. What we'll do is take some shots at these folks, see if that stirs them up a bit. You might not be able to pick targets with the smart rifle's range, but maybe we can get them antsy. Sam, check the north, see if there're any groupings. If it's women or children or old-timers, it isn't them. Hunter, forget about the first floor. If the HNP can't handle it . . ."

"On the way," answered Hunter.

"Download coming, boss," said Sam.

"Sam, get the Ghostriders up and ready to provide support at Delmas," said Travis. "Stan, Jack, you up?"

"We're listening," said Stan.

"If they make a move and you stop them, I want to start putting planes on the ground right away. We have a combat patrol team from First SOW ready to go. I want our C-117 in there ASAP. Then they can start shipping relief supplies or whatever the hell they want. They can't take the airport, guys."

"No problemo," said Stan.

"We'll handle it," said Jack.

"Sam, what have they got to say?" asked Travis.

"Okay. They're going to try and walk right into the airport. Ogun station wants to know if the explosives have been placed. He just found out for the first time that they haven't met up with the guys. Not a happy camper."

"Anything else about Delmas?"

"Ummm, no. Just that they have to take the airport and find some 'tigers.' Nothing about what that means."

"Leopards?" asked Jack.

"No, tigers, according to the translator," said Sam.

"There used to be a Leopard Commando back in the Duvalier days. I remember hearing about that. Maybe Ogun's got himself a private little bodyguard within the MPP," said Jack.

"That'd account for those four hardcores we took down. The sapper team," explained Stan.

"Okay. Stan, you're sure y'all got them before they mined the strip, right?" said Travis.

"They couldn't have been carrying any more C-4. I disarmed the receivers on all the shape charges, disabled the transmitters. No, we got these guys before they placed anything."

"Roger. You guys are off. Stop them," said Travis.

"Erinle station told Ogun it's a walk-in, so I guess nobody's seen you guys or the Gurkhas," added Sam.

"Good. Let 'em think just that," said Stan. "We're out."
"People, let's pick some targets out there. When they get word of what's happening at Delmas, let's see what they do and then we'll go to work."

1430 hours
The roof of the Delmas International Airport arrival building, Haiti

Stan, Jack, and Amblam made their way to the roof of the arrivals building where they had a clear view of the entry road and guard booths of the airport.

"Amblam," said Stan, "we'll see how they enter and how they deploy. When they get to the kill zone, we'll loose the claymores. Anyone standing after that is a target. I'd like to grab the woman alive, so tell your people."

"You got ten guys, right?" said Jack.

"That I do," answered the Gurkha.

"How about you send three of them to cover the service road, just in case. I think these mutts are all gonna come in the front door, but . . ."

"Not a problem," said Amblam. "If you see a red flare, that means the rear guard is in contact."

"We'll know by the sensors, but fine. Then you can shift your remaining squad and we'll handle things from up here."

"Roger," said the cheery sergeant major. "It's been quite some time since these men have had the opportunity to actually fight, you know."

"Yeah," said Stan. "They seemed kinda anxious to go."

"Rather," said the Gurkha as he turned to go.

After the sergeant left, Stan pulled the RF down again. "I see some of them getting geared up in that grove. Lo and behold, they've got weapons."

Jack peered through his RF. "AKs and 16s. Well, maybe we'll get to see how those ever-lovin' claymores of yours do."

"Just wait."

The two TALON troopers watched as armed men moved

to and fro, eventually grouping up. A short, powerful looking man seemed to be the leader; the radio operator was with him and they saw the woman trying to speak to him with what appeared to be little success.

"Looks like the lady's not having much success with this Bobo character," said Jack.

"Good. Probably means she won't be in the vanguard," said Stan. "I'd say NSA and all the other spooks would be reeeeal interested in talking with her for a while."

They watched as the ragtag group of men seemed to be forming into a fairly well-ordered military movement.

"Goes to show," noted Jack. "Can't always tell a book by its cover. As Sun Tzu said, 'All war is based on deception.' "

"Yeah, but let's see how well they shape up under fire."

"One of Sun Tzu's essentials for victory: 'He will win who, prepared himself, waits to take the enemy unprepared,' " added Jack, drawing a shake of the head from his partner. "And these guys sure as shit ain't prepared for us."

When all seemed in readiness, Stan and Jack saw Bobo ordering men into position. A group of about two dozen moved south past the entrance but still on the other side of the road, while another group started the approach, disappearing behind some trees to the north of the gate. The rebel commander remained in sight in the grove of trees, along with the radioman and another group of two dozen. The woman was nowhere to be seen.

"If I'm counting right," said Jack, "and if Amblam and his boys had the count right, we might be a little short. Maybe they're gonna come in the rear as well."

"We'll know damn soon," said Stan.

The group from the south made the first move.

"Trav," said Stan.

"Go," said Sam.

"The festivities are starting. We'll talk to you later."

"Kick some voodoo ass," said Sam.

"Shit man," said Jack. "They're grouped too tight. This is gonna be a turkey shoot."

Jack and Stan flipped down their BSH visors and followed the rebels as they walked in. They came in three groups, staggered over the entire roadway, but with not much more than a meter between them. Their arms were at the ready and they were looking around, but the grouping was going to be their ruination.

"How many you going to let through?" asked Jack.

"I want to get that second group in at least. Let's see what happens."

The second group entered in much the same pattern and Jack spotted the group still in the trees start to move. "Bobo, Erinle, whatever is on the move now."

Six, eight, ten, then twelve men exited the killing zone.

"I think the Gurkhas can handle two dozen, what about you?" said Stan.

"I don't think they'll have a problem."

As the lead man of the second group neared the end of the kill zone, half of Bobo's group had entered it.

Stan took a deep breath. "Here goes." He pressed the ignition button on the transmitter and the four claymores staggered down opposite sides of the road ignited.

A sudden deep-throated *crack!* accompanied by a black cloud of plastique-propelled detritus erupted from where the claymores had been positioned, momentarily obscuring the image of the incoming troops.

The claymore mine is an old but effective weapon on grouped personnel. The progression in the power of plastic explosives—the current C-6 was three times lighter and twice as powerful as the older C-4—had allowed for the device to become even more deadly. Less weight in the charge meant more killing pellets were on board. The effective range had been increased from around twenty meters to forty, and the dispersement of the steel shot was kept tighter closer in. When the smoke of the ignition cleared, none of the forty-odd men who had been in the kill zone were still standing. Most had perished, though they could see several squirming in pain.

Stan had set the first claymore in a vertical position and attached it high on a light pole. The blowback from the explosion had severed the pole, which now lay on the entrance road on top of two bodies and had cast some of its load beyond the road kill zone. Jack and Stan saw men limping and crawling away from the ambush.

The Gurkhas, meanwhile, had not been idle. While the

TALON men had been fixated on the devastation of the ambush, the Gurkhas had taken the remainder of the force under controlled but concentrated fire. Stan and Jack rushed to the back of the roof and looked over.

"Think they need a hand?" said Stan.

"Fuck that," said Jack as he aimed down at one of the rebels. Stan joined in and the fire slowly died off after a furious five minutes. Stan and Jack immediately headed for the stairway and down to the bottom floor of the arrivals building. As they ran out, Amblam rushed up to them.

"My men," he pointed behind them. Stan and Jack heard fire in the distance and looked at the sensor display in the BSH. All had gone active.

"Go!" yelled Stan. "We got this. You see that Bobo dude in that mess?" he asked Jack.

"No. Neither him nor the woman," he said as the two ran toward the airport's entrance.

As they ran through the carnage of the ambush zone, firing coup de graces from the hip at any rebels who indicated they were still alive, they were spotted by what remained of the force that had fallen back and gathered in the grove. The TALON men saw Bobo yelling into the radio and charged the airport's gate.

As the rebels became aware of the incoming fire from the gate they started firing and both men dove to the ground in the ditch on their side of the road. The firing was wild at first, but slowed and started concentrating on their position.

"Shit, almost had them," yelled Stan.

"Left and right, buddy, let's do it," yelled Jack.

Adrenaline always made the BSH commo suite redundant in close quarters.

Both men low-crawled through the ditch below eye level of the insurgents. Stan could hear some yelling, as could Jack.

"Can you make it out?" Stan asked quietly now.

"Nah," said Jack.

Stan crawled about twenty meters, before kneeling and pumping single shots into the grove. As the rebels turned toward Stan's fire, Jack opened up. Two men went down heavily and the rebels broke. Jack and Stan started to clamber onto the road in chase when they saw several black dots arcing through the air. They both yelled "grenade" at the same time and dove into the ditch.

Five of the six fragmentary grenades blew nearly as one. As the smoke drifted across the road and the pitter-patter sound of falling shrapnel could be heard in the grass, the two men arose and sprayed a third of a magazine into the smoke, then disappeared back into the dust, diving into the ditch on the far side of the explosions.

"That was interesting," said Jack breathing heavily.

"As Amblam would say, 'quite,' " answered Stan. "See anything?"

Jack looked up over the edge of the ditch, ducked, moved, and looked again. "Nada, man. You?"

Stan went through the same motions. "Think I got a wounded guy over on the right of that thick tree. Where Bobo was."

"Him?"

"Don't think so. Ready?"

"As ever. On three."

The two men counted together, and upon reaching three, stood, sprayed the woodline with another third of a magazine, and ran toward it. They stopped at the tree where the wounded man was, knelt, and looked in every direction for a target. The rebel had taken several pellets in the left side of the face, and his left eye was either gone or swollen shut. He also seemed to be bleeding heavily from bullet wounds in the arm and chest. He looked up at the two men with a bloodshot eye and spoke in Creole.

"What'd he say?" asked Stan.

"Wants to know who we are."

A slight look of surprise came over what was left of the man's face. "You Haitian?" he groaned to Jack in English.

"No, mon," said Jack. "Just one of de good guys."

"American?" asked the dying man.

"Does it make a difference?"

The man looked at Jack and died.

"So much for Q and A."

"Sam," said Stan. "This is Stan."

"No shit," came Sam's voice. "How goes it, Jack?"

Wise ass, thought Stan.

"Go, Stan," said Travis.

"We hurt them bad here, Trav. KIAs're about seventy or so. No POWs so far. I think . . . hold on." Stan turned up the enhanced hearing function of his BSH to listen for fire from the service road entrance to the airport. He shook his head and said, "Probably about a hundred dead so far. The Gurkhas cleaned up a smaller group from the rear."

"Any sign of the girl?" asked Travis.

"We saw her, but we don't have her. She and maybe a handful of the bad guys got away."

"Get the airport operational. Ghostrider Four and Five are one-zero out. Have them stage at Delmas. SOW is four-five out. As soon as they get the airport functional have them bring the 117 in. I want the Osprey rigged to drop RIBs and you two to take a Hummer and a Wildcat into town as soon as it's unloaded."

"What about the woman?" said Jack. "Shouldn't we track her down?"

"No. Listen. What y'all did out there got these guys' nuts in an uproar here in town. They're panicking and we're gonna start pushing them. Just get here as soon as you can. Out."

Jack walked over to the dead man, kicked his rifle away and put two rounds into the AK's action. He looked around and noticed that people were timidly filtering back into the grove. An old man approached him slowly speaking in Creole. Jack listened, then answered and a sad smile crossed the man's face. Jack patted the old man gently on the shoulder, then turned. Stan jerked his head, questioning what the old man had said.

"Said they knew those guys were bad men because they worked for the spirit of the black Louverture. He meant, like a bad Louverture, not color, know what I mean?" said Jack. "He said thanks and wanted to know if help is coming."

"And you said . . . ?"

"What the hell else was I gonna say. I said help was here, and he and his people would have food soon. I hope so, 'cause these folks look mighty hungry and when they see that C-117 ain't got any chow on it . . ."

"Well, hell. Let's get some food on the way, then," said Stan. As the two men made there way back to check on heir Gurkha allies, Stan was argumentatively demanding C and C arrange emergency food drops from stores at Guantanamo.

Gotta do something besides kill people, he thought as hey walked through the bodies sprawled in the claymores' kill zone.

Chapter 22

September 18, 1545 hours
Cathedrale Ste. Trinite, Port-au-Prince, Haiti

Since LePetit had put the Tigers in the tower and radio communications had commenced it had been absolutely nothing but bad news. There had been no contact with the Tigers at Delmas or at Cap Haitien, though the latter was undoubtedly because of the distance between the two cities and the mountains in between. The relay had disappeared or was unreachable as well. Then Lily's news that she had been unable to re-engage the communications because of a power shortage, and now Bobo, who had never met up with the Delmas Tigers and neglected to mention that fact, had led his men into an ambush by a force that he said was platoon strength or more. Where had a platoon or more of military come from? From the speed and violence of the ambush and the fear in Bobo's voice—not a man easily scared—he figured some type of special-operations force had been launched against him. Well, they may have the airport, but they did not have the capital. And Jean-Guy intended to keep that and the capital's port for himself. The airport was essentially wrecked and of little immediate use anyway.

He had been forced by the constant communications to station himself in the tower at the radio and had heard the reports personally. He'd told Bobo to bring what was left of his men, as well as Lily, who had at least been able to save most of her equipment, to the capital and meet him at the palace. If he could take the palace now all was not lost, and if he could get Lily operational immediately, he could again gain control of the skies and shipping lanes.

"Agwe, this is Ogun. Over."

"Ogun, this is Agwe."

"Sikki, I want you and your men to take the port now. No one is to enter or exit until you hear from me. Make sure you take the docks north of the main pier as well. And make sure the Tigers have mined the area. I want the harbor ready to blow in an instant." With the airport in enemy hands, the piers would be most important, thought LePetit. But no one will have them save I.

"Ogun. What about the post office? Over."

"Send twenty men. It is not as important as the piers. Out."

"Baka. Ogun. Over."

"Baka. Over."

"Ti Rouge. Take the barracks. I want no HNP left, do you understand?" said LePetit.

"It will be more difficult in the daylight, Ogun."

"I know that. Do it and do it fast! No one expects you. Let me know when you are ready." LePetit's voice rose. One of the Tigers looked at the other. Louverture was getting excited; they had not seen this side of his *lwa* before. Not a good omen, thought both men.

LePetit turned to the two Tigers. "Let me know as soon as you hear from Erinle or Yemanja. Find me wherever I am." He spun on his heel and walked rapidly down the cramped stone steps of the cathedral's tower, looking for LeBlanc.

He found the taciturn lieutenant walking the main aisle of the cathedral, apparently deep in thought, and walked up quietly behind him, startling him with his voice.

"Get your men ready," said Jean-Guy. "We wait no longer. We take the palace now."

LeBlanc looked over Jean-Guy's shoulder but addressed him. "Do you think that is wise in daylight?"

Jean-Guy was only partially successful in fighting to keep the anger from showing in his voice. "And do you think it is wise to question what I say we do? We own the city and no one knows it. There is no need to wait any longer. Day or night, it makes no difference."

"There is talk that mercenaries or military have been put against us already," said LeBlanc letting his eyes drift to

Jean-Guy's face. "This force cannot withstand professional soldiers. Some are indeed good. You've trained them well. But many are still just superstitious mountain peasants well fed and armed. You know that"—he looked directly into Jean-Guy's eyes this time—"and so do I."

LePetit looked into LeBlanc's eyes, but the other man did not turn away.

"Tell me the truth, Louverture." There was no respect behind the way LeBlanc said the name, allowing some distaste to creep into the word. "Who are we fighting? And why are we going to do it now, rather than when the advantage of night is with us?" He watched as Jean-Guy's hand went to his pistol, then slowly placed his own hand on his.

Jean-Guy drew a deep breath and stared at LeBlanc. "So you hear things, you think things, you believe we cannot accomplish what we have set out to do. Merely on the weight of words you have 'heard,' " he said, sneering at LeBlanc. "I have worked too long and hard at this. If you wish to leave now, then do so. I will find you and deal with you afterward. But you shall not share in the new Haiti when I bring it forth. You may go back to whatever mountain hole you lived in and remain there until that day when I remember that you lost faith at the crucial moments of our battle."

Jean-Guy continued looking directly at LeBlanc, then made to walk through him. LeBlanc yielded.

"Louverture," he said. The name was said more respectfully this time. "I am with you, but a man cannot help but hear. These others"—he spun his hand in an upward motion—"they have not the education of you or I. You know that. They follow in fear of you or in love of you. I followed you because I thought the plan was good, the rewards great. Simply tell me why we go in daylight."

"And then what?" said Jean-Guy. "You perhaps will fight? Perhaps you will go? What then, LeBlanc?"

"I will fight alongside you, Louverture. But I do nothing blindly. I ask for my own knowledge, man to man. What can we expect? I have done everything you have asked to now. I ask only that in return."

Jean-Guy looked at LeBlanc again. Yes, he thought, this one will have to be one of the first to go. "I know you will fight. A military force has stopped Bobo at the airport. The fighting is fierce, so it will take longer for them to gain control. It may have been the force in the hills and they must have gotten through somehow without Pierre Jeune's men seeing them."

"Or Jeune's men were beaten," said LeBlanc.

Jean-Guy fought back the anger again. Oh, this one would die very soon. "Or that," he answered. "But whoever is there is now tied down at the airport. Let them hold it for now. If we take the palace—and the president—we own the country and it makes no difference who has the airport. It will be too late then. That is why I have decided to take the palace now. There is more risk, true, but there is much to be gained. And the sooner, the better."

LeBlanc looked at Jean-Guy thoughtfully. "Louverture, had I known these things I would have come to the same conclusion," he said. "That was why I asked as I did."

No it wasn't, thought LePetit. "If you hear any more rumors, shoot the man spreading them. On my authority. In the name of Louverture and the new Haiti."

LeBlanc nodded. "As you wish."

Jean-Guy nodded his head curtly at LeBlanc. "Get your men ready, and get me a runner to go to Geffrard. We attack the palace in one hour."

One of the Tigers came running into the cathedral. "Louverture! Geffrard's men are being shot at from the palace!"

LeBlanc whirled around and looked at LePetit. LePetit calmly removed his 9mm and shot the lieutenant in the chest. LeBlanc pawed for his own pistol and LePetit pulled the trigger three more times. LeBlanc staggered backward into the pews, his eyes already glazing over, and collapsed into them as the noise of the shots reverberated around the walls of the old stone cathedral. "A traitor," he said to the startled Tiger. He walked past the man who stood, mouth agape, and headed to the tower, then turned and walked back to LeBlanc. He looked down at him and saw there was still a spark of life in his body and emptied the pistol's magazine into it.

He turned and yelled, "Move!" as he again strode past the stunned Tiger, jettisoning the magazine and slapping in a fresh one.

1540 hours
Palais Nacional, Port-au-Prince, Haiti

"Let's see if we can stir something up," said Travis. "Sarah. Take over from Sam. Pick some likely concentrations and pop a few rounds in. Let's see what happens. Sam, I want you to keep giving me a running account of what's being said on the FM band by our friends. Hunter—have Jen help you launch a Dragonfly. I want an aerial recon of the section north around the cathedral, the entire area to the west, and the piers. President Antoine has alerted the HNP at their barracks, so they're on their own for now. If you've got time—or launch another 'Fly—do a recon down there last priority."

"We can launch two," said Hunter.

"No, you handle it. I want Jen after you launch. Sam, tape down the 'Fly's video as well. No more crawling around. Don't make yourself a target, but let these folks know we're here."

As Travis shot the orders out, the team went into action. Hunter sat with his back against the wall and the control console of the 'Fly on his lap, while Jen hand launched the little drone. Hunter nodded, his eyes never leaving the control screen, and she moved away, taking a position on the west wall scanning the streets and buildings below. Sam wedged himself into a corner of the wall and stairwell kiosk and hummed away as info started coming in from the UAV and the C and C translator. Sarah leaned against an ornate cement cap on the east wall and panned the park looking for targets, Travis alongside her.

"Got a likely looking group," said Sarah. She exhaled, sighted, and took up what little slack was in the smart rilfe's trigger. The high-tech gun discharged and she saw the round blow dirt up in front of an MPP rebel. She saw the man run and scramble around the gear lying by a small smoky fire. He came up with a shotgun, as did his companions. "It's our boys," she said to Travis, who was checking the entire area. Her second shot was low, and she saw the five men moving their heads wildly as they tried to find the source of the fire. Travis looked and saw more men in the park arming themselves. She adjusted for range and windage and went through the sight, breathe, squeeze motion again and saw one of the shotgun-toting rebels go down hard as the bullet impacted his shoulder. She could see the dust puff out of his clothing at the initial impact of the round.

"Use non–armor piercing rounds or we're going to kill an awful lot of civilians," said Sarah.

"You'll lose range," said Jen.

"Round's dropping about an inch at this range. No windage to speak of," she said. "We can take them no problem without the AP rounds."

"Sarah, stay with the personnel loads," said Travis. "Everybody else stay with AP. You've got buildings. Keep it low on long shots. The civilians will disperse as soon as this thing heats up."

Travis scanned the park with the range-finder capability of the BSH and picked out the command post by the radio operator. "Sam, what have these guys been saying?"

"They've reported in to Ogun. And they're waiting," replied Sam.

"Let me know if they get the order to attack."

"Roger."

Travis needed the men out of the park and into the area covered by the arsenal boxes. He needed them to get the attack order. Then he'd attempt to take the radio out. Sarah continued to squeeze off rounds, distributing them throughout the park at different groups as they armed and sought cover. It was a slow, measured fire that—if you were on the receiving end—became increasingly maddening. Travis saw one of the men in the command post point, it seemed, directly at him. "Sarah, get ready for incoming fire."

Travis could see muzzle flashes and then heard the rounds slapping weakly into the building about six feet below them. He aimed the XM-29 at one concentration and fired a single shot. "Sam," he said, "make a note that we always carry a PS-G2 or PM1 sniper rifle from now on."

Sam looked at Travis's back. "Sure, boss," he said shaking his head at the absurdity of military life. I only have four thousand things going on at once.

Travis smiled to himself, and then his lips went to a thin line as he took another rebel under aim and let go a round. He saw the man drop. Return fire was sporadic, and Travis saw someone running from group to group organizing the independent pockets. The return firing slowly ceased and then men started moving toward the palace.

"That's it for now, Sarah," he said. "Any time they slow down, goose them with a round or two."

"Boss?" said Sam. "Ogun told them to take the building. Said he'll be joining them with his people."

"Let's pay attention on the north, Jen," he said as he made his way to the building's west side. "Hunter, anything?"

"They look to be well set up at the waterfront," said Hunter, never removing his eyes from the drone's monitor. "Lot of civilians running away from the piers. En route to the north side now. Gimme a minute."

Jen and Travis peered down at the streets as far as the city layout would allow and saw no movement. They could hear Sarah occasionally fire a round, once popping off a three-round burst.

"Whoa, dudes, surf's up on the north shore," said Hunter. "We got quite a crew moving out of the big church a couple of blocks north. Let's take her down for a closer look."

"Sarah," said Travis. "Take out the radio."

"Will do, Travis," she said calmly.

"C'mon, Hunter, whatcha got?"

"Looking, looking, looking, let's see. Hmmm. We got . . ."

"Ogun's on the move heading for the palace," said Sam. "We're about thirty seconds behind on translation from real time."

"Well, then we just might have Mister Ogun coming out of the church," said Hunter. "Guy with just a pistol, got a radio operator and a couple of other guys in camies with him. Yeah, that must be him. He's giving a lot of orders. The company is splitting up east and west. Hold on a sec, let's see where they're headed."

Travis looked over the north wall, but saw nothing.

"Okay, they're heading south. They split three ways. One

crowd on the road into the north park, two on down the roads that run on the sides of this building."

"I'm losing a bunch of them behind that museum," said Sarah. "Got the radio and the operator though."

"Anything on the west side?"

"Hang on." Hunter flew the UAV over to the area west of the palace. "Lots of people all headed in the opposite direction," he said. "Lemme get back to the north. Travis, part of the group coming from the north have cut off and are swinging out around to the west. Probably come in behind that brown building there."

"Okay. You got time to swing down to the HNP barracks?"

"No. This Dragonfly's about had it," said Hunter.

"Blow it and get another one up and down there, then get it back over us until we need to roll," said Travis.

"Roger." Hunter pressed the self-destruct button on the control console and the UAV blew up like a clay pigeon hit with a good shot from a Purdy. Jen ran over to Hunter and prepared a second Dragonfly for launch.

"They're pretty well all massed behind the museum, Travis," said Sarah.

"This is timing, folks. I don't want the arsenal box on the west side to go off until I say so. I want to make sure we get this attack coming in from the north and west."

"Ogun's been trying to raise Dambala," said Sam. "No luck."

"That's the radio over here. Good, he'll have to use a runner. That'll give us some time," said Travis.

The situation calmed, though Jen and Sarah fired at any targets of opportunity that presented themselves. Single incoming shots rang out from the east side, but nothing from the others. Travis moved to the south wall and scanned the area. The huge lawn at the front of the palace was deserted. He returned to the north side, trying to think of a way to isolate Louverture.

Well-planned ambushes are one of the safest means of inflicting damage on an enemy while absorbing little damage to your own force, as well as the only hope a numerically inferior number have of surviving the battle. While it is possible to defeat an ambush, it's a rarity when the ambush is executed properly. An ambush requires that many variables go a certain way for both sides. Waiting in ambush puts the odds with you, but doesn't necessarily make it any easier to pull off successfully. An ambush is a *danse de guerre* of timing, accuracy, speed, violence, and luck; good luck for one side and bad for the other. The hard—and crucial—part, regardless of size, is waiting. And it was waiting that Travis was concerned about.

He needed the northern group, ostensibly led by Louverture, in the kill zone. Though he'd thought disabling the communications with the eastern force would end up confusing the rebels, he now wished he'd left them in communication so they'd coordinate the attack and TALON Force could concentrate on the northern group and let the arsenal boxes take the eastern group.

Travis was hoping that Louverture wouldn't be in the kill zone when the arsenal boxes let loose, but he didn't want the eastern group to enter the zone too soon. The massive casualties of the arsenal box would spook anything but a total idiot from continuing. And as yet Louverture hadn't shown he was an idiot.

"Travis, the crew on the west looks like it's getting ready to move. They keep looking to the north, so I guess they're waiting on those guys. You have about fifty at that building on the far side of that park area, and another twenty-five or so about a block up just to your one o'clock." Hunter flew the UAV to the east over the museum building. "There's a crowd back there. Looks to be near one hundred or so."

"How's the HNP barracks doing?"

"They got a serious firefight going on, but they seem to be holding."

"Baka keeps calling Ogun and asking him what to do," said Sam, "but he isn't getting any answer except to take the barracks. Sounds a little shaky over there." Sam paused for several seconds then came back. "Stan and Jack are rolling. Ghostriders are rigging the RIBs, SOW is on the ground and should have the airport operational in about three zero."

"Have them head into town. HNP barracks first and break that up hard. Gimme the town map," snapped Travis.

"It's yours," said Sam, downloading it to Travis's BSH screen.

Travis perused the map quickly. "There's a spit at the river mouth on the south of the piers. Have the Ospreys ready to drop the RIBs there on Stan's say so. Tell Stan and Jack to head there after they clear the HNP. I want them ready to roll north. Either we'll meet them there or we'll talk them in."

"Got it," said Sam, as he started relaying Travis's orders.

Three whistle blasts reached their ears, followed by two more three-blasts in return. A distinct yell arose from the rebels and they left their cover and simultaneously headed for the palace.

So much for technology, thought Travis. Whistles! Nice and simple.

"Rock and roll time," said Sarah.

"Sam!" yelled Travis. "Let C and C take over the commo. I want you up here. Call the kill zone and let it fly. Jen, Sarah, free fire on the west side. Hunter, blow the drone, we're gonna get Louverture. Let me know if anything goes folks. We're moving out when the arsenal boxes go."

Sam ran to the north wall. Hunter blew the second Dragonfly and followed Travis into the stairwell. They ran out the front door, past several wired-up and antsy HNP men, then waited at the front west corner of the building.

"Louverture is hanging back. His people are all headed in though," said Sam.

"Good. As soon as you blow it, we're after him."

Travis and Hunter could finally discern what the rebels were yelling. "Louverture! Louverture!" rang out as they attacked. They could hear the firing picking up in intensity as the insurgents neared the palace. Any sounds of XM-29 return fire were lost in the general mayhem.

The arsenal boxes were the TALON Force equivalent of artillery pieces. They could be dropped or parachuted and could be remotely fired by any of the men as long as they could be seen by them. Each box held eight shots and could be pre-loaded with a variety of rounds. In this case the boxes were loaded with antipersonnel ammunition. Firing would release hundreds of bomblets, which exploded upon hitting ground, covering the area of a football field. It sounded like a pack of Fourth of July firecrackers going—firecrackers that belonged to a Brobdignagian-size person, however.

As Travis and Hunter checked their gear and loads, readying for the dash around the palace and into the north of the city, they heard the arsenal boxes let go. The whoosh of the sixteen rounds brought the yelling of the rebels nearly to a halt. The time lapse between the launch and the hit would vary, but in this case would be long because of the severe angle of attack; the arsenal boxes had to be aimed nearly straight up. Travis and Hunter looked at each other in anticipation.

"And three, two, one . . ." said Sam, the end of the sentence drowned out by a series of loud aerial blast as the bomblets deployed, then the deep-pitched crackling of the individual bomblets letting loose. Four seconds later a deathly quiet came over the area and Travis and Hunter flew around the wall and headed north. As they ran up the west wall of the palace they saw four men at a complete standstill in the streets looking to the back of the palace. Their weapons were pointed at the ground. Travis and Hunter went to take them under fire, when the four crumpled in turns from shots that rang out from above their heads. The two men kept running for the north of the city.

They entered the lawn area fronting the north side and through carnage worthy of any image drawn from Dante's *Inferno*. The smoke was thick but bodies, parts of bodies, and things no longer discernible as bodies lay scattered about as they ran through the thinning cloud. They'd covered over 250 meters before they broke out and there—not one hundred feet away—were seven camouflage-clad men and a tall man with a pistol, standing and staring at a future that had become a past so surprisingly fast that their minds hadn't no time to comprehend what had happened.

"Louverture?" said Hunter.

"Good as any," said Travis coming to a stop and kneeling for a shot. Hunter followed suit. When the first Tiger dropped, Louverture seemed to come to life. As his Praetorians fell around him, he spun and headed back into the city without so much as a glance.

"Let's go!" yelled Travis.

Four of the Tigers had snapped out of their daze as their comrades had gone down and immediately dropped to the ground and returned fire.

"Shit!" yelled both men as they dove to the ground.

"I guess these are those hard-core guys Stan was talking about!" yelled Hunter, spraying three-round bursts at the four Tigers.

"Grenades coming in!" said Sam as he fired the launcher on his XM-29.

"Shit!" yelled Travis and Hunter at the same time. Sam was the team's ace when it came to electronics, but neither Hunter nor Travis were real comfortable with him lobbing grenades over their heads. Not at nearly max range.

The first grenade landed behind the two TALON men. "Oh, Jesus," said Hunter, as the second *carumphed* down about twenty feet in front of the Tigers.

"Sam, that's enough!" yelled Travis, as close to panicking as he would ever be.

"Nice fucking bracket," yelled Hunter angrily. "And don't give me that shit again about the Chinese inventing gunpowder."

But Sam's grenades *had* broken the contact and gotten the Tigers moving. All four were headed into town in the general direction of their leader.

"Well, it worked," yelled Travis, getting up and then running after the fleeing rebels.

"Sam, let Jen handle the grenades from now on. Please," said Hunter following Travis's lead. "Oh, yeah. And thanks."

"Anytime," said the little IMS man.

Jean-Guy's mind was racing, crumbling, and screaming all at the same time as it tried to cope with what had just happened. But the survivor inside fought its way to the forefront. It's done, it's finished. All that remains is how it will not happen to you. How are *you* going to get away from this debacle?

Jean-Guy's feet carried him relatively unconsciously deeper into the city, but west to the waterfront. He darted down an alleyway and slid to a halt. People stared, but he was oblivious to them. He still held his pistol in his right hand, but it may as well not have been there. He was still not completely conscious, having seen his dream destroyed in an instant. What in the gods' names had happened? One minute the attack was underway and the next—noise, black smoke, and dead men everywhere he looked. He breathed deeply and took off running again. He exited the alley on a street and stopped again. Where . . . ? Rue Pavee. To the piers. A boat. Cuba. His father had used that island as a refuge and so would he.

"Boss?" said Sam Wong.

"Go," answered Travis.

"Sitrep. The battle, for what it was worth, is over here. Not even mopping up. Whoever was left, and by the looks of things there ain't many, have disappeared."

"So has Louverture," said Hunter, opening his arms in an "I don't know" gesture.

"Jen's flying the last Dragonfly," said Sam. "We'll let you know if we can find anything."

"Smart going, kid," said Hunter.

"I know. Anyway. Stan and Jack broke up the action at the HNP barracks. The cops are out kicking ass. They also said they have a surprise. Wouldn't tell me anything else. Oh, and the ambassador and some pissed off Marine gunny are here. The grunts are armed to the teeth."

"That gunny's probably pissed off because he smells blood and can't get any," said Jen.

"You owed him a kick in the ass, Jen, and there it is," said Travis. "Okay, Sam. Have the Ghostriders get the RIBs in the water and tell Stan and Jack to head to the pickup point, fire up, and head to the piers. We'll take the piers back. Anything on our quarry?"

"The streets are pretty jammed with people, except over by the waterfront, but we picked three or four camouflaged guys heading thataway. They keep disappearing, but we can usually pick them up 'cause they're running and it doesn't seem like anyone else is in a hurry to get anywhere."

"Okay, police up the sensors and thermite the arsenal boxes then get outta Dodge," said Travis. "The fewer people see y'all, the better. Stage at Delmas with the Gurkhas.

We'll meet you back there. We're headed to the piers. Tell Stan and Jack to let us know when they're inbound."

"You got it. Uh, boss?"

"Go."

"Sorry about that first round. I was a bit excited."

Travis laughed. "No sweat. It worked and didn't kill us."

Hunter smiled. "Didn't kill *anyone*, but it did the job, little man."

Chapter 23

September 18, 1645 hours
Palais National, Port-au-Prince, Haiti

Since TALON Force was highly top secret, and since none of the members wore rank or insignia, there were a few awkward moments when the ambassador and his Marine escort arrived at the palace. All were placated by President Antoine, and it was hard to tell who was more startled, the ambassador or the gunny sergeant, when the president addressed Jen Olsen as "Captain,"—and only Captain—and said the gunny owed her an apology for using his foot so harshly. Jen merely nodded, shook hands with President and Madame Antoine, and left to join Sarah and Sam to police up the sensors. The Technologically Augmented Low Observable Networked Force made sure nobody found any of their advanced equipment.

Sarah stood the arsenal box on end and laid a miniature thermite grenade on top of it. It turned into a heap of smoldering plastic and metal in seconds; she did the same to the second. Jennifer and Sam walked the grounds retrieving their sensors, avoiding the bodies still strewn about.

"The cavalry's here," said Stan as he slid the Hummer to a stop in front of the palace.

"Almost done," said Sarah as she walked in from the building's east side. "Policing up. How'd it go?"

"Piece of cake when all is said and done," said Jack as he braked the Wildcat. "Got a bundle inside here." Jack climbed out of the Wildcat and entered the troop compartment and returned with a hooded, bound, and gagged Lily Rebuffat. "We ran into them running down the road toward town. Most of them split except that guy Bobo. He shoulda run. Anyway, we found Miss Hacker here flat on her face about twenty feet off the road. Damn near ran over her tight little ass. She's all yours."

Sam came running around the building with Jen, and slowed somewhat nonchalantly as he approached Stan and Jack. "Hey, Sammy," said Jack, grinning. "I think you know this broad."

"You gotta tie her up like a bale of hay for chrissakes?" said Sam.

"Hey, pretty or not, this chick caused a lot of bad shit. She gets POW treatment, at least until we get airborne. Then you can make your reacquaintance with her."

"Travis wants you and Stan to—"

"You told us already. Relax. We're outta here," said Stan. "Oh. Look for the Gurkhas. They're loggered around the UN camp, but they're probably running around looking for something to kill. The regimental sergeant major's name is Amblam. Good guy. They'll tell you what's what. We pretty much left the airport in their control."

"What about the security clearances, need to know and all that?" asked Sarah.

"Hey, these guys are pros. Hell, they ain't *here* either. They're actually in Belize. Or Aldershot, or on R and R. Or in Tibet or Nepal or some fucking place. They know the routine," said Stan. "They're tough cookies."

"Well," said Jack as he turned for the Wildcat, "see you back at the ranch. Anything further on Louverture?"

Sam noticed the prisoner stiffen and nodded his head toward her. The others watched her.

"The drone malfunctioned, but they got him about five minutes ago," said Sam. "He didn't put up a fight, just folded like a three-dollar suitcase. Gave up the rest of his men, the whole bit."

Stan, looking impressed, held his hand up head high and gave Sam the okay sign. "Yeah, you know how this revolutionary bullshit goes. It's okay to kill everybody as long as it ain't you," he said.

The five troopers watch Lily seem to practically deflate. Then all four gave Sam a thumbs-up and a nod. Jack slapped him on the shoulders, making the small man wince and glare at him in pseudo-anger. He looks like a puppy dog when Jack compliments him, thought Sarah, but that *was* a smart move and will make the interrogation a hell of a lot simpler.

"Later," said Stan as he and Jack climbed into the Wildcat and the other three, along with their prisoner, opened the Hummer's doors.

The Wildcat armored personnel carrier revved up and roared away from the palace, followed by the Hummer and its four occupants. The Wildcat headed west toward the waterfront, while the Hummer turned left for Delmas.

"Wildcat, Ghostrider Four," came over the armored car's com system.

"I thought we were Vikings or something," said Jack.

"I don't know nothing about that Viking shit," said Stan. "This'll do. Ghostrider, go," he answered.

"We're ready to drop,"

"Is the beach clear?"

"Negative. Lots of people about. Civilian."

"Hold the drop until we get there. We're about one-zero out," said Stan. "Step on it," he said to Jack.

"Buckle up."

The XM-77 Wildcat roared through the streets, but people barely spared the boxy black vehicle a second look. They thundered down Guilloux, angled right on Durand behind the sports stadium onto Denoux, finally making a sliding left on Harry Truman Boulevard. They immediately crossed the narrow waterway, jumped the curb, and headed across the sand and dune to the water, scattering people as they forged on.

"Ghostrider, you got us on the beach?" asked Stan.

"Roger, Wildcat. Stay buttoned up and we'll drop 'em at hover. It *is* cold, Roger?"

"That's affirm," said Stan. "Cold as a witch's droopy, shriveled up tit. Don't think there are any bad guys left."

"Roger."

Jack locked down the vehicle hatches and they watched the first Osprey go into a hover. The force of the downdraft threw up an atomic bomb blast's worth of sand, sending everyone running. The twenty-four foot RIB dropped relatively gently into thigh-deep water. The second Osprey dropped its load one hundred yards up the beach, then lifted off. Jack and Stan were out of the Wildcat as soon as the second Osprey went horizontal.

Stan headed down the beach to the second RIB and Jack waded out to the first. They threw the XM-29s aboard before climbing over the inflatable tubes that formed the rails of the craft and fired the silenced, 250-horse jet drives up. Both boats started on the first crank.

"I got a boat down home'll never do that," said Jack.

"I've been in Navy boats that won't do that," laughed Stan.

The rigid inflatable boats had fiberglass hull sections for stability and strength, but their flotation was mainly the providence of the huge hypalon/Kevlar/neoprene chambers that made the craft look like rubber rafts. A cage was mounted over the coxswain's station and mounted atop it was an HID lighting system, twin Stinger missiles, and a single 5.56 electrically fired Gatling gun. The Gatling gun was fed via a corrugated chute that led to an ammunition store at the base of the cox's station. You could empty the eight thousand rounds it held in approximately a minute's worth of sustained fire. Both the gun and the Stingers where aimed via the BSH's aiming system. The two boats spun away from the beach and headed out to sea.

"Trav," said Stan.

"Go, Stan," said Travis.

"We're rolling. Just coming around the point now."

"We're on the north side of the casino, about one hundred yards from the north side of the pier. We've got about ten guards in front . . . hold on a minute."

"Wonder what's up," said Jack as he bounced along at forty miles per hour.

"Well, looks like Louverture showed up," said Travis. "He's hustling down the pier and the guards are getting ready. There are some luxury boats. Couple of mules and some good-size sport fishing boats. He's probably headed for those. We're gonna take the place now. You've got guards the length of it. Clean it up and don't let that bastard get away."

"You got it, Trav," said Stan, slamming the throttles full-lock forward.

"Travis," said Hunter. "These guys aren't the brightest bulbs in the pack. Let's mosey on up a bit before we start shooting."

"You go out to the left." Travis and Hunter headed for the piers, angling to the sides some twenty-five meters apart. They kept their XM-29s pointed down and walked slowly toward the guards, who paid them little attention until they were about twenty meters out. One spotted Travis and started to draw down on him, but Travis raised the XM-29 and squirted off a three-round burst that slammed into the pavement in front of the man. He went down, his legs riddled with bullet fragment and rock. The other nine guards spun toward Travis, who calmly knelt and started squeezing rounds at individual targets. The guards never noticed Hunter, who had closed to within thirty feet before loosing off several three-round bursts from the hip. Between Travis's directed fire and Hunter's close-in bursts, the guards didn't stand a chance. All ten were down in twenty seconds.

The shootout had drawn the attention of most of the guards strung along the pier and some had come running. Travis and Hunter sped through the pier gates and picked off stragglers as they approached and before they knew there was anyone shooting at them. They hunkered down behind some pilings when they heard Jack and Stan say "Clear it" over the com system.

The RIBs would have roared in had their engines not been so well muffled, but fly in they did. Both boats throttled down and whatever engine roar there might have been would have been lost under the incredible tearing/ripping sound of the one- and two-second bursts of their Gatling guns sweeping the pier. Wood, metal, bullets, and bodies flew as the two boats pumped in bursts on the order of eight thousand rounds per minute. The only thing visible, even in the daylight, was the red of tracers, and they constituted only every fifth bullet. Three two-second bursts and all Travis and Hunter could see were survivors slowly rising with their hands in the air.

Both Jack and Stan did showboat high-speed 360s then throttled back down and powered over to where Hunter and Travis stood.

"Nice going, guys," said Hunter. "They teach you that hotdog synchronized-swimming shit in the Navy?"

"Damn right. No different than a barrel roll after a MiG kill," said Stan.

All four men heard the deep-throated rumble of a high-powered boat ignite. "Louverture!" yelled Travis, jumping the ten feet down into Stan's boat, which had nosed to the pier. "Jack, stay with Hunter and disarm these fools," said Travis as Stan backed out and swung the boat west along the south side of the pier.

They cleared the west end of the pier and saw the twin-hulled offshore powerboat flying west.

"Shit," said Travis. "Can we get him?"

"Unless he's real good, we're gonna get him," said Stan. "Grab onto something. Once we get out of the lee it's gonna get real bouncy."

Travs grabbed on and knelt on the deck of the RIB as it seemed to literally come out of the water and fly. Louverture's boat was doing much the same and it seemed to be doing it at a faster rate. "Can we get him?" asked Travis again.

"Wait, Trav," answered Stan. "He's running out of control." He reached down as the RIB started to bounce and managed to push an arming button for a Stinger. "Get one of these off. Even if you don't hit him it'll spook him, and I want him spooked. Aim in front of him."

Travis's saltwater-speckled BSH face shield would have probably caused him to miss regardless of Stan's need for a miss. The RIB started pounding, Travis got a fix on the distance and ordered the missile to fire. The Stinger left its launch pod and streaked one hundred yards in front of the violently bouncing offshore boat before exploding.

"Nice shot," said Stan sarcastically.

But the shot did what Stan had intended it to. The cat swerved ever so slightly and then started to cavitate. They could hear the engine wind up tighter, then they saw the triple screws coming out of the water. The boat launched off a small swell, the air caught under the cat's "trampoline" superstructure, and the boat went into a slow-motion backflip.

They saw a man in the rear holding onto the steering

wheel, a look of utter surprise on his face as it crashed upside down.

"Told you he was going too fast," said Stan, down throttling the RIB and motoring over to what remained of the broken, smoking craft. "Was a nice boat, too."

"I want a body, Stan. This guy was good. I want to make sure."

Stan slowly drove the boat around the wreckage, the two men looking from the water to the still floating pieces of hull. Travis kept his XM-29 at the ready.

"Over there," said Travis, pointing off the RIB's bow. A body in a jungle-green BDU shirt floated face down in the water. Stan threw the RIB into neutral, grabbed the telescoping boat hook off the front of the cox's station, and tossed it to Travis.

Travis screwed out the sections, locked them, and shot the hook at the body. Stan held his XM-29 casually aimed at the end of the hook. The hook grabbed shirt and skin as Travis set it and pulled the body slowly back to the boat. When he got it alongside, he reached down and grabbed the man's hair and pulled.

The body rolled over. Jean-Guy LePetit, the rebel, killer, and self-styled *zanset yo* of the real hero of Haiti, Toussaint Louverture, was dead.

"Fill him with lead and let him go down. Sharks'll take care of the rest," said Stan.

"Nah, I think it's better we bring him back. Let the Haitians do what they want to, but I think they'd rather see his body. At least they can say he's definitely dead."

"I don't know, with all this voodoo or Vodoun stuff . . ." said Stan warily.

"This guy had a bunch of people believing," said Travis. "I'm not gonna question it. Besides, he was a pretty good soldier, pulling off what he did with what he had."

"I'll give him that," said Stan. "Y'know, twenty years ago he might have been successful."

"And a lot of people would have died as a result. He'd have fallen anyway," said Travis. "His kind always do, but he probably would have had a hell of a run. Help me get him aboard."

Stan and Travis grabbed the body and hauled it over the low gunnels of the RIB and laid it on the floor.

"Home, James?" asked Stan.

"There's one more job and I want you and Jack to handle it."

"What else . . ."

"Cap Haitien," said Travis. "We know they have people there at the port. I need you and Jack to handle it. I'm thinking it's a smaller crew. Louverture wouldn't have wasted a major effort there. He wanted the capital; everything else would have fallen into place if he had that. Either way, I want that place secured."

"Roger. We'll get Ghostrider to pick us up."

"Sam?"

"Go, boss."

"Get an Osprey to the beach where it inserted the RIBs. Jack and Stan are headed to Cap Haitien."

"Roger, boss."

"We'll need both RIBs ferried to Delmas. Looks like we got Louverture. I want that computer lady to make an ID. Get everybody ready to saddle up. Oh. Sam, download a copy of the Cap Haitien waterfront for Stan will ya?"

"Roger."

"Jack, you copying all this?"

"Yo. I take it there's some unfinished business at Cap Haitien."

"Ten-four, big man," said Stan.

"What're your plans, Stan?" asked Travis as they powered the RIB up and headed back to the beach.

Stan was staring at the map readout in his BSH visor. "Do an underwater assault on the main pier. If I can take somebody alive maybe we can save a shit load of time not having to see if the fucking place is mined. We got short-range subsurface gear in the RIB. Enough to do the job."

"Okay. Lets get this done. The Osprey will probably have to refuel after he drops you. Give me a yell when you're ready for extraction."

Chapter 24

September 18, 1925 hours
On board Ghostrider Four en route to
Cap Haitien, Haiti

"Damn lucky you ain't driving," said Lieutenant Goose Miller. "Damn near double the distance. One-seven-oh by road, but only ninety as the Osprey flies."

"What's the ETA?" asked Stan.

"Figure we'll hook wide west and come in as low as we can. We'll do the drop as far east down the peninsula that the pier is on. Figure to insert at, oh, say twenty-oh-five hours. You'll have daylight left."

Stan handed the headset back to the crew chief and nodded at Jack. Both men broke open two medium-size duffel bags and started donning their dive gear. TALON teams had essentially two sets of underwater units, both based on a CIS-Lunar rebreather design. The full kit was a multi-gas rig set up for deepwater ops, but the rebreathers carried on the RIB were minimalist units. These rebreathers were good for ninety minutes to two hours at depths above forty feet—and depending on the breathing rate of the user. The dive masks were Cochran Heads-up display masks that functioned much like the BSHs did. All the info they'd need to have regarding their breathing mixture, depth, direction, and time was available, as were deco modes, temperature readings, breathing rates, and more. You looked down as if wearing bifocals and the information appeared in front of you, courtesy of a variety of sensors on the rebreather. A weight system was included with the rebreather and the diver could shed weight by removing lead shot. With the units on board the RIBs, the weight was rigged to accommodate the man who needed the most weight to maintain negative buoyancy. Surprisingly, on Eagle Team, this had turned out not to be Jack, but Travis, who floated like a cork. Propulsion was provided by split-blade Force Fins that had turned up leading edges, making them wearable when walking—though no one ever wanted to actually walk anywhere with them on. If the mission had been scheduled for anything other than tropical water, a wet-suit or drysuit would have been part of the gear, but in Haiti's water, their LOCS BDUs would suffice. The TALON armament system had been upgraded to waterproof, but would require a good cleaning as soon as possible after the mission. It took Jack and Stan ten minutes to rig up.

The crew chief waved his hand at both men for their attention and nodded at him when he held both hands up, ten fingers showing. Ten minutes till drop.

They felt the Osprey bank to the left and begin to drop altitude. The pitch of the engines slowed, and the crew chief opened the bay door. They were seven miles west of Cap Haitien and dropping and slowing noticeably. The crew chief held up one hand. Five to go.

They felt Miller start to rotate the wings into VTOL configuration and could see the water rushing up to greet them. The Osprey maintained its forward momentum at approximately twenty miles per hour.

The crew chief held up two hands and started the count-down from ten. When he had two fingers remaining he held a beat and pointed at Jack and Stan, and both slid out the bottom of the craft and crashed feet first into the warm water fifteen feet below.

Stan and Jack remained submerged and struggled into their fins. Stan got his on first and waited for Jack to give the okay. When the signal wasn't immediately forthcoming, Stan slapped the big man on the arm. Jack looked through the mask and gave the TALON number two a Jersey salute. He finished donning the fin and both men headed down to the bottom, which they reached at twenty-seven feet. Visibility was worse than the typical Caribbean harbor by a long shot. Stan estimated it at seven feet max. They checked the digital compass heading in their mask display and headed west until they hit the first upright of the pier.

The first explosion startled them slightly, and both men looked at each other and began finning farther along the pier. Someone had spotted them dropping in and from the sounds of it were dynamite fishing with grenades. There was another explosion. Stan felt a slight pressure wave and saw his heads-up display flicker. Okay, you wanna play, you're gonna pay. He tapped Jack, pointed to his right, and both men slid into the shadows of the pier and headed for the surface.

Jack removed his mouthpiece when they surfaced. "Fuckers saw us drop," he said.

"Guess so," said Stan, spitting.

Another explosion and both men turned and looked out into the dimness. "Missed us by about fifty yards," smirked Jack.

"Wait here," said Stan, who surface swam to the edge of the pilings to look landward, then swam back to Jack.

"About a hundred yards thataway," he said, indicating toward the town, "a gangway and a floating dock."

Two loud splashes drew their attention.

"What the . . . ?!"

"Whatta they got? Depth charges?" said Jack.

"No. Look."

Two heads surfaced, followed by a blast of compressed air as one first stage stuck open. A speargun was raised in the air as the diver silenced the runaway second stage.

"Okay. Two, both probably with spearguns," said Stan. "You take the dock and come in on these fucks from up top. I'll handle these two."

"Be careful, man," said Jack.

"You too."

Both inserted their mouthpieces and headed off in different directions. Stan swam to the bottom, which was now reading twenty-five feet, and made his way in the direction he'd last seen the divers. He stopped swimming and listened. Since the CIS Lunar was a closed-circuit system, there were no bubbles released and no noise to interfere. He heard the bubbles of the two divers before he saw them.

The first diver never had a chance. Stan came at him

from below and on an angle, slammed his trusty K-Bar into the man's midsection, and angled it up, piercing the man's diaphragm. He had taken the last breath he was going to. He pushed the drowning man out of the way and headed for the second diver, who reacted quickly. Unfortunately for him it wasn't quickly enough. The twin-band rock gun the man carried fired harmlessly past Stan, but the man managed to turn and start kicking up and away as he scrambled to pull his dive knife out of its sheath.

Stan got an iron grip on the man's hand as it fumbled with the knife and stabbed upward, going for the abdomen again. The other diver moved and received a deep wound from the knife, but kept struggling. Now it was for his life.

Stan hauled himself up the length of the man's torso and maneuvered behind him. He sliced the second-stage hose, pulled the man's mask off, and pushed him away. Stan jackknifed and headed for the bottom and the dark of the pier shadow before surfacing again.

While Stan was finishing off the two divers, Jack had quietly made his was to the dock and gangway, pulled off his fins, dropped his rebreather and mask on the dock, and unhooked his XM-29 from his harness. He started up the pier.

As he quietly walked up the gangway he saw an armed man appear at the top. The man was looking down the pier in the direction Stan had headed.

"Pssst."

The man turned and looked down, his weapon still carried casually by one hand.

"Asshole," said Jack, firing twice. The man went down without a sound, and Jack ran the rest of the distance to the top of the pier, then knelt along the railing. He grabbed the shotgun the man had held and tossed it into the water.

"Now I wish I had my BSH," he said aloud. He checked both directions, saw no one behind him but did see a group of men down the pier. Twilight had set in and he couldn't see them distinctly. As inconspicuously as was possible for a man his size he headed toward the men, staying close to the railing.

"Ah, what the hell." Jack stood up and yelled, "Lou-

verture!" at the top of his lungs and raced at the group of men.

At the sound of their leader's name, the six men spun around to face the charging Marine. As Jack could distinguish the lineal forms of weaponry he started shooting. Light taps of the trigger produced two- and three-round bursts that hit five of the MPP men between the neck and waist. They went down as fast as Jack got the rounds off. The sixth raised his hands in surrender and Jack lowered his aim and fired at the man's legs. The second round took him in the thigh and the man went down.

"Sorry, pal," he said when he reached the wounded man. He grabbed the wounded man by the collar and dragged him over to his comrades. He patted the man down swiftly, then scanned the rest of the pier. The man moaned.

"What's your name, mon?" Jack spat.

"Erla," groaned the man.

"Well, Erla, me and you gonna have a little talk." Jack pulled out his Randall knife and slammed it into the wooden planks of the pier for emphasis.

Chapter 25

September 19, 0300 hours
Delmas International Airport, Haiti

The Osprey landed in front of the arrivals building and Jack and Stan got out, flipped Goose Miller a salute, and headed inside as he taxied the ungainly craft away.

"Well, the heroes of Cap Haitien return," said Sam.

"Hey, little buddy, how goes it?" said Jack.

"Where the hell is everybody?" asked Stan. "We leaving already?"

"Well, actually we are leaving, but . . . well, I'll let Travis tell you what our gal pals have set up for us."

"Where is he?"

"They're all over near where the Ospreys are gassing up," said Sam.

"What's the story? And where the hell are our BSHs?"

"They should be with your combat gear. Everything else is loaded in one of the Big Birds and gone, though."

"We need a little R and R after this, man," said Jack. "Or is there something we missed?"

"Hey, I want to say good-bye to those Gurkhas," added Stan.

"Jeez. Relax, will ya? Everybody's over by the Ospreys."

The three men started walking toward a hangar on the north end of the airport. Stan and Jack could see traffic controllers in the blown out tower, and they suddenly noticed that most of the essential lighting on the airport was functioning. The sounds of taxiing jet engines, the howl of exiting jets, and the over-rev roar of landing ones made conversation next to impossible.

"What?" yelled Stan.

"I said SOW did a pretty damn good job. They've been pushing some serious tonnage in here. Oh, by the way, Lily identified Louverture, so that's definitely over with."

"Lily," yelled Jack. "My, my," he screamed at Sam, as a C-141 rolled past them. Sam gave Jack a dirty smirk.

"She's already headed back to Washington," yelled Sam.

"Who?" yelled Stan. "Why are we going to Washington?"

Sam shook his head emphatically and waved the two men toward the hangar.

The three men stepped through the wooden door into the relative quiet of the closed hangar and were greeted by the rest of their teammates.

As they traded remarks, Sam pointed with his chin behind Stan, who turned and was greeted by Regimental Sergeant Major Jangbu Amblam with the kind of salute only a British sergeant major could pull off.

"Well, gah-damn," said Stan, shaking hands with the tough little Gurkha. "How ya doing, Sergeant Major?"

"Quite well, Stan, thank you. Yourself?"

"Hangin' in there Amblam, hangin' in there." He turned to Travis. "What's up? We outta here or what? I got some serious stand-down time due me."

"We all do," said Travis, "but we're going to do something a little different first."

"Here you are, Stan," said Amblam, handing Stan a can of beer. "I know you Yanks prefer it ice cold, but the best we could do was soak it in some Av Gas for a bit to chill. Guinness, you know."

"Thanks Amblam." Stan turned to Travis and made a "what's up?" gesture with his hands.

"Jen, you want to let the boys in on the secret?"

"Well, Stan. And Jack. While you guys were off playing Navy SEALs, I did some snooping around. How would you all like seven days R and R on the shore of your very own private tropical mountain lake?"

"I can live with that," said Jack. Stan nodded in agreement.

"Here's the deal. I'll supply the steaks and booze . . ." Both men's eyebrows raised at that. ". . . courtesy of a

young flight lieutenant whose acquaintance I've recently made."

"I'll bet," said Stan.

"You're damn right," said Jen.

"What do we gotta do for all this largess?" asked Jack.

"Well, actually, we get to help Sarah treat a bunch of orphans, and we get to help rebuild a village. For whom the self same flyboy will make sure we get the supplies for."

"Jesus, come on, Olsen," said Stan beseechingly. "Ain't we done enough around this place? I'm dead-ass tired, and all I wanna do is sleep and drink and—"

"You never know if it'll come to that," said Jen with a wink.

"Y'know," said Stan, pointing his finger in Jen's face. "Even on the off chance that maybe, just maybe—"

"Travis, what the hell is this all about. Ain't this what they make engineers for?" said Jack.

"Tell them the rest, Jen. Seems our intelligence operative found out something interesting."

"You might even call it career enhancing, guys," she said.

"Go ahead," said Jack.

"Stan, remember the briefing you and Travis went to at HQ? The bit about the lady doctor?"

"Ah, shit, you gotta . . ."

"Listen, Stan. Seems that doctor is also a nun—she's a Maryknoll missionary sister—and is not only a friend of General Gates . . ."

"Yeah, she's what?"

"She's his sister."

"His sister's a sister? A nun? You must be shitting me," said Stan. "Why the hell didn't he have us bail her ass out of here in the first place."

"You know Gates wouldn't ask us to do that," said Jen. "The only reason I was able to find out was because I pulled in a few past-due accounts that led to General Krauss. I had to twist the hell out of his good arm—figuratively speaking—to get the word."

Stan looked at Jack and shook his head. "I don't believe this shit."

"Look at it this way, guys," said Travis. "We'll get some R and R, build some houses, treat some kids, drink and

eat, relax some, and earn some good points with the Chairman of the Joint Chiefs of Staff. Can never hurt."

"And I got the Brits to cut Amblam and his boys loose for the week, as well," said Jen. "So they're coming with us. An SAS guy I know at Hereford is the brother of the battalion commander's adjutant at Aldershot and he—"

"Spare me the spook shit, Jen," said Stan, surrendering. "Jeez, I'm glad we ain't in Hawaii or you'd have us R and R-in' at a fucking leper colony."

Jen walked over to her combat pack and rummaged inside it. She drew something out and held it behind her back as she walked back to where Stan was standing.

"Tell you what, I'll give you this," she said, holding up a quart of Johnny Walker Black Label, "if you come along quietly."

"I only work for bourbon, sweetheart," said Stan.

Jack's huge mitt closed over the bottle, and he grinned down at Jen. "He'll be working for Johnny Black now, sweet thing, or he'll answer to Black Jack. Why, I betcha ol' Stan here is gonna be the most orphan-loving, hootch-building, nun-salutin' swabby in the whole damn world. I guaran-gah-damn-tee that!"